D1302194

Sunday's Child

Tom Lewis

McBryde Publishing
NEW BERN, NORTH CAROLINA USA

McBryde Publishing
NEW BERN, NORTH CAROLINA USA

SUNDAY'S CHILD
Copyright © 2006 by Tom Lewis

The characters and events in this book are fictitious.
Any similarity to real persons, living or dead,
is coincidental and not intended by the author.

Cover by Liaisin Design Group, LLC
Photograph by Don David

ISBN 978-0-97587007-5

First Printing 2006 By VP Publishing, LLC
Second Printing 2009 By McBryde Publishing

Printed in the United States of America

*This novel is respectfully dedicated to the memory of
every brave man who served in the
United States Life-Saving Service*

And to

My Ila Grey

who always believed.

ACKNOWLEDGEMENTS

Few fiction writers birth a book-baby all by themselves. I believe that nowadays most of us have to be very lucky and lean heavily on the help and influence of others. Many others. This is certainly true for me.

Watching this trilogy come to print, I am quite conscious of owing thanks to so many people I could easily fill too many extra pages doing so. Still, there are some who especially deserve my limitless gratitude.

Long ago, Kaa Byington, friend and mentor, set me on the right track as a novelist and often kept me from going off the rails. Maxine Harker and her pool of lovable sharks taught me, among many other valuable things, how to be my own worst critic. My agent, Lettie Lee, faithfully stuck by me from the beginning. Bill Lupold kept me from breaking down every time my computer did. Bruce and Kim Long unselfishly shared their talent with me for practically no reward. Too many friends to count and every living member of my family never allowed me to lose faith in myself. To all of them, my deep gratitude and love.

And finally, I must thank my publishers and their staff. Ron Pate shared with and included me in his remarkable publishing goals. James Vick worked tirelessly as my literary guide. And I am certain that no other author ever had a better editor than Matt Young, who helped make my work so much better. I am happy to call each of them my close personal friend.

Tom Lewis

March, 2006

Monday's child is fair of face,

Tuesday's child is full of grace,

Wednesday's child is full of woe,

Thursday's child has far to go,

Friday's child is loving and giving,

Saturday's child works hard for a living,

But the child born on the Sabbath day

Is fair and wise and good and gay.

PROLOGUE

AFTER TRAVELING two thousand sea miles, the heavy log had become saturated. Twenty feet long and twelve inches thick at its splintered base, it had broken off from a foundering schooner near Galveston. Floating east, then south in the warm Gulf Stream around the curve of the southern coast of the United States, it meandered just below the surface around Florida, made a slow, unimpeded path northward, and, passing thirty miles east of Cape Hatteras, ploughed headlong into yet another storm. Even though it was a large object, no human eye would ever see it . . .

The message came to the Pea Island Life-Saving Station at 8:20 on the night of November 9, 1918. As usual, the text was brief:

DISTRESS SIGNAL RECEIVED THIS HOUR FROM SAILING VESSEL MARTHA JANE /FIVE ABOARD/ BELIEVED ENTERING YOUR SECTOR NOW/ STAND BY FOR RESCUE/

Standing on the rooftop platform above the Station House, Ben Searcy nodded his silent acknowledgement to the surfman who had read the terse message to him. He raised his binoculars again to the northeast. Although Searcy's official title was "Keeper," all six of his surfmen, and most others who knew him, called him "Captain" out of deep professional respect.

This one, whose name was Clem, shouted through nearly-horizontal rain driven by the full gale that threatened to tear both of them from their perch, "Orders, Cap'n?"

Searcy kept his gaze seaward, but leaned over and away from the wind. "Make ready the boat and send Amos up here. I need a pair of young eyes."

Aboard the MARTHA JANE, when he could catch a quick breath, John Tyler loudly cursed the boat, her owner, the storm, and most of all, his luck. He had *known* this was not a good month to take a boat south, and would not have if he hadn't been so desperate for a job. *Any* job! Now, he was caught up in the worst nor'easter he could remember and, without a reversal of that luck, he might very well die. So might everyone else aboard this stinking tub. But desperate men do foolish things, and for five hundred filthy dollars which would have guaranteed him paid passage back home to England, Tyler had agreed to skipper the tired old ketch from Annapolis to Fort Lauderdale.

The only concession wrung from Jacob Weintraub, the new owner, was that they also obtain the services of a good mate. After haggling for hours, Weintraub had finally agreed and so the MARTHA JANE had set sail with Peter Tomlinson also aboard. Peter was as good a blue water sailor as any Tyler knew, and it was Peter who had kept them all from drowning before now. When the storm first hit them, Weintraub showed that he was nothing more than a bragging amateur who knew next to nothing about heavy-weather sailing and was soon stone-dead drunk. The first time the ketch had heeled over more than ten degrees, taking white water over the starboard rail, his wife had become profanely abusive, then violently seasick, and finally hysterical. The kid, a boy about twelve, was the only one of the family who showed any guts at all. He was small for his age, however, and except for managing to get his miserable parents into life jackets was practically useless.

If not for Peter's help, things would have become critical much sooner. He and John had shortened sail twice already in seamanlike time, and had secured everything fast belowdecks. When they discovered serious water rising in the forward cabin, deducing that the old boat was leaking like a straw hat, Peter had tackled the decrepit bilge pump with a furious passion. His mechanical skills had kept them afloat so far, and as the storm worsened, John had wisely decided to run before it, drogue or no drogue, under bare poles, making for Oregon Inlet.

From there down to Cape Hatteras, there were few rocks ashore, only sand. Blessed sand. If beaching the old girl became necessary, he wouldn't hesitate to do it. The last time he'd had a chance to glance at the chart, just before commanding Peter to send the distress signal, he had fixed their approximate position due east of the Bodie light. Intermittently, he could see it faintly through the sheets of rain as they clawed over the crests of enormous waves. He strained, without success thus far, to see the much stronger beacon of the Hatteras light.

His cursing ceased abruptly when Peter's head appeared in the companionway.

"John!" Peter yelled. "The pump is shot. Gone. We're taking on too much water. No pump could handle it. I sent another SOS."

"Good man!"

"There's more bad news."

"Better tell me."

They paused to ride over yet another massive wave.

"There's a bad crack in the mizzenmast step," Peter yelled. "If the wind gets much worse, I think it may go. Watch yourself. If it does go, it could take you with it. She's sinking, John. Want me to get the others up here?"

"Yes, and tie them down."

Peter's head disappeared back below, and John reached into the starboard cockpit locker for the flare gun. In forty-six years, thirty of them on the water, he had never prayed. Not once. But now, flying before a force 10 gale generated from the very gates of hell, not knowing whether the vessel would make it through one more trough, John Tyler gripped the wheel tighter and began to pray to his Maker at the top of his voice. He paid scant attention to his mate laboriously hauling every moaning member of the Weintraub family into the cockpit and lashing them snugly to the binnacle.

Tyler's last prayer was that they were now close enough to shore for someone—*anyone*—to see the flares. He raised the gun and fired.

Amos Turner saw the red glow first. *"There,* Cap'n!" He pointed directly east. "Can't be more'n a mile offshore."

Glasses in hand, Searcy jerked his head around in confirmation. "Good work, Amos. Let's go."

The other five men already had the lifeboat poised at the water's edge. The moment they saw Searcy and Amos running toward them, they knew they would have to go. All eyes were on their leader, who shouted, "Prepare to launch!" The surfmen stretched hands for position, dug their heels into the sand and bunched leg, arm, and back muscles for his command, knowing they'd have to wait only for the short sailor's prayer. The wind was too strong for them to actually hear the brief verse, but each had known it by heart for years, both the two traditional lines and the two Ben Searcy had added:

"O God, Thy sea is so big
And my boat is so small,
Bring us home safely
Each of us, and all.

Ready . . . *Heave!"*

It took almost half an hour to punch through the roiling surf, and distance covered beyond it was no easier. Every straining man rowed in silence, backs bending backward and forward in a steady rhythm of brute strength. Conserving their collective energy and breathing in unison, they occasionally glanced at the calm face of the man at the tiller, who, in return, gave each a slight nod and smile. No words were necessary; each man knew his job, and not one of them had the slightest doubt that they would succeed this night. They had proved it many times before.

Within another half-hour, Ben Searcy saw two more red streaks rise and fall through the distant fury and adjusted his steering accordingly, not toward where the last one had died, but on a course where the stricken vessel must have headed after shooting the flares. He glanced at his men every other minute with mute pride— and no little affection. They were splendid examples of manhood, strong and quietly brave. When called upon, each hand-chosen man was trained and drilled to perform like six fearless parts of one well-oiled strength machine, even in weather like this. Ben reflected that he had seen worse storms than this one, but not very many, and this nor'easter had been something of a surprise.

Unexpected. Coming right on the heels of the end of hurricane season, too! He raised a prayer of thanks that it was only early November. Water temperature would be bearable for quite a while, and besides, the current was no doubt pushing the warm edge of the Gulf Stream toward them. He wasn't worried about his men or the vessel's crew freezing to death when they went into the water. Still, there were plenty of other unknowns to—
Wait! There's another flare!

"Come on, boys," he yelled. "We're gaining!"

Head-on, the wide end of the log struck the MARTHA JANE six feet aft of the stem, on her port side, bashing a foot-wide hole through the old planks as if they were strakes of cardboard. The force of the blow pushed her bow slightly to starboard just as she buried her nose in the trough between a pair of wild waves, their tops rising thirty feet higher. Her stern slewed suddenly around hard to port, like from a Chinese jibe. That rapid combination of events, which momentarily altered her centrifugal force, wrenched the mizzenmast from its step with massive torque.

The wheel was viciously jerked out of Tyler's hands when the binnacle crashed forward, and the bow of the dinghy catapulted from its weakened stern davits, striking him a glancing blow on his left shoulder as it sailed past him into the maelstrom. Tyler left his feet, pulled in a vacuum that carried him up and out of the cockpit and over the crest of the following wave. Before he was slammed into the dark water, he saw out of the corner of his eye something white. The vision lasted only a split second, yet, as he struggled to the surface with what he knew was a broken left arm, he would have sworn that he had also seen *flashing oars.*

John Tyler heard more than he saw during the next half-hour of his blessedly extended life. From those sounds, however, he vaguely pieced together what was happening around him. The sounds, above the shrieking of the wind, were *voices*. Voices shouting in a strange accent:

"I see one, Cap'n! There, hard a-starboard!"

"I see him. Looks like he's unconscious."

"I'll go over."

"There's two still on board. Hangin' on to the mizzen."

"One of 'em looks like a woman."

"Right. Somebody's got to board that boat."

"She's near 'bout ninety degrees! That boat's gon' *roll*, Cap'n! Five minutes, she's gon' turn turtle!"

"Somebody will have to go anyway."

"I'll do it."

"Take the axe and extra lines."

"Cap'n! There's another one. Looks like a *child*."

"I see him. Get a line to him."

On and on it went. Unfamiliar accent or not, Tyler was certain he was hearing the voices of angels. He knew he was going to be saved. Knew the others would be, too. They would all be saved. And soon. That white boat was beautiful. The loveliest thing he had ever seen. Coming closer now. Tyler felt that he could raise his good arm, and knew better than to try to scream. Still, he tried. And tried again. Of course they couldn't hear him. They didn't see him either. Not yet. But they would . . . wouldn't they?

A different kind of sound gradually filled his ears. A new sound. An ugly sound, and Tyler knew the MARTHA JANE had rolled over and gone belly-up. Men were shouting to get out of the way before she sucked them under as she went down. He closed his eyes and let his body relax. In spite of the pain in his arm, a kind of peaceful resignation began to settle over him, as if he were simply floating in a quiet, warm pool. *If it has to be, well, it has to be.* Then, strong hands were reaching out to him. A line was snaked around him under his arms, and the pain of the broken one made him cry out and faint.

When he came to, he realized he was in the bottom of the boat sent from God Himself, tangled among feet, legs, and whole bodies. He saw six men manning the oars. Six angels, all clad in yellow foul-weather gear. All wearing sou'westers. He looked up into the face of the angel at the helm, then quickly back again at all those other men. Though the light was almost nonexistent, he nevertheless saw that every single face of the boat crew was . . . *black! Black as the night around them!*

Tyler had just enough strength left to ask the helmsman, "Where'd you people come from, and what the devil are you doing out here in this mess?"

The black man smiled down at him. "We're from Pea Island, mister. Doing our duty."

CHAPTER 1

November 12, 1918

BENJAMIN ABRAHAM Searcy smiled. Unless there was a bad storm, you could set your watch by Tom Kinch's independently operated ferryboat, delivering supplies, mail, news, and gossip from Elizabeth City, Manteo, and Wanchese on her way to Hatteras Village and Ocracoke. The official government boat came in only once a month, and was often late with their pay and whatever staples Searcy had requisitioned, but Ben could always count on old Tom Kinch and the sturdy vessel Tom so ably piloted.

Searcy called for two of his men who were playing cards, "Joe! You and Clem go on down there and see what he's got this time. And, mind you, if there are any newspapers, don't let them get wet."

Ben Searcy was by far the most learned man at the Station. Having finished high school—far beyond the average for a black man—Ben had advanced his education considerably by reading everything in print he could get his hands on since. Weekly and day-old papers were precious. It irritated him when one of his surfmen got uncharacteristically careless, and it was still raining hard now. The northeaster had mostly blown itself out, leaving in its wake the usual cold, depressing days that Ben despised: cold as a man's corpse, and dark as his funeral.

Yet, there was good news. On the wireless, Ben had heard that an Armistice was signed the day before over in France, which meant that there might now be less chance of bodies washing up on shore and perhaps fewer shipwrecks. He hoped and prayed the Armistice would hold. Because of that news and the fact that his men were still exhausted from their most-recent labor, he had given them the day off except for taking turns as lookouts.

Sighing, Ben walked to the dining-room window. Through the double panes and rivulets streaming down the outer one, he watched his two men work their way down to the landing, a narrow finger pier which stuck out forty yards into the choppy, slate-gray sound. It was hard to see much of anything that had real form, even the outline of the pier, and at first Ben wasn't sure exactly what he was staring at. With a short blast from her whistle, and a belch of smoke only slightly darker than the moisture it displaced, Tom's boat was pulling away from the dock, sure enough, but it appeared he was leaving one man behind. Not one of Tom's crew was that tall, he knew, yet there were definitely three men slogging back up the path to the Station House carrying the crates Tom had offloaded. Puzzled, Ben hurried to the front porch, reaching for his peacoat which hung on the first peg by the stout oak door. He walked out onto the porch just as the three men reached its steps.

Clem Hardison spoke up, "Tom brung you a bunch of newspapers, Cap'n. This here's Slick Everette. Says he wants a job."

Ben's two men climbed the porch steps and flanked their Keeper, leaving the stranger standing alone at the bottom. Hatless, with raindrops bouncing merrily from his shaved head, he was dressed in a soaked blue suit that was much too small, though his boots looked almost new and housed the largest, longest pair of feet Ben had ever seen.

Ben looked the man up and down—had to be six-four, maybe six-five—and Ben was suddenly aware he was gazing into the clear eyes of the handsomest black man he had ever seen. Ben, inwardly a little embarrassed, lowered his gaze from the sculpted ebony face. From one exposed wrist, Slick Everette's equally long fingers clutched a black leather bag similar to those physicians carried, only bigger. The temperature and the rain didn't seem to bother the fellow in the least, and his wide grin showed a double row of teeth that shone like buffed mother-of-pearl.

"How'do, Cap'n Searcy. I'm your new man."

Ben coughed discretely. "You have come a long way for nothing, Mr. Everette. I have no openings. Somebody must have misinformed you."

Everette's grin broadened. "No, sir. I ain't lookin' for no surfman's job. I mean to do your cookin' for you."

All Ben's crew had now drifted quietly out onto the porch, their curiosity as high as the Keeper's.

"Then you are twice mistaken," Ben replied. "We employ no cook, nor do we have a budget for one."

"Well sir, you does now. I'm the best cook they is in five states, and I'm gon' make you a deal."

"Deal?"

"Yes, sir. A fair bargain. Let me cook y'all supper tonight in exchange for a warm place by the wood stove. After that meal, we can talk it over. If you don't like my offer, I can ketch Cap'n Tom's boat back tomorrow."

Ben Searcy was not given to delaying decisions, especially with all his surfmen surrounding him, silent as cypress stumps. Here was a man standing in the cold rain, making an unusual but not unreasonable request: a cot and shelter for the night in return for cooking one meal. In any case, he couldn't let the poor man stand out there all day.

He turned abruptly. "Back inside, all of you."

His tone, which each of the six had heard many times before, brooked no argument. Obediently, they filed back into the house without a word, like chastened children.

Ben looked down at the stranger. "Come on up here, man, before you drown. You must be freezing with no coat on."

"I been colder, Cap'n," Everette said, laughing. "But thankee. I b'lieve I will." He was up the eight steps in two leaps.

"Come with me," Ben ordered. He led the dripping giant inside, down the hall and into the warm, now-deserted kitchen. "Get out of those wet clothes. I'll bring you a towel and some dry ones."

"Thankee, sir."

Ben went to the uniform locker and fished out the largest shirt and pair of pants there, grabbed a towel, and retraced his steps. The stranger had stripped down to his cotton drawers and was hanging his soaked clothes over the backs of chairs. Ben caught his breath; never had he seen such a piece of work. He guessed the man must weigh well over two hundred pounds, and every ounce of it was solid, perfectly formed muscle.

A passing thought occurred to Ben that it was too bad his crew *wasn't* short a man. The basic requirements for becoming a surfman were simple; one had to be sober, needed a strong back, and had to be an excellent swimmer. He must know Morse and be able to use semaphore flags, and a surfman had to possess personal discipline enough to faithfully follow orders. The rest could be learned in a matter of a few weeks, with practice.

Ben watched Everette put on the dry clothes, then walked to the cupboard. Removing a brace of mugs, he poured coffee from the huge, blue-speckled pot that was always warming on the stove.

"Here. Sit down and drink this."

Everette grinned at him again, sat, and sipped. "Ain't bad. Ain't bad at all . . . but wait'll you taste mine."

Ben smiled back. "What's your real name? Your first name, I mean."

"Don't rightly know, Cap'n. I had one, but I reckon I forgot it. Folks have called me 'Slick' ever since I can remember."

"Who are you running from, Slick? The law?"

Slick slapped his huge palm on the tabletop and laughed loudly. "No. No, sir. Worse'n that! I ain't a-runnin' from no bulls, but there's a right purty little black gal up in Norfolk with a real mad daddy, and that's the truth of it. He ain't a big man, but he's got a real big shotgun, if you ketch my meanin'."

This time Ben laughed, too. "I understand. What's in the bag there?"

"My knives and spices. Tools of the trade, y'know."

Ben stood. "I see. Well, Mr. Slick Everette, you can cook us that supper tonight and make yourself a pallet here in the kitchen after you clean up. Fair enough?"

"Fair enough, Cap'n. Jus' show me where the food and the icebox is."

Ben pointed to the pantry door. "Canned stuff's in there. The icebox is out on the back porch. We usually have supper at seven."

"Yes, sir. Seven it is. Say, who does your cookin' anyhow?"

"The men take turns, one week at the time. Pardon me for asking, since it really is none of my business, but why does a man with your, uh, physical attributes make his living as a cook?"

Slick bellowed again. "Well, Cap'n Searcy, my Mammy taught me how. When I was little, she told me a man could break his back and his soul workin' for next to nothin' in cotton fields or cuttin' timber from sunup till dark; but folks have to eat, and a good cook can always find easy work and live a long time doin' it. With the way I can cook, I mean to live me a right long life."

Shaking his head slowly, Ben couldn't help but laugh. "All right. I'll leave you to it, then." Still chuckling, he went to his room, picked up his pen and wrote in his daily log.

Nov. 12, 1918: Rain all day. No sightings.
K's ferry came and went. Gave men one day
off because of Armistice in France. Hopefully,
it will hold, and our country will have peace
again. One that lasts.

B.A. Searcy

There was not a word about his new houseguest.

By half past seven, having been tantalized for hours by the smells permeating the Station, Ben knew he would find a way to make their guest a permanent one. The meal, eaten in a rare silence around the table, was not one they would soon forget. They had all eaten fried chicken before—countless times, of course. They were used to fried fish, too, fresh or salted, with canned vegetables, cornbread, and biscuits. But *nothing* had ever tasted like the feast set before them this night. There was cold buttermilk, sweet tea, and delicious coffee to wash it all down with, and how the man had concocted some kind of miracle dessert from dried peaches was a mystery. Every surfman ate his fill thinking the very same thought: *I sure as hell can't cook like this, and neither can anybody else around this table.*

There was one other thing each surfman thought of: whoever did the cooking had to also clean up afterwards; no easy task in itself, and one they all hated, down to the last man.

Slick Everette showed he was no fool. He chose his moment well. Waiting until every plate had been pushed forward, he reached into his bag and passed a cigar to every man who wanted one, saying, "From the looks of them cleaned-off plates, I ain't gon' have much washin' up to do."

Looking Ben in the eye, he added, "Now, Cap'n Searcy, I understand the word *budget* you used 'cause I've heard it before. I knows you have to spend what the gov'ment gives you and no more. But if each man here chooses to put up two dollars of his pay ever' month, includin' you, y'all got yourselfs a cook. I'll just wait out yonder on the porch with my coffee and cigar while you talks it over."

The giant strode out, and Ben looked around the table into six pleading pairs of eyes.

Coughing once, he said, "All right, I'll leave it to you. We'll take a vote, and it must be all or nothing. If one man votes 'no,' then Everette goes back with Tom tomorrow. All in favor of hiring him, raise your hand."

The vote was unanimous. And, all voted to pony up a full month's wages for November, even though the month was twelve days gone.

Later that night, the men heard Slick's singing, along with the sounds of pots and pans being scrubbed and put away. They all smiled at the rich baritone rendition of the silly old folk tune:

"Old Dan Tucker was a fine old man,
Washed his face in a frying pan,
Combed his hair with a wagon wheel,
And died with a toothache in his heel . . . "

The following morning, after a breakfast fit for princes, Ben sent the Station crew off to their duties and walked down to the pier to meet Tom Kinch's boat. "Thanks for the papers, Tom. Here's my supply list for next week."

Tom took the list and stuck it into his jacket pocket. "Do I have a passenger to take back to Elizabeth City?"

"No. The man's staying here a while. You know anything about him?"

Tom spat over the lee side of the rail. "Some. Waterfront gossip, mostly. People say he's a first-rate cook, and when he ain't cooking, he's a pretty damn good fighter."

Ben raised an eyebrow. "Fighter?"

"Yeah. Known from Richmond to Jacksonville as one of the best bare-knuckle brawlers around. Fights in private clubs, carnivals, barrooms, wherever he can pick up pocket change and free beer, but most say he fights just for the love of doing it. Thinks he's Jack Johnson. Come to think of it, he favors old Jack, don't he?"

Ben returned the grinning boatman's smile.

"Yes, Tom. He does at that. Thanks again for the papers. See you next week."

CHAPTER 2

"TELL US about that little gal up in Norfolk, Slick. Is it true she was jus' fourteen?"

"Tell us again about your fight with Big Bob Angus. You went nineteen rounds with him?"

"Naw, Slick, tell us 'bout them Charleston women. Did you really have two of 'em in one night? Together at the *same time?*"

And Slick would tell them. At least one tall tale practically every night for nearly a year. Slick's adopted home had a ready-made fraternal family—and an eager audience. Within a few months, all seven surfmen became his good friends as well as employers. Three of them, Lonnie Padgett, Nat Poole, and Royce Weeks, were older, close to Ben's age. Lonnie was married, with a family of his own living across the sound over on Roanoke Island. With subtle shaking of their heads and low chuckles, they tolerated Slick's entertaining, boisterous bragging with good humor. ("I been set on this earth for jus' three reasons, boys: good cookin', good fightin', and good lovin'. And be-damned if I ain't good at all three!")

The other men, Clem Hardison, Amos Turner, and Joe Freeman, were all younger than Slick and soon worshiped him like spaniels. They hung on the threads of every fanciful story of his exploits with the ladies, fights he'd had, and the exotic places he claimed to have traveled to as pure gospel. Ben Searcy, also a lifelong bachelor, kept professionally aloof but secretly enjoyed the nightly yarns as much as the others. Slick's adventures helped break the routine and monotony of their lonely existence on Pea Island. Those lazy evenings on the porch after supper included card and checker games, horseshoes, mumblety-peg, and occasional impromptu music with Slick throwing in a decent and enthusiastic job with a pair of spoons for added rhythm.

But this close association was not a one-way street. For his part, Slick was genuinely interested in the unique and colorful history of the Life-Saving Service, their heroic deeds (which he knew were considerable and always understated), as well as hearing about their families and personal lives before they had become surfmen.

One morning, Slick walked the dune ridge beside Ben Searcy, watching the men drill below with the "apparatus cart," which was loaded down with their equipment. From only the briefest of vocal commands or hand signals, the surfmen performed automatically; trundling the heavy cart down half a mile through the sand to the practice scaffolding, setting up the lines for the Breeches buoy, loading and firing the leading line from the powerful tiny brass cannon they called the Lyle gun, then simulating rescuing each other as though they were stranded sailors from an imaginary sinking or beached ship.

"They're good men, Cap'n. Real good."

Holding his watch, Searcy gave him a sideways glance and half a smile. "They have to be, Slick. Tell you what, though, if I ever lose one of them, I want you to train to take his place. Strong as you are, I'll bet you could pull that cart all by yourself."

"Yes, sir. Maybe I could, but I couldn't never be one of your surfmen, even if I wanted to."

"Why not?"

"Well, sir, if you promise not to tell *them,* I'll tell you."

"Tell me what?"

Slick showed his wide grin. "Can't swim."

"You can't swim?"

"Not a lick. I'm scared to death of water. 'Specially the ocean. You couldn't get me to so much as poke my big toe in it, even if you was to hold a gun to my head."

"You never learned how to swim? I can't believe that."

"Well, sir, it's true. I never did, and I ain't about to try to, neither. The other night, when you and the boys took the lifeboat out through the surf, I got cold chills jus' watchin' you. Come to think of it, why'd you do it, anyway? The ocean was mean as a bull with one ball that night."

"Because ships don't usually go aground in nice weather like this. We have to be ready to go no matter what it's like out there."

"I reckon. Anyway, you won't tell the boys what I said, will you? I ain't no coward, it's jus' that—"

"I understand. Every man has his Achilles' heel."

"His what?"

"Means a vulnerable weakness. A fault. There's no man alive doesn't have at least one." Searcy glanced at his watch, frowned, and yelled to the men, "Half a minute too slow! Come on back and try it again."

Slick worked his toes into the sand. He wasn't sorry he'd told Searcy about his whatchamacallit-heel, but he was be-damned if he'd admit to having two of 'em! He made no bones about the fact that his hero was Jack

Johnson. Never had. Hell, everybody knew that, but
nobody knew he shared another of the famous fighter's
traits: he was tired of chasing after black women. They
were too easy. No, the only challenge left for him was to
someday have himself a white woman, even if he had to
do something he'd sworn he'd never do—and so far never
had—pay cash money for his lovin'. Lately, he'd heard
rumors about a pretty white girl working in Miz Pike's
fancy house over to Elizabeth City who might bed down
with a black man, if he had the price. If that was so, Slick
meant to have her, no matter what her price was.
Meantime, for two dollars, he could bribe one of Tom
Kinch's crew to nose around town and see if those
rumors really were true, maybe find out what she looked
like, and take the girl a message from him. Better yet, he
might talk Cap'n Searcy into letting him make a trip or
two to the mainland—to get better deals on their
groceries—and find out for himself!

It took him only one to find the answers to all his
questions. Not only did he see the girl and learn her
name, he politely inquired at the house she worked in
and was told that, for a double fee, a secret backdoor visit
would indeed be possible.

And so, when his early-November work break of 1919
came, Slick Everette was more than ready for it. It had
been a long season, almost like a prison sentence. There
had been no shipwrecks on their stretch of beach, and
though they had been through several storms, none were
of hurricane force or bad northeasters. With little to do
but practice, all the men were just as restless as he was.
They had all become more than a little cranky, too.
Though much of their work was light, they all still
clumped in with huge appetites. No matter how good the

food was that Slick prepared for them, or how much of it he put on the table, it never seemed to satisfy either their hunger or their tastes. But, Slick knew their increased grousing was not because of his own work. Those wise wooly-heads in the government had not yet thought of adding saltpeter to the diet of men serving at lonely posts in order to tamp down their natural restlessness. Slick would not have used it anyway, and he knew exactly what the men needed—none more than himself.

Having no timepiece, he squinted up at the noon sun. Cap'n Tom's ferry would soon heave in sight. Slick felt himself becoming aroused at the thought of the next few days, reaching into his pocket to feel the bills stashed there. He had saved every penny of his pay, and since Cap'n Searcy allowed no gambling and there had been no other way to spend it, he estimated he had more than enough. He knew he would take a mighty ribbing when the other men found out how he was going to spend it, but Slick didn't care what they thought. It was *his* money and he could spend it any damn way he chose to. Who knows, maybe she would give him a discount!

He thought about the girl, relishing the picture of her he had framed in his mind for three months. Amanda Cooper's face was not what you could call handsome; she had two missing teeth, which ruined her smile, but she had long hair the color of a January sunrise and a fine young body that was white and smooth as beach sand. Slick grinned again. Even the older men would have new respect for him when they found out he'd spent a whole day and night in bed with a white girl! Yessir, they'd have a short ton of new respect.

He looked out across the unruly sound to the northwest. The low hull of Cap'n Tom's boat, trailing a mule's tail of black smoke, was finally chugging toward the landing. She was mighty slow, but reliable, and Slick knew that within a few hours and after two stops at Roanoke Island, he'd be in Elizabeth City. *Man, oh, man!* Without realizing it, he began humming, then singing.

> *"Combed his hair with a wagon wheel,*
> *And died with a damned Achilles' heel . . . "*

Ernestine Pike wrinkled her nose and pulled the collar of her fur coat tighter. On the waterfront, the odors swirling like dust devils in the cold afternoon northwesterly were strong. The foul mixture of tar, fish, and unwashed bodies assaulted her nostrils every time she went there, which she did every workday afternoon after making her bank deposit. She was glad it was winter. Summer days around the Elizabeth City docks were much worse because the softer, prevailing southwest breezes carried the dockside smells right into the town itself. It was a nearly unbearable stench until around five of an afternoon when they died down, leaving the stink to settle heavily back down on the harbor like premature morning dew.

She slowed her pace a little, having seen Tom Kinch's boat easing in, and was curious to see what dregs he had brought in this time from the Banks and from Roanoke Island. She made it her business to know who was coming into town, from which direction, and whether they arrived by local ferry, fisherman, steamer, or pleasure boat. New arrivals of the male gender meant potential customers. Cash-carrying customers, and as long as the hot water lasted in her house, some of those same gents would be clean as boat whistles before they ever touched one of her ladies. Most of them objected very little to bathing beforehand, which was an added advantage since their lust and anticipation was heightened measurably. They were therefore usually closeted in her private rooms less time than they might be otherwise, making it possible for a girl to service more of them per hour. Ernestine grunted. It was a matter of simple economics. Water and firewood were cheap, but it was getting harder and harder to find girls young enough who would work for the percentages she demanded. Her clientele tended to range from lumberjacks to boatmen to farmers. There were also the occasional merchants, not to mention policemen and certain town officials who came and went surreptitiously on Sundays, when her house was supposed to be closed for business.

Beneath her cloche and layers of rouge and sachet, she allowed herself a private, red smile of reproach. It had not been that many years ago when she herself had disembarked from a similar vessel, one that had come down the Dismal Swamp Canal from Norfolk. She'd had to get off at Elizabeth City because she'd not had enough money to travel farther. She was thirty-seven that year, and, having been not-so-politely asked to permanently exit the City of Norfolk (and the City of Richmond before that), she had known that Elizabeth City was going to be her last stop. One way or another.

But her luck and her looks had held out at least long enough for her to establish a decent house of twelve girls, complete with a fine bar with a new player piano, a smoking room, and a dining room replete with good crystal, silverware, and china. Plus, since the Great War had ended, there was a better supply—and class—of customers with fresh dollars they were anxious to spend in high style. After expenses and bribes, Ernestine had done rather well. Better than she had expected to. She estimated that another four or five years would be all it would take for her to return to her home town of Baltimore and open a house that would make her a rich woman. Her crimson smile widened. She was already confident she enjoyed as much local status, popularity, and (most importantly) security as had the famous Elizabeth Tooley. Mrs. Tooley was a prosperous widow and tavern owner of an earlier time in the town, which—most people said—was actually named for her and not for England's Virgin Queen.

Ernestine watched the big buck walk down Kinch's gangway, arrogant as the Prince of Wales, along with several other blacks and a few Banks fishermen. With yet another smile, she turned away from the docks and began walking home. She knew perfectly well who the huge Negro was and that Amanda would clean his pockets along with his clock before the weekend was over. That ignorant cook would probably be *happy* to pay double the usual for one night of pleasure with Amanda, and from the looks of him, one night wouldn't be enough. He'd probably be good for two! Well, if Amanda's thin frame and energy didn't hold out, maybe she would take him up to her own apartment for a tumble or two. He was one prime male specimen, black or no, and she'd known a bunch of men in her time—including a few blacks who'd had enough cash. She hoped Amanda wouldn't get carried away like she sometimes did and forget to protect herself. Rubbers were also cheap.

Ernestine suddenly slowed her pace, scowling, wondering if her decision was a smart one. She normally didn't allow coloreds in her house except as servants, and had only agreed to let Amanda encourage this coal-black giant because she'd heard he was a first-rate, dependable cook. She desperately needed one who wouldn't work for three days and leave her high and dry with a tubful of dirty dishes. Well, no matter; whichever way it worked out, she was sure to profit from Slick Everette's clandestine visit and, after all, business was business.

Two nights later, Amanda Cooper went to her second-floor window and watched the figure of the tall man gradually recede as he walked through the shadows down toward the docks. *So you do shrink up after all.* She didn't hear her boss lady come in, and didn't notice Ernestine until she felt a touch on her bare shoulder.

"Oh . . . it's you, Miz Pike."

Both women watched Slick Everette's retreating figure until it was out of sight, then Ernestine spoke, "There goes a genuine, one-hundred-percent man. I wish he had taken the job I offered him."

"I'm glad he didn't. Did you leave him enough money to get back home with?"

"Certainly. We want him to come back someday, don't we?"

"Speaking for myself, not for a while. He wore me out, and that's no lie. Still and all, he was the best man I ever bedded . . . and you know what else? He was also the kindest. A real gent. I can't say that I didn't enjoy myself."

"And, you made yourself a right smart piece of change to boot."

"Yes." Amanda was wise enough not to remark that her madam had pocketed twice what she had.

"You feel up to working tonight?"

"I don't know if I feel anything at all."

"I'm not surprised. Anyway, you deserve a day off. Go shopping. Buy yourself a new frock, or a pair of new slippers."

"Thank you, but all I want to do is take a long, hot bath and sleep for a week!"

Ernestine sniffed. "I think you'll recover sooner than that, but take tomorrow off. I'm curious, though, Mandy, did he ever tell you what his first name was?"

"No, and I guess I really didn't have time to ask him."

Slick hummed bits of *Old Dan Tucker* all the way back to Pea Island. He had no second thoughts at all about what he had done—and spent. Amanda Cooper was everything he had expected, and then some. Sure, she was a whore, but she was a fine, high-class lady, too. Jus' wasn't very much *of* her. The only bad thing was that she had hollered out loud enough to wake up the whole damn town, lots worse than any black gal would have. But, she had also done things with him and to him he had never even dreamed of. Yessir. Amanda Cooper was worth it, all right. Worth every penny of a cool hundred and twenty dollars! There would surely be some mighty juicy stories to tease his Station friends with. Enough to last maybe another whole year!

Thus, Slick settled back into his normal daily, weekly, and monthly chores on Pea Island. By midsummer of 1920, even he had practically forgotten about his Elizabeth City adventures and was just as surprised as the others when on the Fourth of July, after a mammoth noon meal, someone happened to glance out the window and exclaim, "Be damned. Will you look at *that!*"

They all rushed out onto the porch.

Coming up the neat path from the landing where Tom Kinch's idling boat was temporarily moored, wearing a dress much too short to be either fashionable or decent and a hat that looked like a gigantic sand dollar with feathers waving from it, was a woman every single one of them recognized. In her left hand she held a silly parasol which did precious little to protect her from the sun, and in her right she carried a large picnic basket.

Eight pairs of shocked eyes focused on the determination written all over Miz Ernestine Pike's perspiring face, but she had eyes only for Slick.

She stomped right up the steps and held out the basket to him without so much as blinking.

"This is yours, Mr. Slick-*ass* Everette."

Her voice was like the hiss of an angry snake, "We buried Amanda yesterday. Poor thing died bringing this creature into the world. I never want to see your ugly face again. If you ever show yourself anywhere *near* my house again, I'll have you arrested and will hope to God Almighty they lynch you."

With those words, she turned right around and stalked back to the landing where Tom patiently waited.

The brown infant in the basket was asleep, at least for the moment. Nearly another hour would pass before the stunned men of the Pea Island Life-Saving Station would discover it was a girl-child; and they were further astonished to find that, however furious Miz Pike had been, she had also stuffed several cloth diapers in the basket, as well as two full bottles of milk with rubber nipples attached.

Independence Day that year had come on a Sunday. Just before sunset, and after a lot of animated discussion, Ben Searcy suggested that "Sunday" might be a very good name for the sleeping baby.

That vote was also unanimous.

CHAPTER 3

SINCE COLONIAL times, life on the Banks was never easy. Comforts were few. Men and women who lived there always had to be efficient at any number of hard chores necessary for simple survival. Isolated like orphans from the mainstream of the mainland, they had to learn to be their own doctors and nurses, their own carpenters and boat builders, their own butchers, bakers, and, yes, candle makers. They had to make and mend their own nets, sew most of their own clothes, birth and care for their own babies—all the while trying to eke out a living from the waters around them, and each other. Like most other evolutionary beings, many a Banker developed certain additional skills to a high degree. Ben Searcy was himself a former channel pilot. He also considered himself lucky to have his particular surfmen (who were exempt from any other military service). Besides their normal duty, they had numerous extra attributes which contributed to the betterment of all at the Station:

Lonnie Padgett was by far the best and most-experienced fisherman on the Banks, besides being an expert with needle and thread. Nat Poole, one of Ben's oldest personal friends and a former boatbuilder and master joiner, was their in-residence carpenter. Royce Weeks was an expert hunter, a dead shot with both rifle and shotgun, and was also a gifted woodcarver. An artist, really, who sold many of his duck decoys and seabird carvings to mainlanders.

Of the younger men, Clem Hardison was the strongest swimmer, forever challenging the others to swim races. None could match his stamina or his uncanny ability to hold his breath under water for so long. Amos Turner's lively banjo-picking and Joe Freeman's mournful harmonica would have been sorely missed had they not been there.

Most important of all to Searcy, however, was that all six men had one trait in common. They were all six possessed of a pleasant, genial personality. They got along well together.

And each of those talented men unselfishly contributed to the care of their newest responsibility. Sunday Everette had no mother, but from her earliest days was blessed not only with a doting father, but seven adoring godfathers! Nat Poole built her a fine cradle from heart-of-pine. He also crafted a rocking chair, an item Cap'n Searcy had never allowed in the house before. Every man gladly took turns rocking the baby, who was dressed in tiny cotton gowns and booties Lonnie had cut from old undershirts then stitched with dainty care. Royce Weeks carved any number of wooden toys and rattles. Lonnie Padgett also showed Slick how to make a sugar teat—nothing more than a plain, damp handkerchief tied in a knot, containing a mixture of sugar and honey, which served admirably as a pacifier. Not that one was needed often. Sunday was a quiet baby, and cried only when she was hungry or messed. Diapers and a weekly supply of milk were delivered regularly by Tom Kinch, and Sunday's later diet consisted entirely of nothing more than what the men themselves ate—only crushed and spoon-fed to her by her father and the others, taking turns.

From her first day on Pea Island, she was never left unattended. During the short winters or otherwise inclement weather, her handmade playpen stood in one corner of the big dining room, while the rest of the year she romped in the largest sandbox any child north of the South Seas ever had. When she was nearly three years old, Clem Hardison took her right down to the surf where she learned how to swim within two hours! By the time she was four, she seriously toddled after the men every day, watching them work at their drills.

Shortly before her fifth birthday, a wonderful surprise came for everyone. A new, powered surfboat was delivered to the Station! It was a better present than if each man had been given a brand new automobile. There was great rejoicing among all the crew, and they showed it by taking the boat out for hours at the time—more for play than for work—and included Sunday in their three-day celebration. She sat tall on Clem's lap in the bow, laughing into the spray, looking for all the world, as Ben later remarked, like a miniature figurehead. Sunday simply loved every activity the men did (much of which included her), never had reason to even *think* of anything feminine, and never once had anything that resembled a doll.

Sunday also developed amazing eyesight. She could see mastheads and other objects in both ocean and sound long before any of the men could (even Amos), and was soon taking a regular turn on the raised platform on top of the house the men called the crow's nest. She never missed watching Tom Kinch's boat come in and leave either, staring at crew and passengers with the same silent, standoffish curiosity she showed when she saw other rare white visitors, like the important Coast Guard officers or people the Life-Saving crew occasionally rescued. She exhibited no outward fear or concern because their skin was different than hers, and neither was she comfortable showing natural curiosity as to why that was so. Sunday never said a word to any of the others about this, but it was clear that she wondered about it in her secret moments. When she was in one of those periods of quiet contemplation, the men had sense enough to leave her alone.

She grew rapidly. That is, she grew tall quickly, but that was all. She was skinny, with arms and legs like furnace-tempered tobacco sticks beneath a large head. Yet, being thin didn't mean she was weak. Just the opposite, in fact. All the flesh around her long bones was muscle tougher than beef jerky, and her slender legs carried her fast as the wind when she ran up and down the beach. Slick kept her hair cut short, and unless she was running around nearly naked (which she did most of the time), a stranger would have taken her for a boy—especially since her only clothing consisted of drawers, shift shirts, and duck trousers cut down by Papa Lonnie. She went barefoot most of the year, and except for a minor bout or two with colic when she was an infant, was never sick a day of her life. And, it was about age five when she began to ask a million questions, many of which were rather astonishing, proving over and over she had superior intelligence. Each man except Slick did his best to give her answers (some she seemed satisfied with, others not).

Slick took a different tack. He began teaching her how to fight! He was dead serious about it and methodical in the extreme.

"Now, looka here, honey, when we get done with this, ain't nobody gon' ever mess with you and get away with it. First, you gotta learn how to move. How to dodge. Your face and head is the smallest target your opponent will go after, and the hardest to hit, but don't you know, that's what bad fighters always go for first."

Down on his knees he went.

"You learn how to move outta the way of head punches, you stand a good chance of gettin' your own shots in. That's it. Doin' jus' fine. Watch me, now. See? I moves my head jus' a little bit. This-a-way and that-a-way. Come on, try to hit me again. See? Like that. Now you try it . . . "

Days. Weeks. Months went by, and Slick never missed a day teaching his young pupil.

"Best punch in the world is the jab, honey. The left jab. One after the other. Like a lightnin' bolt. Gets 'em off their balance. Then the straight right. To the body first, then to the head. The jab's your snakebite. Then the straight right, with all your weight behind it. That's your mule kick. That's it. Good. Keep it up. And don't forget to move. Yeah! Good girl. You gettin' it! You gettin' it jus' fine. Damn, it's a shame you ain't a boy . . ."

Sunday paid no mind at all to his last statement. For all she knew, she *was* a boy.

A week after her sixth birthday (the men counted the Fourth of July as her day of birth), a monumental occasion came along. Ben Searcy had to attend a meeting of all Station Keepers at the hotel on Ocracoke Island. At the last minute, he decided to take Sunday along.

"It's time you saw something of the world, Sunday. Put on your clean shirt and pants."

The short trip—not so short in those days—was the first time Sunday had been off her beloved Pea Island,

and a first in many other ways as well. On Ocracoke Island, holding tight to Papa Ben's hand, she was awed by the men and women who were dressed in something besides work overalls or uniforms, and was frightened to death by her first sight of a noisy machine on wheels that Ben said was an automobile. And, it was the first time she laid eyes on white children her own age.

That brief visit also marked the first time other Bankers heard of Sunday Everette.

At the hotel, Ben said, "I have to go inside for a little while, honey. I want you to sit down here on these steps and wait for me."

"We gon' spend the night in there, Papa Ben?"

"No, honey. We wouldn't be allowed to, but this is a government meeting I am required to attend, so they have to let me in. I won't be long."

Ben left her sitting on the steps of the hotel while he went inside to register, pausing long enough to chat with a few colleagues sitting in the lobby. When he came back outside, he found Sunday squirming in the strong grasp of the grinning town constable who stood in front of a small crowd of murmuring townspeople. "This here wildcat belong to you, Cap'n?"

"Yes, she's with me."

"She? This here's a *girl?*"

Ben laughed. "Yes, sir, she doesn't look like one, but she is. What has she done?"

"Nothin' much," the uniformed policeman replied, trying hard to stifle his own laughter. "Just beat the livin' shit outta two of them boys over there is all."

Ben looked across the street, where several white boys of about seven or eight stood, glowering back at him, one with blood running from his nose and an ear.

"Popped a couple of 'em pretty good, she did, and near 'bout bit the ear clean off of that big one," the officer reported, wiping tears from his eyes. "A regular little black barracuda this one is, girl *or* boy."

"I'll take her with me now, Constable. I promise she won't give you any more trouble."

More seriously, the officer jerked his thumb in the direction of the crowd of boys across the street. "I doubt those young fellers will ask for any more neither, next time this one comes around, but right now, I reckon it would be best if you took her somewhere else for a while."

It was then Ben decided, on the spot, to buy Sunday a new dress and a new pair of shoes. Sunday eventually wore the shoes out, but she only wore that dress once—during their overnight stay with one of Ben's friends on Ocracoke Island.

The following morning, they walked back around the pretty little harbor to the ferry landing. Ben explained that outsiders had named it Silver Lake, but back as far as anyone could remember, the local people simply called it "the creek." Sunday was barely listening, though, and was nearly frightened out of her new shoes when they met a bent-over, ugly, female figure coming toward them. Though it was the middle of the summer, the woman wore a filthy, gray Confederate soldier's overcoat, and her hair, equally gray, hung down in stringy strands over her shoulders nearly to her waist. Her sallow face was a map of wrinkles, and from beneath thick, shaggy brows shone one blue eye and one brown one.

Both were fastened onto Sunday, who cringed and tried to hide behind Ben as he tipped his hat politely. "Morning, ma'am."

The ancient hag stopped, nodded briefly at Ben, then bent farther over and reached for Sunday's face with long, bony fingers. She squeezed Sunday's cheeks, forcing the child to look into her eyes for a full thirty seconds. Sunday felt like wetting her pants, and held her breath. The wrinkles below the mismatched eyes stretched into a toothless grin, and a hoarse voice said, "You'll be the one."

With that cryptic utterance, the apparition moved on.

Ben had no trouble urging Sunday forward! After a few minutes, Sunday had caught her breath. "Who was *that?*"

"No one knows her name," Ben answered, laughing softly. "I doubt if she does either. Some say she's a witch, and I'll admit she looks like one, but she's actually harmless. Folks call her the 'Old Woman.' Best midwife on the Banks, and knows more about healing people than any doctor."

"I'd have to be mighty sick 'fore I'd go see her! What did she mean, sayin' I'm the one?"

Ben shrugged. "Who knows? Forget it. Come on, Tom's boat is waiting."

On the ferry voyage home, Ben asked her what had provoked the fight.

Sunday's answer came in the form of a recitation:

"Nigger, nigger, black as tar,
Stuck his head in a 'lasses jar."

"Oh. I see."

"Daddy told me the only people can call us niggers and get away with it is other niggers," she added, "And only when they're funnin' each other."

And that was when Ben made a second decision regarding his young barracuda. It was high time he expanded Sunday's education—supplementing what she learned from Slick. The reference to molasses and the skirmish that had followed would also, over the years, bring a smile back to him when the others referred to Sunday's rapidly growing body as "bunches of hemp rope dipped in molasses." He knew it would take his best efforts to keep pace with instructing this wiry tomboy whose mind was also growing faster than a scuppernong vine.

And try he did. On his next visit to the mainland, he bought a copy of McGuffey's Reader, with which, along with nightly passages from the Bible, he did his best to teach her how to read and write. This turned out to be mostly an exercise in frustration, taxing even Ben's patience. Sunday hated to be indoors, and fidgeted constantly until Ben shrewdly turned her classroom into the island itself, using the fresh-washed beach as blackboard. Tracing with a stick, he spelled words and drew lines in the sand, which made sense to his student.

"See, up here is Kitty Hawk and Kill Devil Hill, where the Wright boys flew the first airplane. Down here is where we are, and south of us is Cape Hatteras. Still farther down is Cape Lookout. Many, many, many years ago all this was probably one long island, but the water from the rivers and sounds—plus the bad storms we get push through the sand now and then—that's what causes the inlets. Can you spell 'inlet?' Here. Take the stick and write it out for me."

Sunday progressed—to some degree—but in spite of Ben's best efforts, she showed scant interest in more than the basics of the three R's, let alone any formal or theoretical studies. She was much more interested in the natural world beneath and around her—the island itself, and the waters of both the sound and the ocean—paying rapt attention to the lessons she learned from Mother Nature and her more practical professors.

By the time she was ten, she was an expert swimmer. Clem had taught her to have great respect for the ocean, but not to fear it. He taught her how to relax in the water rather than fight it, and how to deal with the undertow. ("If it catches you, never try to swim directly towards shore. Swim sideways along the beach until you can touch bottom. It may take a while, but you can always make it if you don't panic. Come on, let's try it!")

Sunday had already taken over cleanup after her father's meals, and by the time she was eleven, was also doing a lot of the cooking. She paid close attention to subjects the men talked about during meals, though she had little or no understanding of terms like "the Crash on Wall Street" in 1929, or the "Great Depression" that had followed it. Her life on Pea Island was hardly affected by any of that. She knew her adoptive Papas had always done extra things to supplement their wages, but now they all talked about harder times ahead. She was innately aware, however, of her sense of duty to the Station; of pulling her own weight, earning her keep, and did what she could to help out.

She quickly learned how to mend Lonnie Padgett's nets, working the needle with the same dexterity and speed she had learned the mending of clothes. She had a sore shoulder for weeks learning how to shoot Papa Royce's shotgun, but soon, with her uncanny eyesight, was able to bring home ducks, geese, and other fowl which she also expertly cleaned and soaked in buttermilk for three days before they were cooked. (After which, Ben seized the moment to tell her, "Sunday, the geese come back here every year because they love to eat those wild peas that grow up there by the marsh. That's why we call it Pea Island." Another oblique lesson learned!)

She pestered Lonnie to take her out in his boat to fish. And Lonnie did, teaching her where, when, and how to find the trout, the drum, the flounder, and when the snapper and blues made their runs.

"What do you do with 'em, Papa Lonnie?"

"Why, once we got enough, we takes 'em over to the fish house at Wanchese, those we don't eat or salt down ourselves. You can make right decent money fishin' and crabbin' if you're good."

She quickly became adept at fishing, as well as setting night nets and surfcasting. One day while about a mile offshore, a school of dolphin appeared, playing like puppies around Lonnie's boat.

Sunday was ecstatic. "What are they, Papa Lonnie?"

"Those are bottlenose dolphins, Sunday. Little bitty whales. They ain't fish at all. They bear and nurse their young same as we do, and have to come up to breathe. See? Looky there. They're friends to us humans, 'specially sailors, and may even be smarter than we are. Never ever kill one. You hear me?"

Sunday's response was to instantly strip off her clothes and dive overboard! Lonnie was so amazed and surprised, he sat there motionless for several minutes watching something he would not have believed had he not witnessed it in person.

Sunday was surrounded by a dozen delighted dolphins who took the girl into their midst with obvious joy. "Look, Papa Lonnie!" she squealed. "I got myself a whole bunch of new playmates!"

That night, after Sunday had gone to sleep, Lonnie could hardly contain himself while telling the others about it.

"Y'all shoulda *seen* it! She swam right on down to 'em, and they played with her jus' like she was one of their own. I ain't never seen the likes of it in my whole life. I could swear they was even talkin' to each other. I had one hell of a time gettin' her back in the boat, and that's the truth. God's my witness, I b'lieve that damn kid is about half fish! She ain't scared of *nothin'!*"

Chapter 4

THE FIRST crisis in Sunday's life came on a sultry afternoon in August, almost a month to the day after her thirteenth birthday. Ben had climbed to the crow's nest to check on Lonnie Padgett, who had been known to doze off now and then after the noon meal. This time, however, Lonnie was wide awake, glasses to his eyes, but not scanning the open sea. He appeared to be looking at something down the beach and didn't notice Searcy until the Keeper spoke to him, "What are you looking at, Lonnie?"

"Huh? Oh. It's funny, Cap'n."

"What is?"

"I don't mean funny, I mean strange." He removed the binoculars from his eyes, turned, and said, "That's Sunday down there, just standin' in the surf. Looks like she's cryin'. You reckon there's something wrong?"

"Let me see."

Ben took the glasses and focused on Sunday's motionless figure. She was maybe a quarter-mile south of the house, standing waist deep in the surf without a stitch on, and tears were definitely rolling down her brown face.

"Looks like it. I never saw her cry once in her whole life. I'll keep watch for you, Lonnie. Go on down there and see what's wrong."

Lonnie hurried down to where Sunday was standing, sobbing, her back to him. "What is it, Sunday? What's the matter?"

Sunday turned her face toward him, her chin trembling. "I . . . I don't rightly know, Papa Lonnie. I'm bleedin' but I ain't hurt!"

"Bleedin'? What you talkin' about? Bleedin' where?"

" 'Tween my legs. I think it started this mornin'."

Two thoughts came to Lonnie in rapid succession: The poor child is thirteen years old now, and has got the curse for the first time. His second thought was more critical.

"Sunday, you come outta that water right this minute. Hammerheads smell any blood, they'll be on you 'fore you can move. Get outta there!"

Sunday obeyed instantly, and as she walked toward him, Lonnie noticed for the first time there were two small protrusions on her chest. He also couldn't help but notice a small patch of pubic hair, and sure enough, there was a little red intermingled with the water trickling down her inner thighs. His next embarrassed thought was that Cap'n Searcy was sure to be watching both of them from the crow's nest. He reached into his back pocket and pulled out his handkerchief, hoping to God it was clean.

His voice was now soft. "Here, honey, fold this up and hold it tight between your legs. Where's your clothes?"

Sunday pointed down the beach a few yards. "There. My pants is messed up."

"It's all right." Lonnie retrieved her shirt and stained pants.

"Listen, Sunday, what you're bleedin' from ain't real serious, but I want you to come with me. Jus' hold that handkerchief in place. It's all right, now. No need to cry. Come on."

Sunday followed him back to the house, and as instructed, sat down on the bottom step of the front porch, holding Papa Lonnie's bandana tight against the place where the blood was coming from.

Ten minutes later, Lonnie returned. "Come on, honey, we're gon' take my boat over to Manteo. My wife will take care of you. You're gon' be all right, now, trust me. Like I said, it ain't serious, but there's some female things you have to learn about."

Ben watched Lonnie launch his boat from the finger pier. As soon as her sails were up, and she was headed toward Roanoke Island, he called the men together for a meeting in their dining room, except for Clem who was sent to the crow's nest. When they were all assembled, Slick included, Ben said, "Men, we need to talk about Sunday."

"Where is she, Cap'n?" Slick wanted to know. "I ain't seen her since breakfast."

"I sent her with Lonnie over to Manteo. She's . . . Well, the pine blank truth of it is, she's growing up. She's not a child any more. Another truth is, none of us have ever thought of her as a girl. We've raised her just the way we would have a boy. She's plain ignorant of womanly things, and I fault myself for most of that, but that's as may be. No sense dwelling on past mistakes. What we need to discuss is what to do with her now."

"What are you suggesting, Cap'n?" asked Royce.

"I had a brief talk with Lonnie. As you know, he's got two girls of his own, maybe a year or two older than Sunday is, and his wife Mary is as good a woman as there is on Roanoke Island. What I'm proposing is that she live with Lonnie's family from now on. As a matter of fact, Mary Padgett has complained many a time to Lonnie and to me that Sunday should live with them, and they are certainly not strangers to her. There's a school there, a church, and something of human society. Sunday needs all of that. We should have done this a long time ago, and again, I fault myself. All of you know I'm just as fond of her as any of you are. Anybody wish to comment?"

"Yes, sir," Joe said. "Lonnie's family ain't no better off than . . . Well, what I'm gettin' at is, how can Mary and Lonnie afford one more mouth to feed?"

Ben sighed. "I've thought of that. I'm proposing that each of us contribute a dollar a month. That should help a little. Lonnie assured me that Sunday wouldn't be a burden to Mary and the other children. She'll help out, too. You all know Sunday. She's one smart Banker, and laziness isn't in her makeup. She doesn't know the meaning of the word."

Slick spoke up. "Cap'n, I want to do what's right by my daughter, too, and I agree with you a hundred percent, but I'll tell you one thing, I'm gon' miss her like hell."

"Me, too," came a soft Greek chorus.

"I know," Ben said. "At least we named her well. She's the sun on a cloudy day for all of us, but we have to think of her welfare, and maybe a little of her future. This Station is no place for a young woman."

The men all fell silent.

Ben's words had hit home. Life was tough enough for a man on the islands. Worse by leap years for women, especially ignorant black women. Every one of the Life-Saving crew knew how hardship was made nearly unbearable when compounded by prejudice. They themselves were lucky, and Ben reminded them of it.

"We're fortunate, men. Fortunate to live like we do. We enjoy steady employment and some respect, and you know as well as I do that we're just about the *only* blacks on the Banks who do. But we'd best not forget that it was all earned by those who came over here to Pea Island before us. They bore the worst of that hatred, overcame it and set the example for us. I suppose that's the main reason we're willing to risk our lives out there in the Atlantic for those few government dollars a month. That, plus the natural pride we take in our work."

He let those words sink in before adding, "Still, it's no place for Sunday to grow up. There's a large community of our people at Manteo. She'll be happy there, I'm sure."

The surfmen all voiced quiet agreement. They could very well serve as Sunday's support group and foster family, those descendants of former slaves who had banded together at Manteo, and many had, over the years, more or less prospered. They walked with heads held high, bowing and scraping to no man, white or otherwise. These were families that had produced all seven of them, and surely could be counted on to give Sunday a leg up.

They took yet another unanimous vote.

Mary Padgett sat back in her front porch rocking chair, folded arms over her enormous bosom, spat snuff across the rail, and eyed her newly adopted daughter. It had been only three weeks since her husband had brought the girl home with him, explained the problem, and sailed right back to Pea Island before she could get a word in edgewise.

"What am I gon' do with you, Sunday Everette?"

No answer.

"Seems like everything I try, it backfires on me."

No answer.

"I give you one of Emma's dresses—you won't wear it. Shoes, neither. I try to fix your hair—you won't let me. I pay good money to put you in Miz Carson's school, what do you do? You beat up on half the class jus' 'cause they tease you a little bit. I take you to church, and what do you do? You sit there and giggle all through both services. What was so funny, anyway? Why couldn't you show some reverence? That's God's house, honey. I thought I'd die from pure shame the way you laughed when Preacher Evans and the others got happy and shouted some. Why'd you do that? Huh? Answer me."

"It *was* funny, ma'am," Sunday replied. "I couldn't help it. I don't see how come you have to go in a church-house and do a lot of wailin' and hollerin' to worship Jesus. I liked the singin', though."

Mary rocked a few times. Maybe she was being just a tad harsh on the girl. Sunday had done more than her share with the housekeeping and all. A lot more than her own two girls had ever done, and hadn't complained a bit. Sunday had listened like a mouse when she'd explained the female monthly problems and the sexual facts of life. Had never asked one single question. Not till the end, when she'd said, "So, the man puts his peter-thing in the woman 'tween her legs where the blood comes from, and that's how they make a baby?"

"Yes, honey," Mary had answered. "But they have to love each other first. They have to love each other a lot, and then wait till they get married. That's what the Bible tells us to do."

And then Sunday had asked, "Is that what *cleavin'* means?"

"That's what it means."

"There's another word for it, too, ain't it?"

"Not one decent folks like us uses."

Remembering that earlier conversation with the girl, Mary leaned over and spat over the porch rail again, and sighed. Sunday Everette was smart enough. Real smart, in fact, but she just didn't fit *in*. She hadn't liked it one bit when she'd had to sleep with Emma in the same bed. Well, for that matter, Emma hadn't liked it either, and was not at all unhappy when Sunday took a blanket and went out on the back porch to sleep with the dog.

That was another thing! Sunday and most other human beings didn't care very much for each other. That was as plain as the nose on Mary's face, but every animal that walked on four legs worshiped her. Followed her around all day long. Dogs, cats, even the chickens and the pigs.

And it wasn't that the girl was careless about personal cleanliness. Lord, she'd walk all the way down to the shore once a day and wade right out in the sound to take her a bath, instead of washing like Emma and the others did, out of the wash basin, using soap and a wash rag. And there wasn't no changin' her, that was for sure. It was too late in her life for that. She was what she was, and Mary reckoned she always would be.

Changing the subject somewhat, Mary asked, "What did you think about Josie Smith's weddin' yesterday?"

"Oh, I liked that weddin'. It was mighty purty. Only—"

"Only what?"

"Josie sure didn't wait to do her cleavin', did she? Emma said Josie was, um, what's that word?"

"Pregnant." Mary frowned. It was true Josie had been six-months gone, and she had showed bad, too. Still, Emma had no right to open her big mouth to Sunday like that. "No, honey, I reckon she didn't wait, but at least she did get married."

Both fell silent for a while.

Mary rocked and spat snuff over the rail several times before Sunday stopped her with a statement right out of the blue.

"I reckon Josie and her husband had some of their fun early."

"*Huh?* What'd you say?"

"Fun. Emma told me it was fun."

"Emma told you what was fun?"

"What you and the Bible calls cleavin'. Emma said it made you feel good, too, even if you don't want to make a baby. She said it hurts a little bit the first time, but after that it feels real good."

Mary felt her temper rise, nearly to the boiling point, but she made a supreme effort to hold it. She had long suspected her fifteen-year-old daughter had been fooling around some with boys in the neighborhood on days when she worked for Mayor Tilley, but until now, she'd had no proof, and Emma was an expert liar. Could look you right in the eye and lie through her teeth.

Sunday continued, "She said boys kissin' you and touchin' you on your private parts was nice, and it was fun to touch their peter-things. Is it?"

Mary let her breath out slow. "Emma don't know what she's talkin' 'bout. Other girls tell her stuff and she repeats it jus' like Willie Sawyer's parrot does."

"You're sayin' it ain't true?"

"I ain't sayin' no such thing. What I am sayin' is a good girl, a righteous girl, don't do stuff like that till *after* she's married. Then it's all right to do it, and yes, it feels good, and yes, it is fun, but only with your husband. Anything else is a bad sin."

"But what if you don't *want* to get married? Emma says she don't want to get married. She says it's more fun to do it with lots of boys, and if you didn't have one, you could make yourself feel good with your fingers. She showed me how, and she was right, too. It did feel right good."

Mary now had trouble keeping control. She would have herself one fine talk with her daughter before this night was over! "Listen to me, Sunday, Emma Mae Padgett is a damn fool girl who don't know what's good for her and what ain't. You forget what she told you. One day a good man will come down the road and you'll know what to do, 'cause you'll know he's the one for you. Your heart will go a-bumpin' and a-thumpin' and you'll feel near 'bout sick 'cause he'll be so good lookin' and he'll be a Christian, upstandin' man, and you can do all those things after you gets married in a proper church. Now, I ain't gon' talk to you no more about Emma's foolishness."

Mary got up, spat one last time, and went inside, calling, "Emma? Emma Mae! You come in here right this minute."

Sunday listened only for a minute or so to the ensuing chastisement, slaps, and wailing that came unfiltered through the screen door, knowing somehow she was at fault for what was happening inside. For the first time in her life, she knew the feeling of guilt. She stood and walked out of the yard. Conscious that there was no wind at all, she looked up at the near-full moon for only a short moment before she started moving. With the hound they called Gyp at her heels, she walked, then ran all the way to Wanchese, getting there sometime around midnight. She knew everyone in the fishing village would be asleep; they'd have to be up and on the water by daylight. But she was careful anyway not to make any noise. After twenty minutes of searching, she found what she was looking for, a light skiff somebody had left the oars in. She untied its painter.

"Go back, Gyp. Go on back home," she whispered.

But Gyp merely sat down, wagging his tail slowly, watching her with sad eyes.

"All right, then. If I'm gon' steal a boat, I might as well steal me a dog, too. Come on, get in."

She silently rowed out to the channel. Using the fortunate boost of the nocturnal ebb tide, she and her four-legged crew made it to Pea Island just as the sun rose like the fiery, unforgiving eye of God Himself.

CHAPTER 5

"PLEASE, PAPA Ben, don't make me go back. I'm sorry I stole the boat, and I'll take it back if Papa Lonnie will loan me his to tow it with. Gyp wouldn't go home, so I brought him with me."

"What happened, Sunday? Why'd you run away?"

Ben sat on the porch steps with her, having found her and the dog asleep on the porch just after dawn. That a thirteen-year-old girl had walked more than ten miles from Manteo to Wanchese, and then rowed all the way across the sound, filled him full of both admiration and amazement. Such a trek would have been hard for any one of his *men,* and it had naturally taken him quite a while to wake her up to demand an explanation.

"I couldn't keep outta trouble," she blurted. "Everything I did was wrong, and I got Emma in a lot of trouble, too. Please, Papa Ben. If I have to go back over there, I'll die. My home is here. With you. Miz Mary told me 'bout how free they were, and what a good livin' they all had, but it ain't true. I know they ain't slaves any more, and no white men beats them with horsewhips like you told me they did before Mister Abraham Lincoln came along and freed them after that big war, but—"

"But they *are* free, Sunday. We're all free now."

"You are, and Daddy is, and the others here at the Station; but they ain't. Miz Mary and her oldest daughter has to work three days a week for a big-shot white man jus' so they can have enough money to pay their bills. I went with her one time. His family treated us like dirt. Acted like if they touched one of us, they'd have to take a hot bath or else they'd get real sick and die. His wife called us 'colored people.' The way she said it sounded worse than calling us tar-black niggers! Miz Mary has to bow and scrape, and say 'yes, sir' and 'no, sir' and hang her head down and all jus' the same as if she was a slave. I saw it with my own eyes. That ain't all, neither. Those boys at Miz Carson's school teased me and said my mother was a whore. Said I was nigger trash and a bastard."

"Sunday, you can't afford to look at things that way. You shouldn't even listen to childish tripe like that."

"Who can help it? Daddy told me all about my Mama. Said she was a fine, purty lady and had real nice manners. Said he couldn't help it she was white. Well, maybe my mother was a white whore and maybe I am a bastard, a black bastard, but here on Pea Island with you and my other Papas and out on the water I'm jus' as free as them gulls and dolphins. I'm beggin' you, Papa Ben. Please. If you send me back over there, I'll jus' run away again."

Ben Searcy put his arm around the girl's shoulders. He couldn't answer her right away, because his own throat was constricted. He felt the old choking returning. The gagging return of the resentment he had spent years learning to control if not totally repress. The old bile-flavored bitterness of unfairness that tasted like quinine. Worse than quinine. Worse than anything. He rocked her gently.

After another few minutes, with a low, hoarse voice, he said, "No, Sunday, I won't send you back. You'll have to return that boat you took, and apologize for taking it, but I'll never force you to go anywhere you don't want to go. Ever again."

TOM LEWIS

He paused. Took another deep breath, then added, "Besides, we need a new cook."

Sunday stiffened. "New cook? Why?"

Ben cleared his aching throat. *By God, this is one thing I'm going to do without taking a vote.* "Because your Daddy's gone, Sunday. Sneaked out of here on Tom's boat the day after you left. We haven't seen hide nor hair of him since. I guess he got restless one time too often. He also took the few dollars you had saved in your coffee can. I suppose we will just have to pay you his salary, since you had been doing most of his work anyway. What do you think about that?"

Sunday's eyes filled with tears, partly because of the news about her Daddy, partly because of the job offer, but mostly because she knew she wouldn't be banished again from her precious island.

"What do I think? I think you're jus' as fine a man as Mister Lincoln was, that's what. And I'll be a good cook for you, too. Maybe not as good as Daddy was, but a good one all the same. Thank you, Papa Ben. Thank you. I'll . . . be a . . . good . . . "

Ben started to tell her something else, but realized she was fast asleep again. He picked her up and carried her inside, laid her down on Slick's cot, and after washing his face with cold water, called the men down to the sitting room, wondering how he would be able to relate what had happened without embarrassing Lonnie Padgett.

During the next few months, in order to wrest her mind away from unpleasant thoughts, Ben made it a point to take Sunday with him on more exploratory trips from one end of the Banks to the other. Using the pretext of paying courtesy calls to a few of the other Stations (which he was careful to explain were spaced at more-or-less even intervals of several miles, all the way down the eastern seaboard to Florida), he broadened her knowledge of as much of the Tarheel State as she was interested in. It was a relaxed, easy-to-teach but meaningful lesson, combining history, geography, and sociology.

Leaving the tiny village of Duck, just south of the Virginia line, he took pains to explain how the geophysical phenomenon of the reef of sand evolved.

"It took a very long time, Sunday. Maybe hundreds of years. Look at all the land south of us, between the ocean and the sound. It's hard to believe that all this used to be a big forest. It was wild. All of it was growing in a natural way."

"What happened, Papa Ben?"

"White men came down here. The Indians who lived here first treated the land a lot better than the white men who drifted in here and ran them out. Those men not only cut down all the trees and destroyed most of the other vegetation, they failed to plant anything to replace them with."

"Why'd they do that?"

"Well, they just didn't know any better. They didn't realize it takes a hundred years to replace a full-grown oak tree."

"That's a real shame, ain't it?"

"It certainly is, Sunday. The word for it is 'conservation.' It means you should never destroy something that can't be replaced, at least in a reasonable period of time. Well, Mother Nature covered it all up with sand. And the wind blew the sand, piling it up." He swept his arm south. "It was like a plague. All the way down to Nags Head it was the same."

Ben was certain Sunday could feel the passion of his disgust, but he didn't want her to be sad during the rest of the trip. "Still, not everybody did bad things. Farther south, I'll show you something really good that happened."

At Kill Devil Hill, he led her up the face of the large, steep-sloping dune, feeling the same steady wind that allowed Wilbur and Orville Wright to launch their first flight. "There's talk of someday building a fine monument to those hard-working boys right here on this spot, Sunday. I hope I live long enough to see it."

"Me, too, Papa Ben. That would be somethin' to see. And you'll see it, all right. We'll watch it together."

Ben laughed. "It certainly would. I'll tell you something else good that happened."

"What?"

"My own commanding officer giving me permission to let you live at the Station House. I never mentioned it before, but I can tell you now that I had to do some kind of talking before he agreed."

"I'll bet!"

"You know, on this very trip, you have learned that most of the Life-Saving crews take long work breaks in summer, but at Pea Island, we don't."

"I never thought about it. Why don't you?"

"Because for us, that Station House is *home*. Being black men, I doubt if any of us could find one to equal it anywhere else. Still, all of us need work breaks every now and then. That's why I'm happy to give each of them, by turn, several days off during the slack part of the year—especially Lonnie, who needs the extra time with his family.

"It was a little different with your Daddy. I had no official control over him. You'll remember how he took off on his own every now and then, but not for long, and he always came back. But that last time he stayed gone. I guess we will never know why."

They walked a while in silence, and then Sunday said, "Papa Ben, is that the reason you and the others take so many chances? Because the government gives you a good home?"

"No, Sunday. The reason is because of those brave black souls who went before us. Those men went on well over a hundred successful rescues. No, for us it's that thing called duty, and how we honor them; and besides, we're pretty good at it, or haven't you noticed?"

"It's just that I worry about you. All of you."

"We know that, honey. Hey, are you ready to see some more?"

At Ocracoke, Ben rented a boat and took her across the inlet to Portsmouth Island. Only a few abandoned, rotting buildings and shacks, like lonely gravestones, stood as fading testimony to a once-vibrant community.

He took her with him on a couple of inland journeys as well; one to Elizabeth City, and one to the port city of Beaufort. She didn't think much of Elizabeth City, but was properly impressed with the big ships coming in and going out of Beaufort Inlet. She was also astounded at the sight of actual paved streets, trains, automobile traffic, and, most of all, houses with indoor toilets!

"Sure beats our privy, don't it," Sunday said, her voice feather light. "I won't ever forget how Papa Nat carved that little wooden seat to go over the one-holer so I wouldn't fall in."

On her fifteenth birthday, after they had all polished off the four-layer cake she had baked, Sunday announced, "I'm gon' be a fisherman and a hunter. I'm gon' build me a boat and sell fish and turtles and game to all the folks on the Banks; and when I've got enough money, I'm gon' build me a house right down the beach from here. Pea Island is where I want to live forever."

No one laughed. As a matter of fact, there wasn't one at the table who didn't think she could—and *would*—do exactly what she said she would. But she needed help, and wasn't shy about asking for it.

"Papa Nat, will you help me build me my boat?"

Nat beamed. "In my spare time? 'Course I will, and she'll be one fine vessel, too. But first, you have to save up enough money to buy some good wood."

"I already got some saved. How much will the wood cost?"

"We'll have to first decide on what kind of boat to build, then we'll know how much she's gon' cost. A sloop of some type, probably. Good materials ain't cheap. We'll need cypress for the keel, stem, and ribs, and some quality cedar for the planks. Then there's the bronze fasteners, a fine fir mast and sails, and we'll need to build a steamin' box for bendin' her ribs and planks, and a shelter over her while we work, too. All that costs money."

Ben and the other men knew Nat had gone through this litany to see if Sunday would be discouraged by such a daunting and expensive adventure, but she wasn't. Not in the least.

"When can we start?"

All the men laughed. "By God," Clem said. "She means it! I'm betting my new jackknife that boat'll be the fastest sloop on the Banks, too. Sunday's already a damn good sailor. As good as any man here, and I'll bet she's already picked out a name for it."

"You're right, Papa Clem, I have. I'm gon' name her my *BLACK DOLPHIN*."

Unfortunately, Sunday's grand plans for boat- and house-building were postponed by President Franklin Delano Roosevelt's New Deal. It was on a Monday afternoon in the spring of 1937 when she came running into the Station House, yelling, "Papa Ben, Papa Ben! There's a whole bunch of men pitchin' tents up by the Oregon Inlet. Looks like a whole army!"

Ben sighed. "Calm down, Sunday. I know about them. They are on the island to do some government work."

"What kinda work?"

"Two things, primarily. First though, you remember how I told you about how careless the original Bankers were about conservation?"

" 'Course I do."

"Well, those men are going to try to build up the sand dunes to keep back the natural erosion, build sand fences, and plant grass. The other thing here on Pea Island is to keep some of those professional hunters and all those rich folks' hunt clubs away. If people like that are allowed to keep on killing those waterfowl the way they do now, there soon won't be any birds left. Of any kind. But the main thing is, President Roosevelt is trying to give a lot of young men some honest work. If I were you, I'd just stay out of their way. Ignore them. I doubt if they'll be on the island long. At least, I hope not."

Sunday listened to all this, but knew it would be impossible to ignore the new invaders. Anyway, she had some ideas of her own. The next day, she put on her best shirt and pair of pants, and with Gyp at her heels, walked into their camp. Remembering the hundred times she'd heard how her father had obtained his job at the Station, she politely asked around, and was finally facing Mr. Samuel Kingsley, the foreman.

"Mr. Boss Man Kingsley, my name's Sunday Everette and I'm gon' make you a deal . . . "

Thirty-two-year-old Sam Kingsley was a rangy, stone-hard man from the mountains of Tennessee. He had already bossed railroad gangs, prison gangs, and even bridge-building gangs in his time. He knew how to get the most out of men, even the sorry mixture of runaway farm boys, Negro boys, drifters, and no-accounts he had now. Not more than a half dozen of them could be counted on to actually put in eight honest hours of labor. The rest needed constant supervision and performed adequately only when they thought he was watching them, which he did, all day and most of the night. There was only one thing the thirty-five boys in his gang feared more than his fists, and that was the humiliating kick in the backsides he gave one when they were fired and run off from the camp. That was like being tarred and feathered. Loss of a job, any job, could be the ruin of every man jack among them; and for most, Roosevelt's CCC and WPA camps were the last chance they'd likely get before going on the dole—where indeed many had already been. In return for good (or at least half-decent) work, the government paid them more than the majority of them had ever earned, and Sam paid them with the bonus of a monthly good word. Arguments and fights were rare. He tolerated no nonsense, and did his best to make sure that every single man was too tired at night to do anything more than go to sleep.

Sam gazed at the face of the colored girl who was every bit as tall as he was and smiled. This girl wasn't a hundred-percent Negro. No way! Her language usage aside, she looked like some African princess disguised as a stowaway. She had natural bearing, and aristocratic beauty to go along with it. Her satin-smooth skin was the color of milk chocolate. Her lips were full, but not overly so. Her nose was not flat. Her eyes didn't protrude, certainly not like the bloodshot, watery, tired eyes of hopelessness he had seen in so many black women before. No, this was one proud young woman. And, there was no doubt of her womanhood! The faded shirt and cutoff trousers she was wearing did nothing to hide the splendid, well-formed body beneath, full on the top and slim in the hip—and she was certainly not afraid of him. Probably wasn't afraid of anything.

"Is that so?" he answered, affably.

"Yes, sir. I'm the best fisherman and hunter on this island, and the best cook, too. For two dollars a week, I can supply your crew with plenty of ducks, geese, good fryin' fish, and turtles. For two more, I can cook 'em, too. They'd be the best eatin' these men ever had. Guaranteed! I cooks for all the men at the Station down there. You can ask 'em."

Sam laughed. "Well, now, somehow I believe you, but how could you cook for those men and us, too? You mean every other day?"

"No, sir. Every day. I got it all worked out: if I can borrow one of your wagons and a pony, I can cook breakfast there at the Station, cook yours at the same time, bring it here in the wagon, then cook your dinner up here, take theirs down in the cart, and cook their supper before I cook yours."

"What if we already have a cook?"

The girl named Sunday narrowed her eyes, and cocked her head. When she smiled, she was downright beautiful, with the whitest teeth he'd ever seen. "A real cook?" she said slyly. "Or one of the work gang who prob'ly hates it? Couldn't he be more use to you doin' something else?"

Sam pursed his lips. *Add cunning and shrewdness, Sam.* "You got me there."

" 'Course, now," the chocolate charmer went on, in a more serious tone, "my deal don't include no cleanup. Every man can do his own. There's a big ocean down there, and sand that'll clean any kinda plate and pot. Hey, now, I don't mean for you to buy no pig in a poke. I'll cook you one free supper tonight, and then you can decide."

Sam chuckled. "I don't know if you're a good cook, or not, but you're certainly a pretty good salesman. All right, I'll agree to the test, but I'll tell you what we need more than anything."

"What?"

"Something for these 'skeeters. I've never seen anything like 'em in my life."

The girl's sly smile reappeared. "I don't know why, but they don't bite me, and I know they can be mighty fierce. I'll bring some stuff with me tonight that might help, and I won't charge you a penny for it. Y'all gon' smell like sugar cookies, but it'll keep the little critters off of you."

"Guaranteed?"

"Guaranteed! Then we have a deal?"

Sam sighed in surrender, and pointed to the large tent. "You'll find the water wagon and the cook wagon in there. Help yourself."

That night, singing chorus after chorus of Old Dan Tucker, the tall black girl cooked and served the best fish stew he had ever tasted, with sweet tea and cornbread, plus a wonderful peach cobbler. Better still, she had brought several bottles of vanilla extract, showed them all how to smear it on their exposed skin, and demonstrated how to make small smoke pots to set before their tents at night. Her homespun remedies worked far better than anything they had ever tried before, and the men never smelled better, himself included!

Sam gave her the job.

Her third night in camp, humming along, Sunday was happily up to her elbows in another stew when she felt someone touch her arm. She turned, looking into the soft eyes of a slender, handsome boy as tall as herself, his skin only half a shade darker.

"Excuse me, Miss. Would you like a little help?"

Sunday stopped what she was doing, immediately realizing that Miz Mary Padgett had been a prophet. She felt her heart go a-bumpin' and a-thumpin', and instantly knew that her man had come down the road.

CHAPTER 6

"WHAT'S YOUR name?"

"George. George Harris, Jr."

Sunday forced her concentration back to her job. "Sure, you can help. That bucket of potatoes needs peelin'. Here, use this little knife, and wash each one 'fore you peel it."

With a smile that shook her again to her toes, the boy took the knife and went to work. Not a word more of conversation passed between them until after supper, when he approached her again and said, "As usual, it was all delicious, Sunday. May I walk you back to the Station?"

"Walk? I take the horse and wagon. You know that."

"Then I'll ride back with you, that is if you don't mind."

"What about Mister Kingsley's rules? Don't you have to go to your tent?"

"Curfew isn't until ten. I can be back before then."

"Well, then it's all right, I reckon."

George helped Sunday climb up to the wagon seat, then slid over beside her. Sunday clicked at the old mare, and they drove out of the camp, not noticing that at least two dozen pairs of eyes were watching them leave.

They hadn't covered more than two hundred yards before Sunday stopped. She jumped down, George right behind her. She pulled the reins over the mare's head and began slowly walking, leading the animal behind her.

They walked in silence for a few minutes before George said, "It's a beautiful night, isn't it?"

"Yep." Sunday looked at him. "You don't talk like the other black boys. Where you from, George Harris, Jr.?"

"My home is in Washington, D.C. My father's a doctor there."

"That so? You mean a real *doctor* doctor?"

"Yes. A physician. Eye, ear, nose, and throat."

"Imagine that! Then, what you doin' down here with this bunch of no-goods and white trash?"

George laughed. "That's a fair enough question. I was supposed to start college at Fisk University last fall, but I wanted to work a year first. It's hard to explain, but I wanted to see for myself what really hard work was like, and do some studying at the same time. I plan to do a premed major, and eventually I want to be a psychiatrist."

"What's that?"

"A doctor who works with the human mind."

"I get it. You're studyin' these no-account boys to see what makes them tick?"

"Something like that. It has been quite an experience, too. I've learned a lot."

"They pay you same as the others?"

"No, I wouldn't qualify."

Sunday stopped dead in her tracks, cocked her head at a severe angle, and exclaimed, in obvious disbelief, "You mean you're doin' all that hard work for free? Are you crazy?"

George laughed again. "No, Sunday, but I'm certainly finding out a lot about what makes people go crazy. What about you?"

"Me? What about me?"

"Were you born here? On Pea Island?"

The mare, wanting her oats, nudged Sunday, who stroked her velvet nose. "Patience, Missy, we're goin'."

She resumed her slow walk, and answered George.

"Here? No, I was born over to Elizabeth City, but I've lived here all my life with the Life-Saving crew."

"And how old are you now?"

"Sixteen. How old are you? You talk like you're a hundred."

"I'm eighteen and a half."

They continued down the beach for a while in self-conscious silence. Sunday didn't think there was any need to tell George about *her* parents. This walk under the moon was a dream anyway. She'd probably wake up any minute. Had to be a dream, didn't it? She couldn't remember ever feeling this lightheaded. Light-footed, too. It was like she could walk with him like this all the way to New Inlet. Maybe even walk right *across* it all the way down to the Hatteras lighthouse! After a few more paces, she willed herself to stop.

"This is halfway home, George. You'd best turn around and go on back or you'll get in trouble with Mister Kingsley's curfew."

"You're right. May I walk with you again tomorrow night?"

"Why? So you can study *me?*"

"No, Sunday. Because I like your company. The days are full of work that's hard, as you know, and most of the time with unpleasant men. Like I said, these are beautiful nights, and I would enjoy them a lot more with a beautiful girl. It's just that simple. Good night, Sunday. See you tomorrow."

Three nights later, after finally coming home, not realizing that a slightly worried Keeper had been waiting up for her, she gushed, "Papa Ben, he's the purty-est damn thing I ever laid eyes on! He smart, and he's educated. Talks real fine, like you do. His daddy's a doctor and he's gon' be a doctor, too. A head doctor, and he's got beautiful manners, and he talks to me like I was a *lady*. I want to be a lady, too, Papa Ben. You gotta help me."

"Whoa, Sunday. Slow down. You are a lady. A young woman already and every bit a lady."

"Oh, you know what I mean. I ain't refined and all. I sound like a dumb nigger gal when I talk. You gotta help me. Please."

Ben sighed. "Well, I'll try. First off, you don't call a man pretty. Men call women pretty—and that's 'pretty,' not *purty,* and women call fine-looking men handsome. Next thing you can do is stop saying *ain't* all the time. *Think* a little before you say something—make that something without profanity."

"Profanity?"

"Curse words. It doesn't take much effort to do that."

"I will. I'll do better. I promise."

"You might also do more reading. You can read quite well. Your problem is, you simply don't do enough of it. Never have. But I don't see how you have time enough now to do anything extra. You're working day and night, seven days a week. That's too much, even for a sixteen-year-old, strapping six-footer like you. I think I'll have a talk with Mr. Kingsley myself about that. You go on to bed. You need to get as much rest as you can. You don't want to look like the Old Woman of Ocracoke before you're twenty, do you?"

And Ben did have his talk with the CCC gang boss. Both agreed that Sunday should have one day a week off from both jobs, on her name day. In the days that followed, he was more than pleased that when she had two, five, or fifteen minutes to spare, her nose was in one of his books, a newspaper, or in Webster's dictionary! Better late than never, Ben thought. He painfully remembered how dismal a failure he had been with her before. She didn't shirk her duties, either, and he and his men were mildly amused at her new, more feminine ways, even though she made no mention of anything so drastic as sewing or wearing a dress! Each of them knew perfectly well the reason for Sunday's sudden change. That the girl was in love was written all over her face. Ben privately, wisely, cautioned each of them not to tease her or embarrass her about George Harris, though there wasn't a one of them who thought her infatuation with the doctor's handsome son would last more than a few weeks. A month at most. Surely not longer than the end of summer, and when the boy went off to school, Sunday would probably forget about him in no time at all.

They should have all known better.

On the fifth night, again about halfway between the camp and the Station House, George casually reached for her hand, and not more than ten minutes later, Sunday stopped, turned to face him and said, "Would you like to kiss me, George Harris Jr.?"

George replied, in a husky voice, "You know I would. More than anything in the world."

Their first kiss was tentative. Chaste. Only a meeting of closed lips that lasted a mere two seconds, but it was enough to set Sunday's insides on fire. She somehow sensed to do more would bring her trouble, and him, too, but when she pulled away from his embrace, she said, "That was the nicest thing I ever felt. Did you feel good, too?"

"Yes. It was wonderful, Sunday. And so are you."

"Can you swim?"

"Yes. Of course I can swim. Why?"

"Ever been sailing?"

"No. I've been on boats before, but never on a sailboat."

"Tomorrow's Sunday, and I don't have to work, thanks be to Papa Ben and Mister Kingsley. Come on down to the Station House 'bout eight tomorrow morning. I'll borrow Papa Lonnie's boat and take you out. There's something I want you to see."

They were lucky with the weather. George quickly forgot how badly Lonnie's boat reeked of fish, just as rapidly forgot his initial nervousness at being so close to the water, and marveled at the way Sunday handled it, expertly racing south and then through the New Inlet into the open Atlantic. It seemed as though the ocean, just for them, was on its best behavior as well, with not so much as a single whitecap as far as the eye could see. The Atlantic was dressed in its Sunday best and minding its manners. It was as if God, resting again on the Sabbath, had commanded the seas to do likewise. The water reflected the gorgeous colors of the sky, and on a sweet breeze of no more than five to eight knots, they were soon a few miles offshore, a little south of Pea Island. Only the hint of the beach could be seen. The Station House and dunes looked like a toy building set among anthills.

A few screaming gulls followed them, hoping Sunday would be fishing, and that they might get the scraps. Sunday *was* fishing, in a way, but not for frying fish. She kept up a steady stream of conversation with George, keeping one eye on her sail trim, and the other one somewhere on the horizon.

They hadn't been out two hours before she discovered what she wanted George to see.

"There they are! Hold on."

She tacked, and sailed right into the path of a pod of gamboling dolphins. They instantly changed course, as if they recognized her, and began their joyful antics. They adjusted their lightning-fast speed to the much slower vessel, jumping high out of the water, and performing incredible acrobatics. It was as though they were competing with each other, showing off their individual skills.

Laughing, Sunday seemed to forget about her passenger, and tacked time and time again. Each time she did, the streamlined animals also changed direction, coming so close to the boat George could have reached out and touched them. It was an experience he wouldn't have thought possible had he not been a part of it.

What happened next was something else he could never have believed. Not in his wildest imagination. Sunday hove to, put the sail aback, and stripped off her clothes. Before George could react at all, she was over the side. He caught his breath, and held it, first in fear for her, then in total awe as she actually swam with the handsome animals, her own brown body almost as supple and sleek as theirs. George watched in near disbelief when she grabbed the dorsal fin of one of them, who took off at an amazing clip, with Sunday holding on for a breathtaking ride. The dolphin took her perhaps a quarter mile away to the south, turned in a wide arc, and brought her back to the boat. It occurred to George that she had done this before. Perhaps many times.

Sunday treaded water two feet away from the boat.

"Come on in, George. These are friends of mine. They won't hurt you. It's fun!"

George could see right away that Sunday was breathing quite rapidly, but quickly saw that it was from exhilaration and not exhaustion. Before thinking twice about it, George found himself stripping down to his underwear, and in the next instant, jumped overboard. The following half-hour would be burned forever into his memory: those graceful, sculpted shapes with their sympathetic, nearly human eyes, now almost cuddling, now darting away—never in a threatening way—accepted him into their midst as well! And with them, the absolutely unbelievable form of Sunday Everette, nude, innocent, smiling, and unashamed, and uninhibited as were her sea-cousins swimming around them both. George had no idea when he lost his shorts, but he gave it no thought whatsoever. He knew he was feeling a kind of freedom and happiness not granted by the Almighty to very many of the human race.

Eventually, they climbed back into the boat. Back into reality, and after catching his breath, George realized he was staring at her nakedness with full and complete understanding that what he was looking at was a female body in its most perfect form—a living anatomy class he could never have envisioned, and one he could barely comprehend. The next thing he became aware of was that Sunday was looking at his body as well, her eyes showing something more than mere curiosity. They moved toward each other then, and beneath the caress of the early summer sun, took the first sure steps of the kind of spontaneous, irrevocable courtship God had provided His air-breathing creatures with since time began. Mere words had never been necessary, nor were they needed now, at least not many. Only three were whispered— three of the oldest in any language.

And from the crow's nest, Ben Searcy slowly dropped his binoculars, tears forming in his eyes. He turned away from the Atlantic and faced the gentle breeze, knowing full well that even if he'd had the right to, he could no more have stopped Sunday's surrender that fine morning than he could have held back a major hurricane.

CHAPTER 7

THOSE SUMMER days of 1937 passed rapidly. Too quickly for sweethearts, but George and Sunday managed, in spite of her work and his, to spend every minute they could together. George missed his curfew more times than he made it, but Sam Kingsley looked the other way, knowing exactly what was happening, also aware that if he put his foot down, George Harris would simply quit the crew. George was a special case. Not actually a regular anyway, but he had always pulled his weight with the best of them, and Sam would not have wanted to lose him.

For his part, Ben Searcy hinted to his men that each might pitch in to help Sunday with her after-meals cleanup, which they all did quite willingly, and without teasing her. They all knew the CCC crew would be gone by October, and none wished to deny Sunday an ounce of a happiness that could only be temporary.

For George and Sunday, their precious weekly free day was usually spent on the water, farther and farther away from land, and they managed to also find a spot close to New Inlet, behind a dune ridge that was high enough to block the afternoon sun. There, they made love on a blanket, drank sweet tea, and talked in the universal language and tones of lovers. Sunday told George of the heroic deeds of the Life-Saving men past and present. George read to her short stories of O. Henry and Poe. And, they talked softly about their future.

"It'll be a long time, Sunday. It takes eight years to become a doctor, and I won't be able to earn money enough to support a wife until then."

"I can wait. I love you, George Harris, and I can wait right here on Pea Island until you get done. And, you'll be proud of me, too. I'll sew me some fine dresses and learn how to talk right, and let my hair grow out—"

"And wear shoes, too?"

"Yep. Shoes and stockings jus' like a regular lady."

"I love you just the way you are, but . . . "

"But what?"

"Like I said, it's a long time."

"Well, you can come back every now and then to see me, can't you?"

"Nothing could keep me from it. You know, I wrote to my father about you yesterday."

"You did? What did you tell him?"

"That I had met the most amazing, the most wonderful and beautiful girl and that I was hopelessly in love with her."

"I hope you didn't tell him everything!"

George laughed. "Not likely. He'd kill me if he knew we had . . . you know. He'd cut me off for sure. Maybe disown me."

Sunday frowned. "I don't see why. It's all right if we love each other ain't it?—I mean, *isn't* it? Someday we're gon' get married, in a real church and all."

George stood and stretched. "Well, I can only hope he will understand. Come on, let's go swimming. I'm burning up—in more ways than one!"

They ran from their private beach into their private ocean, wishing their summer of discovery could last forever.

It was to last barely two more weeks. On the first day of August, Sunday drove to the camp and began cooking the supper meal: cured ham, string beans, cabbage, mashed potatoes and ham gravy, cornbread and biscuits. She had brought ten sweet potato pies she had baked at the Station House. Halfway through serving the pie, it dawned on her that George wasn't there. *Maybe he's in his tent. Could he be sick? Asleep? Surely he wouldn't sleep right through supper. Maybe he really is sick.* She kept on working, noticing many of the boys who were usually so talkative were eating in silence. Few spoke to her. She finally knew something was terribly wrong. She put the pie pan down, and walked to the head of the big table where Sam Kingsley sat, stirring his coffee, his eyes averted.

"Where's George, Mister Kingsley?"

The large man heaved himself up, took Sunday by the elbow and led her away from the tables, down toward the surf. In the short time he had known this amazing girl, he had developed genuine affection for her, and tremendous respect. He hated that he had to be the one to give her bad news. After a few dozen steps, he stopped, turned to her and gently said, "He's gone, Sunday."

"What you mean, gone?"

"His pa came and got him right after three this afternoon. Cleared out his tent and they left on the mail boat. I imagine they're well on their way to Norfolk by now."

"Gone? Jus' like that? And he didn't leave me no message?"

"No, Sunday. I'm sorry. Truly sorry."

Sunday nodded, looked down at her toes for a moment, then trudged back up to the camp. She climbed up to the wagon seat and drove away from the camp without a word. Halfway home, she stopped, waded out into the surf, and allowed herself to cry. It was only the second time in her life she had, and was the next to the last time she ever would.

Without being told, Ben and the others knew what had happened by looking at her face the next morning at breakfast. By turn, each man glanced at the Keeper for a cue, but Ben gave each of them a slight shake of the head that told them to say nothing. Late that night, long after Sunday had returned again from cooking at the camp, Ben looked into the kitchen, but she had moved her cot. He found it, Sunday, and Gyp up in the crow's nest. She wasn't asleep; just lying there, looking up at the stars, the dog at her feet.

He sat down beside her, Indian fashion, and waited a long time before she finally said, "It hurts, Papa Ben. It hurts bad."

"I know it does. Hurts like a shark bite, but it will pass."

"I don't think so."

"It will. It did for me, and it will for you, too."

Sunday turned onto her side so she could look at his face.

"What you talkin' about?"

"I also lost someone I loved deeply. Therefore, I know what you're feeling right now, and I also know it will eventually go away."

"Who was it? Some girl you was in love with?"

Ben nodded. "Yes. A long time ago. Remember Miss Carson at the school at Manteo?"

"Yes. Was it her?"

"No. Her sister. A wonderful woman named Edith. She died a few years before you were born, and I thought at the time I would too, but as you can see, I didn't. I suppose losing her is yet another reason I chose to live here the way I do. Listen to me, Sunday, I'm not going to tell you that you will quickly forget George Harris. No one ever forgets a first love, but the pain of loss will fade into your memory like a scar from a fish-scale cut. We each of us have a built-in strength we never know about until it's needed. Yours has already kicked in. You just don't recognize it yet. It's that kind of resilience that allows us to get on with our lives. You're a strong girl, Sunday. Tough as an oyster shell, and this misfortune will only make you tougher. You'll see."

"You reckon there'll ever be another George?"

"Probably, but there's never any guarantee."

"Why'd he leave without seein' me or at least leavin' me a message?"

Ben sighed, dreading telling Sunday now what he should have told her years ago. About the *haves* and the *have-nots*. Of class structure. Of the way things are in the real world, away from her sheltered life on Pea Island.

"My guess is his father came for him, threatened him, and didn't give the boy any choice in the matter."

"Because I'm what I am and he's a rich boy?"

"I doubt if George's father is all that rich, but I do happen to know that a year of college at a good school like Fisk can cost more than a thousand dollars a year. Still, basically, you are correct. It is because you're what you are and he's what he is. You come from two different worlds. The only thing that would have made it worse is if one of you had been white. Our place in this thing we call society, civilization, especially here in the United States, is determined by money and the color of our skin. However harsh, unfair, and unjust that may be, that's the way it is. It has nothing whatsoever to do with a person's character, except to build it up, I suppose; and in the end it's who you are, not what you are that counts the most. This you already know. Given time, you may forget George Harris, but you will never forget that."

"You think he will ever come back, Papa Ben?"

Ben looked at the hound who was watching him with one sleepy eye. "No. The George Harrises of this world never do. Now, you find a man who loves you like old Gyp here, he'd come back. Wouldn't he, Gyp?"

Ben was rewarded for his words by one halfhearted thump of Gyp's tail, one lovely smile, and a squeeze of the hand from Sunday, who turned over and instantly fell asleep.

Sunday, Ben, and the others at the Station were taken by surprise when Sam Kingsley sent word they were all invited to a party he was throwing for the CCC men on Labor Day.

The younger surfmen opted to go that Monday evening, at least for a while. Sunday was also given the day off since the men of the camp were barbecuing two pigs, but she volunteered to furnish the *fixin's*—brown beans, cole slaw, and cornbread. There was one other rare treat the gang boss had provided for the occasion: two barrels of beer. None of the men were used to having alcohol available at camp, and by late afternoon—a very hot one—most of them were well on their way to feeling no pain. Joe, Clem, and Amos were forbidden to so much as taste it, of course, and soon left. By the time the men had tired of their wrestling matches, swim and foot races, and a pickup baseball game, they were ready for the huge meal, what they called a *pig-pickin'*.

Sam helped Sunday serve, and during a short break, said, "Those barrels are almost empty. I set their curfew back two hours tonight, but it won't matter. I'm betting they'll all be passed out by then, and most of them will work tomorrow with whoppin' headaches. Ever tasted beer, Sunday?"

"No, sir, I never have, and Papa Ben would thrash me if I did."

Sam chuckled. "Well, honey, you haven't missed much. You want to stay on for a while? Some of them are still sober enough to play some music, and I happen to know the boys all want to hear you sing *Old Dan Tucker,* all the way through. I do, too."

Sunday grinned, highly pleased at the compliment. "Sure. I don't mind."

After supper, a huge bonfire of driftwood was built. Sunday performed as asked, and lingered on well into the night listening to the ghost stories, other yarns, and not a few slightly off-color jokes many of the men told. No one noticed that four of them, one by one, had quietly slipped away from the camp. Nor had anyone, Sam included, known that one of them had somehow managed to smuggle in a bottle of whiskey.

Calvin "Bummy" Keene had planned it carefully. His three tent mates, all a year or two younger, had enthusiastically gone along with his scheme. With the projected promise of an illicit reward far better than booze, they were ready and willing to perform their parts to perfection. They met at a predetermined spot behind a tall rise in the dune, about halfway between the camp and the Station House. With courage growing from each swallow of the whiskey, along with Bummy's whispered words of challenge, they nervously waited. A little after midnight, they saw the horse and wagon coming.

"Okay boys, here she comes. Everybody know what to do?"

Three affirmative grunts answered him.

"All right, then. Let's do it."

Bummy and one of the others moved into Sunday's path. Bummy grabbed the reins. "Hey, Sunday, ready to have a real party?"

Sunday looked down at the two boys. "Y'all better get on back to the camp. It's curfew time and I'm on my way home."

"Aw, don't be in such an all-fired hurry. C'mon down here and have a drink with us."

Sunday didn't notice the two others sneaking up behind the wagon, but Gyp did. Growling, he jumped off the wagon and began barking at them.

They stopped.

Through his teeth, Bummy hissed, "Somebody shut that dog up!"

Sunday turned around on the wagon seat in time to see the flash of a butcher knife blade, one that she'd been missing for two days and had thought misplaced. She didn't have time enough to react when one of the boys grabbed the old hound by the ears and, in one quick motion, the one named Bryce cut his throat. A split second later, she felt hands grab her by the arms, and the next thing she knew, she was being dragged off the wagon and thrown down on the sand.

It took all four of them.

Sunday fought fiercely, but they were just too many for her. She smelled the whiskey close, now, and struggled even harder as she felt their hot breath on her face.

"We want some of that dark meat you gave away to George Harris."

A handkerchief was stuffed into her mouth, and she caught another glimpse of the knife blade as it cut away

her trousers and drawers. Fast hands ripped her shirt off. "Christ, boys, look at those!"

"Quit fightin' us, Sunday. We know you like it."

"Hell, she loves it."

Sunday squirmed with all her strength, but they pried her legs apart.

"God's sake, boys, hold the black bitch *down*."

She saw Bummy Keene's sweating face, then watched without blinking as he stood, tugged at his belt, then dropped his pants. "Me first. Goddammit, hold her still, why don't you!"

None of them had dreamed it would be so difficult. She was stronger than any of them would have ever thought, but after a while, she tired, and Bummy managed to get inside her. His enjoyment was all too brief, however, and he stood, embarrassed and laughing. With feigned bravado, he exulted, "Damn good stuff, boys, dark meat or not. Who wants it next?"

"Me," said the one named Coley. "Jesus, she's strong. Regular tiger bitch. Here, Bummy, hold this arm."

Bummy started to, then suddenly turned. "Hey. Shhh. Y'all hear something?"

A moment passed, then they all heard it.

"It's Sam Kingsley's truck," Bummy whispered. "Shit. He must be coming down the beach."

"Damn! We gotta get outta here, Bummy."

"Hold on just a fuckin' minute. Where's that bottle?"

"I got it."

"Hand it to me."

Bummy took the bottle from the boy named Eddie, and poured the rest of the whiskey in Sunday's face and over her breasts, thinking that if they did get caught, they could maybe lay the blame on her. He threw the empty bottle as far as he could toward the surf.

"Listen to me, boys. When I count three, let her go and high-tail it. Everybody knows his own route back to camp. Ready?"

"Damn, Bummy, I didn't get none!"

"Me neither."

"Shut the hell up. We gotta go. You want Kingsley to catch us like *this?* Ready, one, two, three, *go!*"

They were gone as fast as they had appeared.

Sunday picked herself up and yanked the gag from her mouth, spitting. She glanced around, found her pants and put them back on. She made no sound whatsoever, but walked over to Gyp's bleeding body, picked it up, and put it in the back of the wagon. She fastened her shirt with the one button left, gathered up the reins, climbed back up on the wagon seat, and slapped the mare's rump with the reins. She had also heard the sound of Sam's truck, but it had apparently stopped. Maybe Sam had spotted one of her attackers.

With clenched teeth, Sunday drove back to the Station House, put the mare up, then walked down to the surf. She stripped, waded in, and washed herself until she was raw.

She climbed the stairs to the crow's nest and laid down, but got very little sleep at all that night. Lying there beneath the stars, breathing deeply, she knew with ice-cold certainty what she would do. George Harris may have taken her virginity, which had surely been an important thing, but now seemed a small matter. It had been freely, lovingly given. But four half-drunk white men had robbed her of what had been left. Something far more precious. Her innocence. And for that, they would pay.

When dawn broke, she got up, channeling all her hatred into energy, and prepared herself for war.

CHAPTER 8

SAM KINGSLEY got up in a sour mood. His sleep had been restless, and he had awakened with a feeling of foreboding. As from a sixth sense, he smelled trouble, and knew exactly why. His luck with this particular gang had been good all summer, which was one reason he had decided on the party the day before. He should have known that his luck couldn't last; something always went wrong. With only the one month to go, he had thought he was home free and had looked forward to a rare bonus.

Dressing, he felt like kicking himself for going against his experience and intuition regarding those barrels of beer. Those were a mistake. He'd had to take the truck up and down the beach, picking up several boys who had passed out. Plus, he had smelled something besides beer in one of the tents when making his final bed check. Well, it wouldn't be the first time; although this time, he had no one to blame but himself.

He left his own tent and went to the mess tent, glancing at his watch. Already eight o'clock, and Sunday hadn't arrived yet. Wondering why, he cursed himself silently for oversleeping, and looked around. Not another soul was up, either, and there would be a camp full of hangovers when they did wake up, that was for sure. Sighing, he put on a large pot of coffee, knowing it would be the only medicine any of them would get.

He walked down to the surf and lit a cigarette. He looked at the horizon, squinting under and over the sun, which was already high. Today would be another hot one, and he knew it would take all his skill—and patience—to goad these boys into anything resembling work. He flipped his cigarette into a receding wavelet, turned, and went back to the campsite. Taking a final deep breath, he grabbed the knotted cord of the bell clapper and began ringing, his own ears offended at the unholy sounds.

Men began stumbling, cursing, and crawling out of their tents in various stages of undress; some in only their shorts, few with their boots on. In ten minutes, Sam managed to coax barely half his crew from their tents, and was considering dousing the rest with seawater when he spotted the wagon coming up the beach. Sam straightened, his bad mood growing worse by the minute as he noticed that Sunday wasn't alone. The Station Keeper was sitting alongside her, and there were two other men in the back of the wagon—all three of them holding shotguns! *They're bringing trouble, sure as God made little green apples.*

He began running through the row of tents, yelling at the top of his voice,

"Get the hell up, and get some clothes on! All of you. Now!" Jamming his own shirt into his trousers, he tried to put on a calm face as the wagon approached.

Sunday drove the wagon up next to the mess tent, but didn't get down. Captain Ben Searcy didn't either, only touched the tip of his cap and said, "Morning, Mr. Kingsley. I'm afraid there will be no breakfast today. We have some unpleasant business to take care of."

Sam's frown stretched deeper, but he kept his voice even. "What's the problem?"

"Rape's the problem. Tell him, Sunday."

Sam looked at Sunday, whose face seemed a thousand years older than yesterday. "What happened, Sunday?"

"Four of your men stopped me last night on my way home. They killed my dog, and pulled me off of the wagon. I fought 'em hard as I could, but they cut my clothes off of me and one of 'em raped me."

Sam tried one weak parry. "You're not fooling me about this are you, Sunday?"

Searcy said, "Sunday doesn't lie, Kingsley, and you know it."

Sam looked down at the tips of his boots, wishing all of a sudden that the sun had never come up this morning. He looked up at Sunday again.

"Do you know which ones did it?"

"Yes, sir. Bummy Keene was the main one. Coley, Eddie, and Bryce helped him."

"You're sure?"

"Yes, sir. I'm sure."

Sam turned around. A dozen or more of his boys had clustered behind him, and had heard every word. They were beginning to make subdued noise, and a decision had to be made right now. He shouted, "Roust those four men out here on the double. Move!"

They moved. Fast, and in another minute or two, the accused boys were pushed into the forefront.

He turned back and said, "Captain Searcy, if this is true, I will keep these boys under wraps until the law can deal with them properly. You can be sure—"

"The law is a long way from Pea Island," Searcy quietly interrupted. "We're going to deal with this ourselves. Right here and now."

Sam watched as Searcy and the other two surfmen now stood up with their shotguns. From the looks on their faces, they meant business, too.

Sam felt control of the situation slipping away from him. "Now look here, Captain," he said, "I can't allow this kind of thing in my camp. If those boys did what Sunday says they did, they will be tried in a court and punished accordingly. We don't have vigilante law in this country any more."

Again, the Keeper's voice was soft. "You and I both know justice would never be done. The word of one colored girl against that of four white men? No, sir. They'd all get off scot-free, and we're not going to allow that to happen."

By now, the entire camp had assembled in a tight semicircle around the wagon. All were now stone cold sober, and all silent, waiting to see what would happen next. Sam was beside himself with rage, but was not about to call the bluff of the three grim looking surfmen with loaded shotguns. If he didn't think fast, and make the right decision, this instant, blood could be spilled. With superhuman effort, he kept his own voice level. "What do you suggest, Captain Searcy?"

Searcy ignored him, raised his shotgun to waist level, and said, "You men back off some. I don't intend to harm one man here who isn't guilty, but you're on my territory now, and by God, I'll blow the head off anybody who interferes." He glanced back down at Sam. "That includes you, too, mister."

Sam nodded. He was helpless, and saw nothing was to be gained by further argument. "What are you going to do?"

Ben Searcy's granite facial expression hadn't changed an iota. "Me? Nothing. But Sunday will." He turned. "Which one do you want first, honey?"

Sunday pointed to a thin, pock-faced youth who was trying his best to hide behind a larger man.

"Bryce."

The moment she said that, Sam remembered exactly which tent he had smelled the whiskey in. He made no argument as Searcy ordered, "Come on out here in the open, boy,"

Hands shoved the miserable, protesting boy into the center of the large half-circle which closed around him. Sunday got down from the wagon and walked toward him. It was only then that Sam noticed her hands. They were wrapped with tape.

"Put your fists up and fight," Sunday commanded.

The boy looked at Sam and bleated, "I ain't gonna fight no *girl*."

"Suit yourself," Sunday said, throwing a right hand that split his lips and knocked him down. Before he could recover, Sunday was on top of him, twisting his arm, and turning him over on his belly. In unbelieving shock, the confused men of the camp stood stock-still and held their collective breath as she reached behind her and drew her filleting knife.

In a flash, she sliced the shirt off the boy's back, leaned over and hissed, "You cut my dog's throat. How does it feel?" With those words, and faster than any of the mute witnesses could have imagined, she carved a letter "S" on his back; not deep enough to cause real damage, but sure to leave a permanent scar. Bryce cried out in acute pain, jerking as he felt the blade.

Sunday stood up over him, gave him a vicious kick in the ribs, and said, "Git!"

As the sniffling youth scurried on hands and knees back through the legs of his camp mates, she looked around the circle, seeking her next target. She pointed to Coley Mason.

"You're next. Come on out here and fight."

Coley was game. He swaggered into the circle.

"I'll fight you, you lying bitch, but not while you've got a knife."

Sunday grinned. She walked slowly backwards to the wagon, passed Ben her knife, then strode back into the circle.

"All right, white trash . . . come on."

Coley was stocky. Barrel-chested with stumpy, muscular legs, he was one of the best wrestlers in the camp. A few of his pals shouted encouragement, and confidence in the form of a smirk showed on his face as he moved, crouching to his left, hands up and ready.

Sunday eyed him carefully. Coley made a fast lunge at her, but she deftly sidestepped him, delivering a punishing blow under his right ear in passing and sending him off balance. He stumbled, and his momentum left him sprawling in a heap in the sand. He picked himself up quickly, hearing a few snickers behind him. Lowering his head, he spread his arms and charged again.

Sunday feinted to her left, ducked to her right with deceptive speed, and sent a hard left hand to his ribs, down low. Coley grunted, twisting; but before he could regain his balance, Sunday's right fist, with all her weight behind it, blasted into his nose, squashing it like a ripe plum. Coley fell back, his hands moving automatically to his broken nose, feeling blood.

Sunday moved in then, pounding him with short, powerful jabs and hard rights, rapidly reducing his face to red-smeared welts. Humiliation in front of his peers no longer a concern, Coley retreated and tried to dodge the steady rain of punches, covering his face.

Sunday delivered her right fist just below his belt, doubling the boy over as she moved out of his way.

Coley lowered his head again, and with a hoarse howl like that of a wounded bull, used it to make one last headlong charge at his tormentor.

Fast as a rattlesnake strike, Sunday dipped and picked up a handful of sand. She flung it in his face and slipped sideways again. Methodically, she pummeled his face and head until her helpless victim fell to his knees, crying through shredded lips and broken teeth, "No fair, no fair . . . God's sake, no fair."

Sunday wasn't even short of breath as she leaned close. "Was what you done last night fair?"

Straightening, she kneed him in the face hard as she could. Coley went down and stayed down.

Sam, watching the debacle, slowly realized that the girl had been *trained* to fight—clean or dirty. Probably by a professional. He couldn't help but wonder at how cool she was, and was astonished at the merciless punishment she was able to dish out. He crossed his arms, to show he would not even try to interfere.

Sunday looked around.

Her third victim, Eddie Conway, didn't wait to be called. Having seen what she had done to the strongest boy in camp, he turned tail and ran down the beach, fast as his skinny legs could take him, not caring a damn about the hoots and catcalls coming from his former friends. He didn't get far, though. He was no runner, and Sunday caught up with him before he'd covered fifty yards. She tripped him, squatted on top of him, and beat his face to pulp. Then she left him there, bawling like a baby in the sand, and calmly retraced her steps back to the camp.

An eerie stillness settled over the circle. Every man there knew who was next. But, Bummy Keene had no desire to exchange a single punch with the black she-devil. He had always relied on his cunning, not his inadequate brawn, and was desperate to use it now.

He made his way into the center of the circle, looked defiantly at Sam, and proclaimed, "Boss, she was the one started it. She pulled up her shirt and teased us like the devil, and she had a bottle of whiskey, too. It wasn't our fault, I swear. She egged us on worse than any whore."

At that moment, Sam Kingsley—knowing now for sure exactly where that whiskey had come from—also knew without a shadow of doubt that these four boys were guilty as hell. In spite of himself, he couldn't wait to see what kind of whipping Sunday was saving up for this lying bastard.

"That so?" He raised his voice, "Any of you boys believe that?"

A lusty chorus of negative answers thundered forth as Sunday walked through them, past the wary rapist, to the wagon. Without a word, she took the long-barreled goose gun from Royce Weeks.

Seeing what she now had in her hands, the stunned gang boss instantly feared something far worse than a whipping was about to happen in his camp. Sam ground his teeth, but remained standing where he was. Bummy Keene also froze in place, helpless to speak or move. Lowering the barrel of the shotgun, Sunday took careful aim and shot him in the crotch.

The blast knocked the youth backwards onto his back. In total disbelief, he sat up, then stared down at the spreading red stain between his legs. Before fainting, he heard Sunday growl, "Be a long time 'fore you rape another woman, you son of a bitch coward."

In a louder voice, she addressed the stunned crowd, her eyes on Sam.

"Don't worry, he ain't bad hurt. That shell was half-packed with rock salt. I took half the shot out. If I hadn't, he'd be dead. Now, if you'll give me the pay I got comin' to me, I'll be on my way. You can find somebody else to cook for you, I reckon."

Five minutes later, Sam watched the four of them walk back toward their Station. Finding someone else to do the cooking for another month was the very least of his worries. *I've got a man lying there with maybe his dick and balls shot off, some evictions to take care of, and a report to make out.* No, on second thought, he wouldn't actually write the report. When the time came, he'd simply give a verbal accounting of the morning's fiasco, and he knew he had thirty willing witnesses who would back him up all the way.

He moved forward toward the small crowd kneeling around Bummy Keene, who had regained consciousness and was squealing like a stuck hog. The thing Sam Kingsley didn't know, of course, was how many times in his lifetime he'd be prodded to tell about it all.

CHAPTER 9

ON THE same early October day the CCC men broke camp and left the island, Nat Poole broke Sunday's month-long lethargy. "Come on down to the beach with me, honey, I want to show you something."

Sunday followed him to the water's edge.

The tide was out, and had left behind a damp, smooth blackboard plenty large enough for Nat's idea. He'd brought a stick to draw with, but started by asking, "How much money you got saved up in that coffee can?"

"Almost two hundred and fifty dollars."

Nat gave a low whistle of surprise. "That much? Really? Then I reckon you've got plenty for your boat. All right, let's see how much you know. What kind of hull goes best in the ocean and why?"

Sunday gave him a look as if he had asked a ridiculous question, but she had way too much lifelong respect for her Papa Nat to give him a sarcastic answer.

"A round hull. Flat bottoms are fine in the rivers and the sound, but you need a round bottom boat for ocean work. Steadier in rough weather and high waves."

Nat nodded. "Good. Still, round-bottomed hulls are hard to build and real expensive to boot. I think your first boat should be a compromise, something in between."

"You mean a dead rise hull?"

"Right. They are fairly easy to build, and ain't too expensive, and with the kind of sailing know-how you have, she can be handled in open water just fine. Now looky here . . . "

With the stick, he began drawing lines in the sand.

"I think this is the type of boat we should build. I thought about a sharpie, or maybe a kunner, but finally decided the best for you would be a shad boat. Ain't nobody yet that's improved much on old man Creef's basic design, and we ain't neither; except we're gon' give her considerable freeboard, 'cause I know you want to fish by yourself in the ocean as well as the sound."

He watched Sunday's face come out of shadow into sunlight as he scratched life-size lines of a graceful vessel into the hard, wet sand. The craft would be twenty-four feet long, with a carved centerboard and rudder; would have a freestanding mast, and a normal spritsail rig.

"You'll be able to haul more than five hundred pounds in her, Sunday, and as long as you stay away from Diamond Shoals, you ought not to have no trouble handlin' her by yourself."

He smiled as the old gleam slowly came back into her eyes. "And, I know where we can find some good cypress tree stumps for her frames."

"Where? I didn't think there was any left on Roanoke Island."

"There ain't, but there's still some good-sized ones left up the Albemarle Sound, close to Edenton. I done took the liberty of getting dibs on some real good cedar planks, too. At least enough for your boat, and I made a deal with Tom Kinch's boy to bring 'em over here. He also found us an old boiler in Bo Jenkins' scrap yard at Elizabeth City we can buy for three dollars. That'll do fine for your steamin' box."

Sunday grinned. "Sounds like you been right busy."

Nat chuckled. "I ain't the only one, and well, none of

us likes much grass to grow under our feet. So, what about it? You ready to do some hard work?"

"I'm ready, and you know what else? I love you to pieces, Papa Nat."

"Don't talk too soon, honey."

He pointed to the sand drawing. "I'm gon' work your tail off, 'cause I'm bound and determined this here shad boat's gon' be the prettiest one on the Banks—and built strong enough to last you your whole life. We'll take our time, 'cause every join, every fitting, and every plank's gon' be perfect."

"Perfect . . . my *Black Dolphin*."

"Oh, yeah. That's what you wanted to name her, wasn't it? All right, let's walk over to the sound side. I found a good spot right down from the pier that'll be fine for buildin' the shed for her."

Nat was pleased to no end when Sunday bounded ahead of him, the fawn-like spring once more in her legs, humming *Old Dan Tucker* as she went.

Ben Searcy, standing in the crow's nest alongside Lonnie Padgett, who was also watching the boat-drawing scene, smiled and remarked, "I believe she's going to be fine, Lonnie. She'll be just fine."

By the end of October, they had laid the keel, stem, and garboards, and were busy steaming frames when Kinch's ferry docked at their pier. Tom's son, Robert, who had taken over the business from old Tom three years before, walked down to the boat shed.

"Sunday, I'm sorry to bother you, but I got a message for you."

Sunday straightened. "Message? From who?"

Robert Kinch reached into his pocket. "From the Old Woman. She told me to give you this, and said she wanted to see you. Wants you to come down to Ocracoke for a couple days."

Sunday looked at the gold coin Robert handed her. She glanced at Nat, at Robert, than back at Nat again.

"Why, this here's a twenty-dollar gold piece!"

"Uh-huh," Robert nodded. "And she said if you show up down at her place tomorrow, there'll be another one to match it. Hell, she gave me two dollars just for deliverin' the message."

Sunday stared at the coin, thought for a minute, then looked at Nat, her face full of confusion. "What on earth you reckon she wants with me? I didn't even know she was still alive."

Nat scratched his head. "No idea, Sunday, but for forty dollars, I'd damn well go see."

He spread his hands. "This can all wait, I reckon. Ain't no hurry."

Sunday turned to Robert. "I'll be ready when you come by tomorrow."

Sunday spotted the old woman before the ferry docked. She was sitting on one of the benches on the landing, dressed either in the same old overcoat, or one just like it. Her hair was even longer, but, except for that, she looked the same as when Sunday had seen her before, almost eleven *years* before. She waited for all the others to disembark before walking down the gangplank.

The old woman stood, and Sunday politely said, "Ma'am. You wanted to see me?"

The ancient one nodded, crooked her finger, and said, "Come with me."

Sunday matched her stride for stride all the way around the "creek," past the hotel and shops, past the sturdy residential houses, finally down a footpath which led to a high spot overlooking Ocracoke Inlet. The house there had to be one of the oldest on the island, and was built up against a grassy dune, protected from northwesters. Chickens and a few hogs scattered as the old woman led Sunday past the well, and up the three steps to the porch, which boasted a rocking chair and swing. She took the rocking chair and pointed to the swing.

"Sit down."

Sunday sat, but kept her feet still, so that the swing didn't move. Two or three minutes passed, and the old woman still had said nothing, so Sunday raised her head, fished the gold piece from her pocket, and handed it to her.

"I can't take this. It's a lot of money, and I haven't done anything to earn it."

The old woman took it, rocked a while longer, then said, "Tell me what you know about cures and medicine."

Sunday shook her head. "Not much. I know you're supposed to swallow a drop of turpentine in a teaspoon full of sugar if you've got a cold."

"A drop of kerosene works just as well, and kerosene helps clot blood on a cut, too. What else?"

"I saw Mary Padgett give her boy a mustard plaster when he had the flu."

"Works good for pneumonia, too. What else? Why do we put a boll of cotton on the screen doors in the summer time?"

"To keep flies and mosquitoes out. They carry sickness wherever they go."

"Good."

"And I know how good castor oil is when you're plugged up, even if it tastes bad, and how you can rub a coin or a frog on a wart to get rid of it."

"That's all you know?"

"Yes, ma'am. That's about it. I ain't never been sick much."

"I know you haven't."

"Ma'am, why are you asking me all these questions?"

The old woman didn't answer right away. She stood, smiled down at Sunday and said. "Would you like something to drink?"

"Yes, ma'am. That'd be fine."

The woman went inside the house, came back less than two minutes later with two mugs, and handed one to Sunday before settling back down in her rocker. Sunday took a tentative sip, then another.

"Taste good?" the old woman asked.

"Yes'm. A little bitter, but good."

"It tastes bitter because I didn't put any sugar in it."

"What is it?"

"Tea. My special brew. Now let me continue with your testing."

"Testing?"

"I brought you here today to give you three tests. You passed the first one by giving me the money back. That showed you have integrity. You just passed the second test, too, by telling me you don't have much knowledge of medical things. That showed me honesty. And, when you finish your tea, we're going into town for your third test."

The old woman reached into the pocket of the overcoat and extracted a large pocket watch, which she opened. "Nearly four. We need to be where we're going by four-thirty."

"Why?"

"Because Alicia Quinn's baby is due."

Sunday felt like asking another dozen questions, but kept silent. She took her time with her tea, which really did taste good, and seemed to calm down her initial feeling of nervousness. The old woman said nothing further, and when Sunday handed her the empty mug, she took it back into the house. When she came out, she was carrying a bag slung over her shoulder and in her hands she held a pair of what looked like giant slingshots.

"Here, you take these; I'll take the birthing board."

She went back inside and returned carrying a board that was about four feet long and two feet wide, only an inch thick. Holes had been bored in both ends, and it was immediately obvious to Sunday that the two "slingshots" fit into those holes. But what was it for?

Still, she refrained from questioning the woman, who set off at a brisk pace. Sunday was amazed at how fast the white-headed old woman moved. They walked into the village to one of the low frame houses where a man and three children of various ages were sitting on the porch. The old woman marched up the steps, Sunday right behind her.

"Y'all get on out of here," she told the man, who didn't need to be told twice. He and the children took off down the street, not looking back.

"Come on," the woman said, and led Sunday into the house, straight to the kitchen. Sunday was surprised to see stacks of towels and sheets already folded and waiting on the kitchen table, along with three wash basins. The neatly arranged linens seemed to please the old woman.

Turning to Sunday, she said, "Take that bucket out to the well, fill it up, and put it on the stove. Soon as it boils, pour some in each one of those basins and bring them in the bedroom."

Sunday did exactly as instructed, not failing to notice that inside the woman was hurrying all through the house opening every door and window. Sunday carefully carried the first pan of water into the bedroom, and saw that the old woman had screwed the slingshot contraptions into the board. Together, they slipped the board under the legs of the huge, moaning woman on the bed, then pushed several pillows up behind her. Sunday helped lift Alicia Quinn's fat legs up, resting them behind the knee in the fork of each slingshot.

"These are stirrups, Sunday," the old woman said. "I used to use a birthing chair, but this works just as well; and it isn't too heavy to carry around with me. Bring some more water."

Sunday hurried back into the kitchen, hearing the old woman tell her patient, "All right now, Alicia. Push. One, two, three—push! *Push,* I said." In an hour it was all over. Alicia Quinn had a new baby boy, and Sunday had witnessed the most incredible sight of her life.

Walking slowly back to the old woman's house, she said, "It was . . . a miracle."

The old woman laughed. "New life always is. This was an easy one. Alicia has dropped three young'uns in the last four years already. And I'm glad to see you passed your third test, too."

Sunday had forgotten all about that. "I did?"

"Yes. You didn't faint. Didn't so much as flinch, not even when the afterbirth came out. I was right. You're going to be the one, sure enough."

Sunday remembered the first words the old woman had said to her, so long ago, but said nothing until they reached the woman's house.

"Want some more tea?"

"Yes'm."

A minute later, Sunday was sipping another mug of the bitter brew, trying to think of how to ask the first of a hundred questions. But she wasn't given the chance to ask even the first one . . .

"Child, I know you're wondering why I've brought you here, and why I've given you those simple tests. You're young, and you're strong. Strong in mind as well as in body. I'm going to die soon, and I want you to take my place."

Sunday almost dropped the mug. She opened her mouth to reply, but nothing came out. She simply stared at her hostess with eyes that didn't blink.

"Don't worry," the old woman said with a cackle. "It won't be right away. I'll give you plenty of time. But there is one thing has to be taken care of today. Right now. Stand up and come over here."

Without knowing why, Sunday obeyed.

The old woman placed her hands just below Sunday's stomach, and asked, "Missed your monthly this time, didn't you?"

"Yes'm, but how could you tell?"

"Because I know things."

She probed a little more. "Sunday, you're pregnant. Not with a love child, either. Your womb has been planted with devil's seed. This baby can't be allowed to be born. He would be a child of hate."

"I was . . . I was raped."

"I know. Do you trust me, Sunday?"

"Yes ma'am, I do."

"Then come on inside. I'll give you some more tea. Stronger tea, and pretty soon, you won't feel a thing. Tomorrow and the next day, you're going to be a little sore, and will need to stay in bed, but after that, you can go home and finish building your boat. Come Christmas-time, I want you to come back here. You have a lot to learn."

CHAPTER 10

WORKING FROM dawn till dusk, Sunday finished building her boat on the first day of December, 1937. It was painted—black, of course—caulked, soaked, and launched. She passed her sea trials with flying colors, filling Sunday with yet a new pride of accomplishment. But, instead of sailing out to celebrate with her dolphin friends, Sunday headed straight down to Ocracoke Island, having gotten permission from Ben Searcy to be away for a while. Sunday found an unoccupied slip for BLACK DOLPHIN on the extreme south end of the harbor tied her up snug and walked to the old woman's house. She knocked on the door and was ushered in with a warm hug.

"Want some tea?"

"Yes'm, that'd be fine. It's cold out there today."

The old woman handed her a steaming mug, told her to take a seat, and said, "I saw you come in. That's as pretty a shad boat as I've ever seen, and from the way you brought her into the harbor and through that crowd of boats, I'd say you're a good sailor, too."

"Thank you."

"How are you feeling?"

"Me? I feel good as I ever did, thanks to you."

"Ready to start?"

"Yes'm. What you want me to do?"

The old woman got up, walked to her kitchen, and brought back two knives, a tablecloth, and a basket of roots. "Help me cut these up."

"What are they?"

"Sassafras roots. Good for lots of things, including that tea you're drinking."

Sunday watched the ancient one, and copied her actions. After perhaps fifteen minutes, she couldn't help blurting, "Are you a witch?"

The woman smiled.

"Some say so, but what I am is a healer. It doesn't matter what people think I am. As long as they have faith in me, faith in my powers, they heal a lot faster. Remember this, Sunday Everette, *believing* they're going to get well is half of what *makes* them well."

"What's your name?"

This time the old woman laughed loudly. "You know, you're the first person in thirty years to ask me that. It's Susan. Susan Bearclaw. They say that when I was born, both my eyes were dark brown. 'Like a black-eyed Susan,' they said. Went blind in my left one some years ago. That's why it's gone blue."

"Bearclaw's an Indian name, isn't it?"

"Sure is. My grandpa was full-blooded Lumbee. I'm part white, part black—like you—but mostly I'm Indian. It was my grandpa taught me most of the things I know. You see, I was a seventh daughter. Seventh daughters are sometimes born with special gifts. You're one, too."

Sunday stopped what she was doing, her face instantly flushed with indignation. "I am not! I'm the only daughter my Daddy had."

"That you know of. Only one he knows of either, I'm guessing. Sunday, I happen to know that from Baltimore to Savannah, Slick Everette fathered six girls before you, all by different mothers, and two more after he left Pea Island. You're his seventh daughter, and like it or not, that's a fact."

Sunday was stunned at this information, and though she didn't want to believe it, she was certain old Susan Bearclaw had not lied to her. Why would she have?

In a subdued voice, Sunday asked, "You think I have some of those gifts?"

"I believe so, but I don't know for sure. Not yet. Time will tell. Depends on how much you learn and how fast you learn it. I started when I was about ten. You're almost twice that old now. Got a lot of catching up to do."

Sunday nodded. What the old woman said made sense. "Can I ask you how old you are?"

Susan Bearclaw squinted at her. "I'll be ninety come Christmas."

"You were born on Christmas Day?"

"That's what they told me. I don't quite remember the occasion."

Sunday laughed. "I reckon not."

"Poke that fire some, will you?"

Sunday got up, walked to the hearth, reached for the poker, and pushed the back log farther over.

Turning back around, she took stock of Susan Bearclaw's sitting room for the first time. By the light of the fire and two oil lamps, she saw that it contained an old horsehide sofa and two mismatched armchairs, a low table, and an animal skin rug of some type stretched out on the plank floor. Most noticeable of all was that every wall was shelved, and light reflected as from a thousand tiny mirrors. The shelves were loaded down with hundreds of jars, clear and colored bottles, and clay pots—all full of things she didn't recognize—and none wore labels.

"What's in all these jars?"

"Herbs and medicines. It'll take time, but I'll teach you about every one of them. First, though, I want you to help me deliver three or four more babies. Aside from talking out fire, new life is my most important work."

"What's 'talking out fire?' "

The old woman sighed.

"That's hard to explain, child. It's a very special gift. Those of us can do it just . . . just talk it out. When somebody gets burned real bad, we rub our hands over the spot, and talk the fire out. The pain goes away and the burned people heal up without scars. There's only a few fire talkers around anymore. Closest other one I know of is a young woman living in Fountain, over in Pitt County, name of Dupree. But don't you be disappointed if you never learn how, Sunday. Now. Let's go in the kitchen. There's another root I want to teach you about right away. It's called ginseng . . . "

Thus, Sunday began a new education. By spring, having helped bring four more children into the world— one by herself, under the watchful eye of her teacher— she was well on her way to learning the fascinating basics of southern folk medicine. She was surprised at how quickly the time passed, and was truthfully reluctant to tell Susan Bearclaw she had to leave.

"It's March already, Miz Bearclaw. I have to go back and start work."

"You've learned a good deal, Sunday. Can you come back this December?"

"Yes'm. I sure will. Are you going to be all right?"

The toothless smile reappeared. "I'll be fine."

The men of the Station were happy to see her. They all knew where she had been, but none questioned Sunday about what she had been doing all winter. They were further amazed at how she wasted no time putting her new boat to work, and how rapidly she became modestly successful at fishing. She sold her first catch at Wanchese, and with the money she got, promptly bought half a dozen crab pots. By the end of the season, she had accumulated two dozen of them, which increased her profits considerably. She was so busy she forgot her seventeenth birthday! Occasionally, she would sail *BLACK DOLPHIN* all the way out to the Gulf Stream, simply for the sheer joy of it, pausing once in a while to take a quick swim with her finned friends, sensing they were a last link to a childhood that was now practically a distant memory.

At night, dog-tired, she'd lie on her cot in the crow's nest and study the stars. Ben showed her how to recognize the northern constellations, and later, began teaching her celestial navigation, not in the least surprised at how fast she learned the use of his sextant.

"There'll come a day when you have a large boat, Sunday, maybe a big trawler, and do your fishing far out in the ocean. You'll need to know how to shoot the sun, the moon, and certain stars. You already know a lot about reading tides and currents. This is the next step."

"How am I doing?"

"Fine so far, but it's easy up here. On a pitching deck, it's a lot harder. Next week, I'll go out with you a few times in *BLACK DOLPHIN*, so you can work on it under actual sea conditions. Once you master all the dead-reckoning skills—most of which you already have—and learn how to navigate under all kinds of weather conditions, then you'll be an Honest to God saltwater sailor."

By the time Sunday reached her eighteenth birthday, there wasn't one of the seven men at the Pea Island Life-Saving Station who didn't think she was capable of sailing right around the world had she wanted to; but, sensibly, none of them mentioned that, for fear she might actually try it!

Sunday's apprenticeship as a healer took three years. From 1938 until 1941, she gradually became known from one end of the Banks to the other, especially to café and restaurant owners who depended on her to bring the best and the freshest fish, turtles, and game. And through that period of time, without really noticing it happen, Sunday watched the communities she visited grow, most of their inhabitants being dragged, kicking and screaming, into the twentieth century. A road from Duck to Nags Head, plus the bridge across the sound at Elizabeth City, brought more and more curious people, vacationers, and a few small businesses. Hatteras Village now boasted a full-time school. A future bridge over the Oregon Inlet was even contemplated.

Without realizing it, Sunday's delivery stops became increasingly longer as people practically lined up to have their minor ailments, cuts, and bruises taken care of by the obliging young fisherwoman. As well, Sunday found that the short winter months studying with and assisting Susan Bearclaw soon stretched into longer periods of time. By the third year with the old woman, she was spending half the year on the water and the other half at Ocracoke. She was delivering babies, setting bones, and gathering roots and herbs. She now knew most of them intimately, as well as how they all worked. No one could put a finger on the exact date Sunday stopped cooking at the Station. The men saw her coming and going, but that was all.

Lonnie Padgett put it best one evening as Sunday's black-hulled boat came gliding in. From the crow's nest where he was watching, he nudged Ben Searcy.

"Here she comes, Cap'n. Funny. Seems like one day she was a skinny little kid, and the next day she's a grown woman. Hard to believe."

"I know," Ben replied. "But you know what, Lonnie? We all did pretty well by her. She's made friends all up and down the Banks and on Roanoke Island, too."

"That's true, Cap'n. You know what else? She's making pretty good money at it! No tellin' how much she's got stashed in those coffee cans by now."

Ben laughed. "You think she'll ever buy a dress with any of it?"

Catching Searcy's meaning, Lonnie laughed along with him. "I doubt it. And even if she did, what man could keep up with her?"

Except for the brief period after George Harris was kidnapped by his father, Sunday had never known the feeling of loneliness. Until late in November of 1941. She had delivered a baby at Wanchese, and had sailed directly to Ocracoke, noticing how cold the wind had suddenly become, portending a nasty winter. She tied her boat up in the slip, and walked to Susan's house, looking forward to the warm hearth and a mug of hot tea.

When she opened the door and walked inside, she was struck with a chill of a different kind. Something was wrong. She looked around. A strong fire was going. Nothing was out place. Everything seemed normal, but Sunday felt the hair rising on the back of her neck. She went into the bedroom and found Susan in bed, wrapped up in two quilts, her face pale as her hair.

"What's the matter? Are you sick?"

The old woman smiled weakly at her. Her voice was like a faint echo. "My time has come, Sunday. Listen closely to me, now. I want you to go right this minute into town and see Mr. Simon Teague."

"The lawyer?"

"Yes. Go right now, and come back soon as you can. I'll be fine till you get back."

Worried, Sunday hurried into town, to the modest frame house where Simon Teague also had his law office. Teague opened his front door as soon as she knocked.

"I've been expecting you, Miss Everette, please come in." He showed her into the book-crammed office and pointed to the single chair facing his desk. "Please sit down."

Confusion now replaced Sunday's anxiety.

Reading it on her face, Teague smiled to reassure her. "Young lady, do you know what a *will* is?"

"No, sir."

"Well, when people die, they leave a written document, usually with a lawyer like me, carefully stating what is to become of their estate."

"Estate?"

"Yes. What they own."

"Oh. You mean like a house?"

"Exactly. House, and any other property. I've been Susan Bearclaw's attorney for as long as I've been on the island, and she wanted me to disclose that everything she owns will pass on to you after her death. It's a little unusual, of course, since wills are generally read and executed afterwards, but in her case, she wanted me to inform you of this before she passed on."

He picked up a brown envelope that had been lying on top of his neatly arranged desk. "This is her will, Sunday. She's leaving everything she owns to you."

Sunday could only stare at the bespectacled, middle-aged man whose thin, expressive face clearly showed how fond he was of his oldest client.

"But she's not dead. I just came from there. She sent me here."

Teague nodded. "What else did she tell you?"

"Told me to see you, then come straight back."

"Then do as she asked. You may come back to see me later. After—"

Sunday didn't wait to hear more. She jumped up, ran out, and back to Susan's house as fast as she could.

Out of breath, she rushed back into the bedroom, knelt down by the bed, tears in her eyes, and said, "You're not going to die, Susan Bearclaw! I won't *let* you die. You hear me? You've still got a lot to teach me, and you've been the only mother I ever had."

Her strength fast ebbing, Susan reached for her hand. In nearly a whisper, she said, "Hush, child, and listen. You know that place over on Portsmouth Island I showed you last year? The place where my mother is buried? I want you to take me there and lie me down next to her. Please don't argue with me, just do as I ask. Now, Sunday."

Sunday hesitated only a moment. She looked down at the withered old face, saw such a serene smile and look of contentment in the one brown eye; she knew the old woman was in no pain, and was actually looking forward to making her final trip. Sunday picked her up, quilts and all, surprised at how light she had become.

Shriveled as she was, Susan Bearclaw couldn't possibly have weighed more that sixty-five or seventy pounds. Still, it was all Sunday could do to carry her all the way down to her boat—allowing no one she met on the way to help her. She made Susan as comfortable as she could in BLACK DOLPHIN's narrow cockpit, then pushed away from the slip, hoisted sail, and made for the inlet thanking the good Lord she would be crossing at slack tide.

Forty-eight hours later, Sunday was once again in Simon Teague's office.

"I buried her next to her mother, Mr. Teague. She didn't die until we were standing on Portsmouth Island. Last thing she said was, 'I love you, Sunday Everette.' It was the hardest thing I ever had to do, and I've never been colder in my life. I shook to pieces the whole time."

"Did you say a prayer over her?"

"Yes, sir. Best I could. It was the Twenty-third Psalm. First one I ever learned."

"I'm sure it was quite enough. Now. Will you stay here in . . . ah, your house?"

"No, sir. I couldn't sleep a wink there all last night. I'll try to come back here often as I can to treat her people, but there's no way on earth I could live in that house."

"I understand. So you're going back to Pea Island, then?"

"Yes, sir."

"I'm sorry to delay you, but you'll have to stay on Ocracoke for at least a few more days while I attend to probating her will. If you like, I can arrange for you to get a room at the hotel."

"Hotel? They won't let me stay there, Mr. Teague."

The kindly lawyer's face turned beet red. "Oh. Yes. Well, please be my guest then. I have a spare room upstairs. You'll be quite comfortable there."

"Thank you, sir."

"Not at all. By the way, you might wish to open an account at the bank tomorrow as well."

"Why?"

"Because she left you some money, too. Almost five thousand dollars, all in gold coins. Miz Bearclaw never trusted paper money—or banks. It's in my safe."

When Sunday finally found her voice, she thanked Teague and asked him to leave it where it was for the time being. She excused herself, walked out into the street, and wandered aimlessly around Ocracoke Island the rest of the day as in a thick sea fog, not able to fully comprehend either her loss or her gain.

In time, Sunday returned to Pea Island, only to find the men all in a bad mood. There were two reasons why.

First, Ben informed her the country was at war. "The Japanese bombed Pearl Harbor, yesterday, honey."

That news didn't make much of an impact on her, given the mood she was in. But the second thing Ben told her did:

"There's someone in the kitchen you probably ought to see."

Sunday walked to the kitchen and nearly fainted.

Standing there, warming himself by the stove, weighing maybe fifty pounds more than when she'd last seen him and with the sleeve of his shirt pinned up where his left arm should have been, was her father.

"Daddy?"

"It's me, all right. Old Slick himself. Hey, don't worry none 'bout this missin' arm. I can still cook better'n most with jus' one. Come on over here and give me a big hug."

CHAPTER 11

THE FIRST Friday in January of 1942 brought yet another unpleasant surprise. A high-ranking officer of the Coast Guard came unannounced to the Station, huddled up with Ben Searcy for an hour, then left in a hurry. Ben called all of them into the sitting room.

"I'm afraid some changes here must be made."

He looked first at Sunday. "Honey, you know that the Life-Saving Service has been a working arm of the Coast Guard since 1915, before you were born. As long as we enjoyed peacetime, nothing much was said about your living here. But we are at war, now, and I've been ordered to evict all nonmilitary personnel from the Station."

"That means Daddy and I can't live here any more?"

"That's true. I'm sorry, Sunday. There simply was no way I could talk Commander French around it. That isn't all of it either."

He transferred his gaze to the men. "Joe, you and Clem are going to get transfer orders within two weeks. I have no idea where they are going to send you, but you will probably be given active duty at one of the new Cutter Stations. We will screen replacements they send to take your places as soon as possible."

"What about me, Cap'n?" Amos wanted to know.

Ben smiled. "You've been recently married, son. You'll stay here."

Sunday said, "Looks like I'm going to have to build me a house after all."

"Can I still cook for you, Cap'n?" Slick asked.

"I'm afraid not."

Ben looked back at Sunday. "I was able to get you two weeks grace before you have to move out. Maybe the boys can help you at least get a shelter built by then."

He glanced around. "Any volunteers?"

There were plenty.

And none of them, the Keeper included, had ever worked harder. Totally against regulations, Ben allowed Nat Poole, who headed up the building team, to use most of the spare lumber they had stored, including many of their often-needed heavy timbers. Those went into the raised foundation. The next time Robert Kinch's ferry stopped, Sunday dug deep into her coffee cans, and Robert was given a commission to buy and transport lumber and shingles, as well as a medium-sized wood stove which would also serve to heat the little house.

Within a week, the basic frame was standing, situated on a high dune close to where Sunday and George had enjoyed their trysts so long ago. By the end of the second week, one room of the two-room shack was roughed-in; enough for the stove and stovepipe to be installed, the roof and sides shingled, and a pine board floor laid. It didn't look like much, but the men, under Nat's close supervision, made sure it was solid enough to withstand a major storm—and foundation timbers were added to the south end for a second room, which could be built later.

There was a single door and two small windows—for which Lonnie sewed temporary burlap curtains. Inside there was barely enough room for two bunk beds, over and under. The only other furniture consisted of a sturdy table and two chairs. The bunks reached practically from one wall to the other because of Sunday's and Slick's height. All in all, the interior of the one-room cabin measured no more than ten by sixteen feet, but with the new stove installed, was cozy enough, and Sunday and her father moved in a day before the deadline. No one gave any thought as to whether the house-building project was legal or not! Pea Island belonged to whoever lived on it.

"When spring comes," Sunday told Nat, "I can start on the other room, but this will do fine for the winter. I really appreciate your help, Papa Nat. All of you have been so good to us."

"Least we could do, Sunday. Ben tells us we're likely to be real busy from now on. The Germans are in the war now, and Ben expects submarines will be just as active off the coast as they were during the last one, but I'll help you all I can. You'll need to dig a well and build your own privy next spring, too, but Cap'n says you can use ours in the meantime."

Sunday hugged him, sent him back to the Station House, sat down and thought about how to solve her other big headache—her father. Slick had cheerfully cooked for the men during the two-week period of grace, but with only one arm, was totally useless regarding the carpentry work. But that was not what bothered her. Her problem was potentially serious. Midway during the second week of construction, during a coffee break, Royce had taken her aside and quietly said, "Sunday, I caught Slick counting the money in your coffee cans yesterday. When he saw me watching him, he grinned, put the money back, and told me he had no idea what a 'rich little gal he had raised.' Raised? Hell, all he ever did was to teach you how to fight. Don't forget that he stole your money the last time he took off. I wouldn't trust him not to do it again, either. I talked it over with Cap'n Ben, and we moved your money into his cabin."

"Thanks for telling me, Papa Royce. I'll take care of it."

All during the last day of construction, Sunday thought carefully about what Royce had said. She loved Slick, and decided to remove him from any temptation. By the light of the ship's lantern that night, she said, "Daddy, I'm going down to Ocracoke tomorrow. I'll be back in a day or two."

"What you goin' down there for? It's freezing cold on the sound."

"I'll be all right. Don't worry."

With long johns, wool pants and coat beneath her foul-weather gear and under short-reefed sail, Sunday weathered the biting cold and chop of the sound, reaching Ocracoke shortly after noon. She made straight to Susan's house, built a fire, made some strong tea, had a bite to eat, and then walked to Simon Teague's office, carrying her savings.

Teague let her in, smiled, and said, "Sunday! What a nice surprise. Come in, come in. What can I do for you?"

"Mr. Teague, I need your help."

"Anything. Just name it."

"First, can you help me open that bank account? I brought all my money with me, and I need to put it in a safe place."

"We can put it in my safe. Anything else?"

"Yes, sir. I need to talk to Mr. Ramsey at the hotel. He's a friend of yours, isn't he?"

"Yes, a good friend. We can go right over there now if you like."

"Fine."

Teague led the way to the hotel, told Sunday to wait on the porch for a moment, then went inside. Sunday stood there in the cold for a full five minutes before he came back, scowling. "Let's go round to the back, Sunday. He's, ah, in the kitchen."

Sunday swallowed her sudden anger, and followed the embarrassed lawyer around to the service door. John Ramsey let them in, offered them seats at the kitchen table, looked at Sunday and said, "Simon told me you want to see me about something. What's on your mind, girl?"

Once again, Sunday bit back her rage.

"I want you to give my Daddy a job. He's the best cook in the whole state of North Carolina, and he needs a job bad. I know your restaurant's a good one, and you know I've been prompt about supplying you with good fish and game. Also, you might remember that Miz Bearclaw and I helped your wife with her last little girl, for which you never paid either one of us."

Ramsey glanced at Teague, his face turning red, then back at Sunday, and with a sheepish grin, replied, "I see. So, you figure I owe you a favor. That it?"

"Well, yes sir, you do. If you'll give my Daddy that job, I'll sell you your fish and birds from now on at half-price and then we'll be even."

"Sounds like a good deal, John," Simon Teague put in.

"Humph. Sounds more like blackmail to me, but I reckon I can give the man a try. When can he start?"

"I can bring him down here next Wednesday on Robert Kinch's ferry."

"Fine. It's a deal."

"Shake hands on it?" Sunday said, mindful she had a witness.

Ramsey stood and put out his hand. "Sure."

Sunday shook the man's hand, then turned, and without another word, walked through the kitchen to the hall and out the front door!

Simon Teague burst out laughing. "Serves you right, John. You should see your face."

Ramsey grinned back at him. "I swear, that colored girl's grip was stronger than any man's. She's something, isn't she?"

"Yes. Quite something."

The following Wednesday, Sunday installed Slick in Susan Bearclaw's house with firm instructions not to touch anything except the pantry. She took him to the back door of the hotel, made the introductions, and left him there, smiling as she heard him singing *Old Dan Tucker*.

As expected, February and March were unseasonably cold. Raw, wet days and nights that made any kind of outdoor work difficult if not impossible. Nearly every night, one or another of the surfmen would walk down to Sunday's shack, keep her company for a while, share a cup or two of the marvelous tea she made, then leave. She kept busy with reading, and studying Morse code and semaphore—tedious tasks, but Ben had suggested she learn them, and helped her with it almost daily.

"These are good things to know, Sunday. At sea, especially now, there's no telling when both might come in handy. Besides, every competent seaman is an expert with such things, whether with flags or signal lamps."

Sunday knew that Ben Searcy had never given her bad advice, and gladly took on the new project for want of something constructive to do, and after a while, became quite proficient.

One night in late February, she walked up to the Station House to bring a pie she had baked for the men. None of them were to be seen! She climbed the stairs to the crow's nest. They were all there, bundled in watch caps and peacoats, their eyes to the east. It didn't take her long to discover what they were looking at so intently. Two distant orange and red glows were visible on the horizon.

"What is it, Papa Ben?"

All the men turned toward her, then looked back to seaward. "Burning ships, Sunday," Ben said. "Enemy submarines at work."

"This close to shore?" Sunday asked.

"Yes. More bodies for the Graveyard of the Atlantic. We'd best watch our own beaches these days. No telling what may be washed up on them. On a clear night, with glasses, you can see ships' running lights going back and forth around the Cape. Downright stupid, if you ask me. All the Germans have to do is simply lie out there and pick them off like ducks on a pond. A lot of good men are dying out there tonight."

"I . . . I brought y'all a pie."

Ben turned back to her. "Thank you, Sunday. We appreciate that." He cleared his throat. "All right, men, show's over for tonight. Go on down and have a piece of pie. I'll be down in a few minutes."

All the men left, and Ben said, "Sunday, I know you'll be anxious to get back out there to fish once this weather breaks, but before you do, it would be a good idea to dye your sails black. I don't want any of those subs shooting at you. Best not to take any chances."

"You think they'd shoot at *me?* Just a poor fisherman out trying to make a living?"

"It's been known to happen. Just be careful is all I'm saying. Keep a sharp eye out all the time, and I'm not talking about for dolphins, either."

Sunday remained quiet for a few minutes, then said, "Those submarines don't play fair, do they? I mean, hiding under the water like that, then shooting at helpless merchant ships and all."

"Fair? It's war, honey. Nothing fair about it. We have subs, too, and our boys do the same thing. But one of these days, our Navy bosses had better get smarter, and put those ships in convoys with escorts. Otherwise, it's going to be a real slaughterhouse out there. Already is, I reckon." He smiled. "Anyway, thanks for the pie. What kind is it?"

"Your favorite. Apple."

"You think those greedy boys saved me a piece?"

Sunday grinned. "They'd better, or I'll torpedo 'em myself!"

The only useful thing Sunday could do during that stretch of bad weather was wait for a sunny day, bundle herself up, and tend her crab pots. She made a few dollars selling them at Wanchese, and stayed over each time she went, treating colds and other minor illnesses.

On one trip, in early March, she genuinely enjoyed making a side trip to Manteo, where she delivered Emma Padgett Hines' first baby, a healthy boy, Papa Lonnie's first grandchild. She was happy to see the Padgett family again, and happier still that Emma had actually gotten married before she had become pregnant.

In early April, the weather finally broke, and she immediately began work on the second room of her house, grateful that Nat Poole sneaked down every other day to give her a hand. By the middle of the month, they were ready to put the shingles on, and were taking a lunch break when they spotted someone walking down from the Station House.

Sunday jumped to her feet. "Mr. Teague! What on earth are you doing here?"

Teague didn't have a happy look on his face. "I'm afraid I have some bad news, Sunday."

"What bad news?"

"It's . . . it's your father. He's . . . well, he's in jail. He lost his job at the hotel, and got drunk one night a week ago. It appears he got careless with the fire, which caused your house to burn down. I think you'd best come with me back to Ocracoke."

CHAPTER 12

THERE WAS nothing left of the house. Nothing at all. The scorched chimney stood like a mocking gravestone over the still-smoldering mound of ashes. Sunday stared into the ruins, wondering what had become of the pigs and chickens, then realizing they were the least of her concerns. Every pot, every bottle and jar, with all their valuable contents, had also been consumed. The fire must have been a fast one. And furious. How had her father escaped unharmed?

With a deep sigh of discouragement, she trudged into town to the jail, where Simon Teague was waiting for her.

An hour later, after a short trip to the bank for money to pay Slick's fine, she led her shuffling, slumped-over father down to the ferry landing. They boarded and took seats as far aft as possible, out of earshot. Sunday was grateful there were only a few other passengers aboard, who were not paying them any attention anyway.

"All right, tell me what happened."

Slick looked up into her face, then totally broke down, his wide shoulders shaking as he blubbered like a baby.

"The demon of drink, honey. I got in a argument with that redneck boss man, and he fired me. I reckon I was feelin' sorry for myself. Anyways, I got me a bottle and went back to the house. The fire was almost out, so I put more wood on it and more kerosene than I ought to,

I guess. Then I went on into the kitchen and started in drinkin' and 'fore I knew it, the place was goin' up like Roman candles on the Fourth of July.

"I don't even know how I got out. With the good Lord's help, for sure. Trouble was, I still had that bottle in my hand when I ran out. They come up a big crowd of people, and the constable hauled me in and locked me up. I'm so sorry, Sunday, and so ashamed. I reckon you're right disgusted with me, ain't you?"

Sunday nodded, put her arm around his shaking shoulders, and said, "Don't cry about it. What's done is done."

Between sobs, Slick said, "That's what happened to my arm, too."

"What? I don't understand. You mean a fire?"

"No. Whiskey. It was down at North Charleston. I got in a bar fight after I'd had a few too many. They was a whole bunch of 'em ganged up on me. One of 'em cut me real bad with a busted bottle, and I passed out. Next thing I know'd, I woke up in the hospital with jus' one arm. Oh Lordy, what am I gon' do?"

"What you're going to do is come home with me, but this time, you'll have to follow my rules."

"Rules?"

"Yes, sir! You'll do the cooking, and if you ever steal money or anything else from me again, I'll cut your other arm off."

"Now wait, honey, that ain't no way to talk to your Daddy."

Sunday snorted. "*Daddy?* You're not my Daddy. My Daddy was a strong man. A good man. And, he was a *sober* man. Look at you. You're nothing but a fat old drunk, wallowing around in your own dirt and shit like a sow. A tubful of black lard. And you know what else? You're a damn coward."

Sunday watched her father's face, knowing that was the one word he hated more than any other. He turned away from her in abject shame, knowing she had spoken the truth.

And Sunday didn't let up on him.

"I'm never going to call you my Daddy again. Not until you show me you can pull yourself out of that hog pen you fell into and be a man again."

Several minutes passed before Slick whispered, "I can change, Sunday. If you help me, I can do it. Jus' like Cap'n Ben helped you learn how to talk right. I jus' wish I hadn't lost my bag in that fire."

"Bag? You can get knives and spices anywhere."

"I don't mean them. I'm talkin' 'bout my Bible."

"You had a Bible?"

"Yeah. I've always had one."

"What for? You can't read."

This time Slick, showing a glimmer of self-respect, raised his head and looked her in the eye. "Yes, I can. My Mammy taught me more than jus' how to cook. I can read right good. Always could. I jus' didn't never tell nobody."

This was astonishing news to Sunday, and it gave her a new idea. She sat there for a while, thinking it all through. By the time Robert Kinch eased into the pier at Pea Island, she got up, walked up to his wheelhouse, and handed him some money.

"What's this for?" he asked.

"A Bible. Robert, next time you stop, please bring me the biggest Bible you can find."

Robert Kinch knew Sunday Everette well enough to know when she was serious and when she wasn't. "I'll try to bring you one by next Wednesday, Sunday."

Her newest project took considerable time away from finishing the house and the new privy, but she managed both. It also cut into her fishing time, but Sunday, in typical fashion, was relentless. She goaded Slick. Teased him. She insulted and ridiculed him, but within a month he had lost ten pounds. Try as best he could, he could not catch her, but stubbornly chased after her every morning at sunrise and every evening at sunset until he fell. Yet he ran longer sprints up and down the beach each time. His stamina grew. Every night, to measure his growing strength, he arm-wrestled her, losing half the time. She laughed at him, sneered at him, infuriated him daily, but he made steady progress.

Within three months, most of his flab had disappeared, and his muscles began to reappear and resemble their former tone. Slick's wind and appetite got better, too, and every night, after he'd had the required bath, he sat with her in the new south room reading the Bible Robert had dutifully brought—from Genesis to Revelations. Occasionally, they'd pause to listen to the distant rumbling of explosions that echoed ashore, straining to see still another glow on the eastern horizon that signified the death of still another ship. They would close their eyes, say a soft prayer for the lost seamen, then turn in, only to repeat the same rigorous training regimen the next day.

The surfmen all knew what was going on, and watched, shaking their heads in wonderment. Each passing day, Slick Everette looked more and more like the man they had first known, and they were all soon convinced Sunday would eventually get her "Daddy" back. Ben Searcy smiled when Sunday took Slick out in her boat, knowing that the one thing she'd never manage would be to teach her father how to swim. There was a limit even to miracles.

He was right, of course. Slick never did learn how to swim, but Sunday at least got him to wade into the water up to his waist, walking against the tide and undertow to help strengthen his legs and lower back. More than a few times, he'd stumble and fall, but she was right there to pull him up, laughing. "Now you're baptized, too, old lard-belly. Come on, try harder! Move!"

By October, Slick was in "right good shape" as he modestly boasted, grinning at his nodding daughter, and now whipped her quickly at arm-wrestling. His reward, after he'd bathed, and after they'd eaten and cleaned up the dishes, was, "Why don't you read some more about King David and Saul, Daddy. I love that story, and you read it so well."

The following morning she said, "Eat a good breakfast. We're going to the mainland."

"What for?"

"I have to go shopping, and I need a guide."

They took the ferry to Elizabeth City. Before they landed, Sunday touched Slick's arm. "Can I trust you, now?"

"Sure you can, honey."

"Here, then." She handed him a wad of bills. "I want you to do the paying. It would be more natural-looking."

Slick nodded, counting the money. "Damn, Sunday, there's over two hundred dollars here! Where we goin'? to *California?*"

"No," Sunday laughed, "but farther than I've ever been, and you know your way around."

She didn't tell him she had two hundred more in twenty-dollar gold coins enclosed in a leather pouch she had prudently hung around her neck and wore beneath her shirt.

Slick bought tickets at the Trailways station, and two hours later, they boarded a bus to Greenville, in Pitt County, by way of Edenton, Williamston, and Washington. Suffering in silent humiliation at being shunted to the back of each bus, and forced to eat and drink at separate facilities along the way (which, to her surprise, didn't seem to bother her father), Sunday hardly enjoyed her first trip to the interior of the state. At Greenville, they took a local bus to Farmville, then one to the village of Fountain, where they sought out Miz Dupree, the healer and fire talker Susan had told Sunday about.

"So you're Sunday Everette. I've heard of you," the tall, reed-thin woman said, offering a tanned, narrow hand with bony fingers; a hand that seemed more like a plover's claw. "What brings you way out here?"

Sunday could not have guessed the woman's age, but her deep-set blue eyes were full of warmth, as was her wide smile. Sunday told her about Susan Bearclaw's death, and the fire that had destroyed all her medicines.

"I need to stock up again, and I was wondering if you could spare some of yours. I'll be glad to pay you a fair price."

"I might. Let's see your list."

After haggling good-naturedly over prices, Sunday made a deal with the kindly woman to ship jars and bottles to her in care of Kinch's Ferry, at Elizabeth City. The list was extensive. Miz Dupree promised that her sixteen-year-old son, Jacob, who had a beat-up old Ford pickup truck, would deliver a year's supply of ginseng, comfrey, yarrow, aloe, purslane, lamb's quarters, dock, pennyroyal, plantain and elder. Sunday told the woman she could find no end of spiders and webs, dandelion, turpentine, collard leaves and lard (for burn pain) around the Banks, and was fairly certain she could also locate purple foxglove, horsemint, and grapevine roots closer to home.

"I think I can get the rest from the Lumbees down at Lumberton. That's where we're going next."

"Most likely," Miz Dupree agreed. "Y'all are welcome to spend the night here." She smiled at Sunday. "You ought to let your hair grow out."

"Why?"

"You're so young. Long hair will make you look older. Folks will have a lot more respect for you when they meet you for the first time." She gave Slick a sideways glance. "I hear you're a right good cook when you're sober. How are you with rabbit stew?"

Slick grinned broadly. "Jus' show me the rabbits and the pot!"

While he was building a fire beneath the cast-iron cooking pot, he whispered to Sunday, "Boy, that's one skinny gal. You sure she's a woman?"

Sunday noticed the old twinkle in her father's eye. He was his old self again, for sure. "Of course she's a woman."

"Couldn't prove it by me. Got a voice like a man's, got no titties at all, and if it rains, she could stand under a clothesline and never get a drop on her! Want to help me skin these two rabbits?"

They were halfway through the meal when Jacob's pickup came roaring up the drive to the rear of the house, kicking up a cloud of dust and scattering the chickens as he braked hard. He jumped out, yelling, "Help me, Mama, it's Albert Johnson's little sister. She's burned real bad!"

Sunday and Slick watched what followed in helpless, total awe. Nothing the Dupree woman did, in sequence, was hurried. At no time did she raise her voice, nor did she seem the least bit nervous. Just the opposite. Her quiet deliberation showed she had seen many such emergencies before.

She walked to the rear of the truck, telling her son in a calm voice that he had done the right thing by placing the child, who looked to be about ten or eleven and rather stout, in the truck's bed rather than on the seat. Together, she and her son lifted the girl up and gently laid her on the ground. The poor thing had not lost consciousness, but had long since screamed her voice out. All she could manage was a hoarse simper. The Dupree woman produced a pair of scissors from her apron pocket, and cut away the charred cotton dress as well as her panties—what remained of them—from the chubby girl's body, revealing horrible-looking, red-raw skin from her waist to three inches below her buttocks.

"Bring the lard, Jacob," she said, then to Sunday, she added, "This looks worse than it really is. She'll be fine."

The boy hurried inside to fetch the lard bucket, and Miz Dupree immediately set to work. Sunday was totally fascinated. The fire talker began a kind of chant, almost like soft singing, as her birdlike fingers began hovering, circling over the blistered flesh, then stroking it with feather-light touch.

> *"You fire, you, get away,*
> *You burn, you, go on home,*
> *You heat, you, cool on down,*
> *You pain, you, get away,*
> *You pain, this ain't your day,*
> *You get on now, while I pray . . . "*

Sunday held her breath, for minutes at the time. The woman's voice was gentle. Caressing. Hypnotizing. Sunday lost track of the repetitions or the odd verses of the chant-song, although she was aware that the boy had brought the lard, which his mother spread slowly over the awful wound, using only the tips of her slender fingers.

Sunday pieced together what had happened. In a fit of rage resulting from some kind of argument, the girl's older brother had pushed the child backwards into a red-hot heater and had held her there long enough to do the damage, but then had presence of mind enough to realize what evil he had done, and had run out to the yard screaming for help. Jacob had often seen his mother take care of burns like this, and had known exactly what to do.

" . . . *You fire, you, get on out,*
You pain, you, leave this child,
You skin, you, heal on up . . . "

Over and over the woman sang-talked, her hands never stopping, her eyes rarely blinking. For two solid hours!

Sunday did not notice when the child stopped crying, or when her body ceased writhing beneath the fire talker's strokes. Neither did Slick, who leaned down and whispered into Sunday's ear, "Is she dead?"

"I don't think so, Daddy. Looks like she's asleep."

"It's a miracle."

"Sure is."

The next time Sunday looked up from watching the operation, she saw that the child's family had appeared, and were standing stiff as statues by the car they'd arrived in. At last the Dupree woman straightened, then stood. She turned to the white-faced mother and father.

"She'll be fine. You can take her home now, and keep her still for the next day or two."

To the mother she cautioned, "Keep lard on her for seven days, then wash her with warm water. I'll give you some stuff to put in with it."

When the Johnsons had carefully loaded their sleeping daughter into the back seat of their car and were gone, Miz Dupree turned to Sunday with a wan smile. "That takes a lot out of a body. I'm hungry. Any more of that stew left?"

Satisfied that the fifty dollars she spent was a fair price for the supplies she would get, Sunday and Slick made the longer trip down to Pembroke and Lumberton, close to the South Carolina line. It didn't take Sunday long to make friends with the genial tribal healer, who informed her he was distantly related to Susan Bearclaw, and would be—for a reasonable fee—willing to ship to her plenty of rabbit tobacco, pine, sassafras, pokeberry, wild horehound, John-the-Walker, red oak bark, mandrake, and a number of other items she had on her list. She paid him with three of the gold coins from her pouch, but politely turned down his offer of sharing a strong pipe. With a sly wink, Slick quietly told her that refusing the pipe amounted to a major insult, and promptly volunteered to take her place and make amends. Sunday was still laughing when she fell asleep that night.

And the following morning, as she had with Miz Dupree, she bargained with the old man for a steady supply to be sent to her annually. The pipe-smoking episode was Slick's only backwards slide during their trip, and Sunday rewarded her father by stopping at Goldsboro on the way home, and buying him a new suit, two shirts, and a new pair of shoes.

They had been away from Pea Island more than a week, and Sunday was anxious to get back home, but their final ferry ride was postponed by a short social visit to the Padgett family at Manteo. They arrived there late in the afternoon on Sunday, October 28th, 1942, and that night, Sunday and Slick went to church with Mary Padgett.

Sunday, now in her early twenties, behaved herself this time around though the fervent shouting and wailing was no less amusing than it had been before. Her mood soon turned serious, however. When the pleading call to the altar came, Slick Everette, tears in his eyes, was the first to fall on his knees before the cross, and was promptly saved!

To Sunday's amazement, the born-again Slick Everette told his daughter the following morning that he'd had a vision the night before. He gave her the rest of her cash money back, and informed her he was going to stay on Roanoke Island. "I've got the callin', honey. Next time you see me, I'm gon' be a full-time evangelist. Praise the Lord!"

Sunday, her own eyes wet, hugged him once fiercely, then turned away before she could argue with him, whispering, "Amen. Amen."

When Sunday got back to Pea Island, she went straight to the Station House and climbed to the crow's nest to let the surfmen know she had come home. All seven were gazing at the eastern horizon, where a red-orange halo arched over four more distant, dying ships. They didn't hear her approach, and Sunday had the shock of her life when she heard Cap'n Ben Searcy do something she had never thought possible!

He suddenly raised, then shook, his fist at the dark Atlantic and cursed—at the top of his voice, "God damn you, you yellow-bellied German sons of bitches. God damn you every one to hell!"

CHAPTER 13

TWO DAYS before Christmas, Sunday had a visitor. She was busy organizing the shelves in the south room with her new supply of medicines when she heard someone knocking at her door. She opened it and was stunned to see Sam Kingsley standing there, dressed in the uniform of a United States Marine, and holding a squirming brown puppy.

"Mr. Kingsley? What a surprise! Come in, come in."

Kingsley came in, shook hands, and said, "It's Sergeant Kingsley now, Sunday, and I've brought you a Christmas present. He's only eight weeks old."

He held the puppy out to her.

She took him and held him up so she could get a better look at him. "Well, now, Mister Christmas Present, what kind of dog are you?"

"He's half Lab and half German Shepherd," Kingsley said. "Friend of mine raises them. Says this mix is great because they're easy to train, very loyal, and love the water like a fish. I thought of you, and so, here he is."

Sunday remembered her manners. She put the puppy down, and said, "Can I offer you some tea?"

"Sure thing. Some tea would be great."

Sunday hurried to put some on, the puppy scrambling around her feet, his tail wagging so fast it shook his fat little body. She glanced down at him. "Looks like you haven't missed many meals so far, Gyp." She instantly realized she had called him Gyp before she had thought about it.

"That was the name of your other dog, wasn't it?" Kingsley said.

"Yes, sir. I reckon it's good enough a name for this one, too. It's real nice you came to visit, and thank you for Gyp, but where on earth have you come from, just to see me?"

"Jacksonville. Camp Lejeune. My unit's going to be shipping out pretty soon, and I had a few days leave, so I decided to bring this little feller and see how you're getting along. No telling when I might come this way again."

Sunday poured the tea, really touched by Sam Kingsley's gesture. "I'm getting along all right, Mr. Kingsley. Just—"

"Please, call me Sam."

"All right. Sam. It's been a long time. Wonder whatever happened to all those boys in your camp?"

"My guess is most of them are in the service now. I joined right after Pearl."

"The country's in a real mess isn't it?"

"Not for long. The Japs and Krauts picked on the wrong folks this time. It was rough right after Pearl Harbor, but we're turning the tide now."

"Where do you think they'll send you?"

"Probably somewhere in the Pacific."

"I wish I could join up."

Sam laughed. "Now, that would be bad news for the Japs for sure. They'd probably make you a whole platoon all by yourself! What are you up to now? Still cooking?"

"No. I fish and crab for a living, and for extra money, I do what I can to help sick people. I also help women with birthing their babies. I've brought twelve of them into the world in the last few years. Haven't had a bearcat yet, knock wood."

"What's a 'bearcat?' "

"A birth you can't handle."

Sam sipped and nodded. He shifted his feet, bit his lip and tried to think of what next to say. It was an awkward moment for both of them. At last Sam found his voice again.

"I swear, Sunday Everette, I don't think there's anything you couldn't do if you set your mind to it." He paused for yet another thirty seconds, and in almost a whisper, added, "You know, I never did get around to apologizing to you for that terrible mess back in '37, but I—"

"That wasn't your fault, Sam. Anyway, it's all in the past. Like my Papa Ben would say, it's ancient history." Sunday gave him her best smile, reaching over and lightly touching his arm. "Still, I really do appreciate your taking the trouble to come all the way out here to see me, and I'm sure Gyp and I will get along just fine. I'll think of you every time I look at him. Say, can you write me a letter every now and then?"

Vastly relieved, Sam promised he would, and soon left.

Sunday started to go back to her work, but looked down to see that little Gyp had proudly produced a small puddle on her floor.

Sunday frowned, promptly rubbed his nose in it, and said, "No, *sir!* This'll be the last time you do that, mister. You'll do your business outside from now on."

She picked him up, deposited him unceremoniously out the door, and went back to her work, unmindful of the pitiful wailing he instantly set up. But after a while, a pang of conscience attacked her. She relented, let him back in, fed him a little canned milk, and except for that one instance, he never left her side again.

To her dismay, however, Sunday quickly discovered that Gyp was a talented and indiscriminate chewer. The World Champion chewer! Anything he could reach, he would gnaw on. Nonplussed, Sunday mixed up a batch of bitter herbs, which she diluted in water, and used it to paint the bottoms of table and chair legs, brooms, her boots, and everything else the puppy could get his tiny teeth onto. Gyp got the message, right away, and was happy to exercise his teething needs on the discarded spools and the occasional soup bone she tossed on the floor.

Experimenting, Sunday found, to her delight, that Gyp liked oatmeal. That, plus a mixture of cornmeal and ham gravy served admirably as his staple dog food. Sunday was careful never to feed him from her table, and Gyp slept under her bed or napped by her feet when she read from the books Ben loaned her. The edges of the sound and even the Atlantic were, almost from the beginning, never too cold for him to play or swim in, and when he was three months old, he got his sea legs aboard *BLACK DOLPHIN*.

The middle war years between that Christmas of 1942 and 1944 were busy ones for Sunday and her canine crew. Escorted convoys had finally stopped the carnage off the Atlantic coast, and from her own boat, Sunday often saw great numbers of ships coming and going around the cape. She never failed to wave at them, or at the men flying low in the little yellow Piper Cubs out of the new airfield on Roanoke Island. Usually, the civilian volunteer pilots would wave back at her, or waggle their wings, then continue on in their search for German subs. Sunday's days were filled, as before, with fishing, occasional duck and goose hunting, and doctoring people from one end of the Banks to the other.

Gyp rapidly grew into his feet, and proved Sam's prediction over and over. He loved the water almost as much as Sunday did, had no fear of sailing with her out of sight of land, and would wait patiently at the door of whatever family Sunday called on with her medicines. The only time he acted strange was when she took him with her to put fresh flowers on Susan Bearclaw's grave. Sunday never could figure out why he'd get but just so close to her grave, and go no farther. He'd sit or lie down and simply wait for her to start back to the boat. For her part, Sunday, from their first day together, patiently and thoroughly trained Gyp, so that he walked at her side and at her pace when she was in town, was never tempted to chase after any other dog or cat. He was docile as a teddy bear around children, though he had grown into a huge, rather frightful-looking animal.

Gyp also went with her back to Elizabeth City in the summer of '44, when Robert Kinch told her that Ernestine Pike was dying and was begging Sunday to come see her before she did. Totally perplexed, Sunday was too curious to refuse, made the trip, and commanding Gyp to *stay,* walked into the big house, having been let in by a black woman dressed in a maid's uniform.

Following the black-clad woman up two flights of stairs, Sunday's nose instantly told her the entire old house had taken on the smell of death. As she walked into the bedroom, whatever preconceived notions she'd had about the infamous madam gave way to pity when she saw the wasted figure propped up with half a dozen pillows on top of a monstrous four-poster bed. Sunday walked slowly to the bedside and peered down at the wrinkled face.

Ernestine Pike's eyes were sunken back into her skull, but the stretched lips were smeared bright red. A few remaining strands of her hair poked out from beneath an old-fashioned bed-bonnet. The red smear parted and a paper-thin voice rasped, "Thank you for coming."

The words cut across Sunday's nerves like a wood file. "Miz Pike, I—"

"Oh, I didn't ask you to come here for some of your famous treatment. There's nothing any doctor can do for what I've got. Pull up that chair and sit down for a minute."

Sunday pulled the antique Windsor chair close to the bedside and sat.

The dying woman wheezed, "There's something I want you to have. Look in the drawer of that table. There's a picture in there."

Sunday opened the drawer and removed a framed sepia photograph of a slim young woman with long blond hair, pretty eyes, and full lips, which were set in a faint smile. Sunday immediately knew who the girl was without being told.

"That's right, child. She was your mother. I thought you might like to have it. Either you or your father. No matter what you or anybody else may think about her or what she did, Mandy Cooper was every inch a lady. She had grace, wonderful manners, and the kindest heart of anyone I ever knew. I thought of her as if she was my own daughter. Maybe nobody else loved her, but I did, and I believe you would have, too."

Ernestine went into a bad coughing spell that lasted what seemed like five minutes, while Sunday sat there, helpless and not a little embarrassed, breathing through her mouth because of the odors wafting in waves from the bed.

After she finally recovered her voice, Ernestine said, "Anyway, I think Mandy would be proud of you and what you have done with your life. I know I would be. Now, go. Go on back to your precious island and let me die in peace—and with a clear conscience."

But Sunday didn't get up right away. She reached for the dying woman's hand and whispered, "There's a story in the Bible about how Jesus tells people who were about to stone a woman who sold her body, 'Let he who is without sin cast the first stone.' I reckon I won't throw any either. God bless you, Miz Pike, and thank you for the picture. I know somebody else who would like to see it, too."

Sunday squeezed the frail hand gently, then stood, turned and left, anxious to be out the front door and able to breathe fresh air again. She took the photograph home with her and placed it in her dresser drawer to give to her father when she saw him again.

One Tuesday afternoon, Ben brought her a military-issue envelope containing a letter from Sam Kingsley—from "somewhere in the South Pacific."

Dear Sunday,

I thought I would have more time to write letters, but I don't. We are kept pretty busy out here, building roads and airstrips. My crew is a swell bunch of boys. Sure are a lot different than that bunch I had on Pea Island. Speaking of Pea Island, the skeeters there are pigmies compared to the critters on this island. I remembered how the vanilla extract worked so well there, and put in for some out here, but it has not come yet. It is mighty hot out here, too, but we can go swimming about every day if we want to. It helps a little bit, and sure makes the boys smell better at night. Me, too I guess.

Our boys out here are really giving the Japs a bloody nose. It looks like we will not need you to come out to help us after all. Ha Ha. How is everything with you? Are you having a hard time with the rationing and all?

I know there cannot be much chocolate left in the U.S. any more. It is all out here. And we have plenty of smokes, but I miss home a lot, especially the grub. I do not know how many times I have told my buddies about you and how good your cooking was. Just about every one of them wants a picture of you, and your address!! But do not send them. We Marines do not want any deserters out here!!

Well, I am running out of time and paper.

Write soon if you can.

Yours truly. Sam

Succeeding letters from Sam arrived regularly, about every two months, saying much the same kind of things, and barely disguising his homesickness. Sunday answered each one, telling him how big a dog Gyp was, how many babies she had delivered that month, and that her fishing and crabbing business was doing well and making her a little money. Sam's letters stopped abruptly in the autumn of 1944, and Sunday didn't have to be told why. In denial, she mailed a last one to him anyway, commenting mostly about the lack of tourists and vacationers.

This was true, and the bad hurricane eastern North Carolina had that season didn't help. The big hotel at Nags Head had very few guests, and the one on Ocracoke Island closed down completely. Sunday wasn't sorry to hear that John Ramsey had gone broke, but the lack of customers there and elsewhere on the Banks caused a sharp reduction in her income, although her reputation as a healer grew steadily. Sometimes people could not pay her, but those who did made up some of her financial loss.

She bought a small radio and kept up with the war news all through the nasty winter of 1944, often sitting with Ben Searcy over a cup of tea and talking about it. She couldn't help but notice too, that Ben seemed despondent in spite of better and better news coming over the radio and printed in the newspapers. Finally, in mid-January of '45, he told her why:

"Sunday, they're going to close the Station down."

"*What?* When?"

"I don't know exactly when. Seems like this war will soon be over, and the Coast Guard has new Cutter Stations all over the coast now. Far as they are concerned, the Life-Saving Service is no longer needed. We're all dinosaurs. Extra expenses they can do without."

"But what's going to happen to you? And Lonnie and Royce?"

Ben smiled. "Haven't you noticed? We're all getting a bit long in the tooth. Old men, practically. I'm sure they're going to retire all of us. Hopefully, with full pensions. God knows they never paid us much to begin with."

"What will you do?"

"I don't know that, either. I'm too old to go back to sea. I'll find me a front porch of my own, I guess; get myself a pipe and some slippers, and sit there all day telling old stories. Won't be long before you'll be the only resident on Pea Island. You and Gyp here."

Gyp, hearing his name, raised his head and thumped his tail on the floor.

"Anyway," Ben said with a sigh, "Have you got a little bit more of that peach cobbler left? I'd sure like a spoonful."

Their retirement orders came on March 1st. In only one week, the surfmen were all gone, except for Amos Turner, who was given the lonely duty of patrolling the beach between the Oregon Inlet and New Inlet. Against regulations, he took most of his meals with Sunday, and since there was no one to monitor him, he usually lingered far longer than he should have. He was with her late the night of April 12th, when the news of President Roosevelt's death came over the radio. Both of them sat there in silence, not quite knowing what to make of it, yet feeling a strange, even personal sense of loss.

The following morning, Amos came running down to catch Sunday before she and Gyp headed out to check her crab pots. "Sunday, Cap'n Searcy's on the telephone. He wants to talk to you. Sounds important."

Sunday followed Amos to the Station House, not failing to notice how rundown Amos had allowed everything inside to become. It also occurred to her that this was the first time in her life she had spoken over the telephone!

"Papa Ben? What's wrong?"

"You heard the news?"

"Yes, sir. Last night."

"Sunday, if you can get away, I'd like for you to come right over to Manteo. Estelle and I are taking her car inland to see President Roosevelt's train. We'd like it if you could come with us. It's all right if you want to bring Gyp, too."

"Estelle Carson?"

Sunday heard an embarrassed laugh in her ear. "Yes, honey, there is another little bit of news. Estelle and I got married last Saturday over in Edenton. Aside from her two cousins who live there, she didn't want a big crowd, so we didn't invite anybody else."

Sunday shrieked in joyful surprise, remembering the prim schoolteacher whose sister Ben had once loved. *How about that! Ben found his front porch after all. Good for him!* "Well! Papa Ben, that's the best news I've heard in years! Congratulations. I'm happy as I can be for you. Her, too. And I can't wait to hug your neck!"

"Thank you. Then you will come over?"

Sunday didn't hesitate. "We'll be there by noon."

She and Gyp spent the night in Estelle Carson Searcy's spare room. The following morning, early, Sunday helped prepare a large picnic basket to take with them all. She and Gyp climbed into the back seat of Estelle's spic-and-span '39 Chevy, and by mid-afternoon, Estelle drove into the bustling town of Rocky Mount.

Ben explained, "Honey, this town has a lot going for it. It's on the main rail line between New York, Philadelphia, Washington, and all points south to Florida. Matter of fact, the Atlantic Coast Line railroad has its main shops here. Lots of troop trains come through here almost every day."

Estelle drove from the south end of town to the north, and added, "There are dozens of tobacco warehouses here, plus a factory. And, there are two major textile mills. Plenty of work for those who want it."

She turned back and drove down the retail center of Main Street—split by the railroad tracks.

"Funny, isn't it, Sunday," Ben said. "Half the town is in one county, and half in another one. Say, you know that radio program we like so much, 'Kay Kyser's Kollege of Musical Knowledge?' Well, Kay Kyser was born here." He pointed. "Couple blocks down that street."

By dusk, they found themselves waiting in a silent vigil with hundreds of other black people (and a sprinkling of whites) on the north end of town, by the double tracks. Ben was looking south. "The train will have to slow down there, before it gets to the station, and won't speed up again until it passes by us here."

Every hat came off, many white handkerchiefs fluttered, and many a reverent tear was shed as the train carrying the body of the dead president passed by, slowly enough for them to see the honor guard inside the crepe-draped car carrying the casket. Long after it was out of sight, creeping north, the huge crowd stood fast, some talking quietly, others crying unashamedly.

On the way back to Manteo, Ben remarked, "Many hated him, but most think he was a great man and president, and his wife is a true friend of black people. It's a damned shame he didn't live long enough to see the end of this war."

"You think it's about over?" Sunday asked.

"Yes. I don't think it will last too much longer. According to the news, Hitler is practically finished, and the Japs, stubborn as they are, can't last too much longer either. Your old friend Kingsley was right. They picked on the wrong country, and now they're paying for it."

That night, there was a prayer service held in memory of Roosevelt at the church, and Sunday was delighted to see her father there.

"Daddy," she said, after it was over, "I have something for you. A present. Can you come with me back to Pea Island for a day or two?"

"Sure I can, honey. What is it?"

"You'll see."

Slick cried real tears when she gave him the photograph of her mother. Not so much because of his remembrance of a white prostitute, but for the understanding and forgiveness of his daughter. Sunday had long since vowed never to tell him what Susan Bearclaw had said about her being his seventh one! She wasn't about to throw stones in that direction either.

They spent four pleasant days and nights together, catching up on all Slick's newest adventures, and were enjoying a cup of good coffee when Amos came running down to her house, his face contorted with anxiety.

"What's the matter, Amos?"

"It's my wife, Sunday. She just called me and told me her water's broke and she's in a lot of pain."

"But that baby isn't due for another two weeks."

"She's in a bad way. Can you—?"

"Of course. I'll get my things and sail right on over there. Try to relax. Everything's going to be all right. I haven't lost one yet."

"I'm going with you."

"Amos Turner! You can't. You'd be—what do they call it?"

"AWOL. I don't care. Ain't nothin' *happenin'* on this island anyway, and she *needs* me. I'm goin' with you, and please don't you try to talk me out of it."

Sunday saw there was no use even trying to. The man was clearly sick with worry.

"I'll stay here till you get back," Slick offered. "I got nothin' else to do for a while. Take him with you, honey. I'll mind the store for you."

"We might be gone several days . . . "

"Don't matter. I can get caught up on my sleep and readin'. I ain't had much lately."

"All right then." She looked at Amos and gave him a smile. "But if you get in trouble with the Coast Guard, don't blame me. Let's go. Come on, Gyp, we have a baby to deliver."

The baby was Sunday's first bearcat, but she had presence of mind enough to call for help, thanking God there were now two real doctors living and practicing at Manteo. In the end, however, nothing could be done. They managed to save Amos' wife, but the baby was stillborn.

Not waiting for daylight, Sunday sailed back home to Pea Island with a heavy heart. She hadn't slept in more than twelve hours and was exhausted. Under the moonless sky, she allowed herself to doze off from time to time. She tied up at the pier somewhere around two in the morning, and with Gyp at her heels, began walking home. Halfway there, Gyp suddenly stopped, a low, visceral growl coming from his throat.

Still preoccupied, Sunday stopped, too. "Gyp? What is it? What's wrong?"

This time Gyp didn't look up at her the way he normally did. He laid his ears back and growled again. Louder.

Chapter 14

"STAY!" SUNDAY commanded, her voice low.

Gyp instantly obeyed, though his face showed he was not a bit happy to.

Sunday bent over to a crouch, and crabbed her way to the top of the dune ridge. An inch at the time, she raised her head over it, looking in the direction of her house. There was no light coming from the windows, but at this time of morning she hadn't expected to see one. Still, she knew there was something wrong. Her skin was crawling, and she knew Gyp hadn't growled the way he did for no reason. His sense of smell and hearing was far greater than hers, but she knew her eyesight was better. Without moving her head, she glanced left and right, straining to see what was out of place.

Everything seemed normal, and she was almost ready to stand and call her dog when she saw something she'd missed. Leaning up against the north wall of her house was a shovel. Not hers, either, or one that belonged to the Station House. It had a short handle, almost like a toy spade. She had never seen one like it before.

Then she noticed something else. The sand around her house looked different. It was smooth as ever, but it seemed to be piled up a little higher! *Somebody's been digging around the house. For what? Could Daddy have been looking for something? Money, maybe?*

With renewed disgust, she was again about to stand up and call Gyp when she heard the door open. She couldn't see it from where she was lying, but her heart nearly froze when she saw a man walk around the corner, cup his hands carefully, and light a cigarette. He was tall, but not nearly as tall as her father, and he was wearing what looked like a military uniform—one she didn't recognize. *Who are you, mister? And what are you doing in my house?*

The tall man walked a few steps toward the surf line, stopped, and proceeded to make water, turning rapidly away from the south breeze as he did. *Well, whoever the hell you are, friend, you're no sailor. Any fool who grows up around the water knows better than to pee upwind. What are you doing here, and where did you come from?*

Sunday was trying to think of what to do when she heard something. She raised her head a little higher. The sound was coming from the ocean, and getting closer. It didn't take her more than a few seconds to recognize it—powerboat. *Surfboat? No, that's not the sound of a surfboat. Sounds like . . . outboard motors? Was the lit cigarette a signal?* She wished she was a little higher, so she could see better. If only—*Wait a minute. The Station House, of course! From the crow's nest, I can see everything.*

Carefully, like a turtle, she eased her head down, and backed away from the dune. She hurried back to where Gyp patiently waited, and whispered, "We've got strange company, Gyp. Come on, and be quiet!"

The dog at her heels, she backtracked to the edge of the sound, followed the path to the Station House, and climbed the steps. Inside, she snatched a pair of binoculars from the shelf by the door and flew up the stairs. She told Gyp to sit, and knelt by the rail. She raised the glasses, first to her house, then down to the beach where the stranger was standing, looking out to sea. *Where the devil is Daddy?*

Less than a minute later, she saw him! Half a head taller than the rest of the men in the two boats coming through the surf, there was no mistaking him, but he was—blindfolded? Gagged? Tied up? Why? Where had he been?

Fascinated, confused, and fearful all at the same time, she leaned over and whispered, "Gyp, you be quiet. Don't you make a peep!"

She turned back in time to see the men beach both black-painted boats, realizing several things at once: First, those boats would be almost impossible to see in the water on such a moonless night. Second, they had to have come from a bigger boat farther out. And third, the men who were in them were certainly not seamen. Real sailors would have jumped out the instant their boats touched sand, and would have grabbed the rails and pushed hard, adding their own strength to the boat's momentum, thereby carrying it farther up on the beach.

Sunday silently counted heads. Two men and her father in one boat, and two more in the other one. *That makes five, counting the real tall one.* Hardly daring to breathe, Sunday noticed that from the way a short, chunky man in the second boat jumped out and began gesturing and talking to the tall one on the beach, he must be the one in charge. Sunday adjusted the binoculars, to get a closer look at him. He had a mean-looking face, one that meant business.

She shifted the glasses so that she could see her father. The tall man was removing his blindfold.

"Bet you a dollar that big guy is the assistant boss man, Gyp."

Apart from being tied up and gagged, Slick didn't
seem hurt, and Sunday instantly wondered how much, if
anything, he had told those men about her, or maybe
where she was. When had they kidnapped him? Where
had they taken him—some ship out there?

Logically, she raised the glasses and stared out to
sea. She swept the horizon, but saw nothing. If there
was a ship out there, it had to be a long way offshore. At
least twenty, maybe thirty miles offshore. Either that,
or—*a submarine?* She shifted her gaze back to the beach
in front of her house. *Germans?*

The stocky one was now giving more quiet orders.
His men were unloading small wooden boxes that had
rope handles, stacking them on the beach. From the way
the four men were straining, those boxes were mighty
heavy. What could be in them that would weigh that
much?

"Okay, Gyp," she whispered, "I guess now we know
what that shovel was for. They're burying whatever's in
those boxes around my house. And they're mighty
careful about it, too. See how they've fixed the sand back
so it looks the same?"

Done with the offloading, the tall man left the boats
and climbed to the top of the dune behind the shack.
Sunday now noticed that he was wearing what appeared
to be a black rubber suit. *Well, Mister Lookout, you
should have blacked out your face, too. Don't need a
moon to see it.*

She caught her breath as she saw the others untie her
father who, with a gun to his back, was put to work,
carrying box after box to the privy.

"Look at that, Gyp. They're dropping some of them
into the Station House privy! Smart. Nobody would ever
think to look in *there!*"

Sunday lowered the glasses, crept back toward the stairwell, and tried to think all this through, whispering to Gyp as if he understood every word.

"All right. Those men are hiding something, and going to a lot of trouble to do it. It's pretty plain they have been here at least once before, since they took Daddy with them and left the big guy in his place. How many loads of boxes have they brought ashore already? Will they be bringing still more? Whoever they are, they most likely will take Daddy with them when they leave, *if* they leave. No matter what, they're not about to let him go free to tell about it. We better get some help out here, and right away, too."

She slipped downstairs, heading for the telephone. She picked it up and immediately saw that the line had been cut.

"Damn, Gyp. They've already been in here!"

Sunday noticed her hand was shaking. She replaced the receiver and climbed back to her perch on the crow's nest. The men were still working, her father doing most of it.

"Gyp," she whispered again, "Daddy's in a lot of trouble. So are we if they catch us here. All of them except that little scrawny one are carrying guns. We wouldn't have a chance. But how can we—"

Another frightening series of thoughts suddenly flitted through her mind: those men were doing their secret work under cover of darkness. That meant they would have to go back to their mother ship before sunup, and dawn wasn't more than an hour or two away. They wouldn't dare take those boats out during daylight. One of those little Piper Cubs out of Roanoke Island could spot them easily. Maybe their submarine, too. Or . . .

Or, maybe they'd spend the daytime here, laying low. But then, if they did, where would they hide those two boats? The only place they could possibly stash them would be—*Lord! Right under the Station House!*

"Gyp, we'd better get out of here right now. If one of those men comes up here, he'll spot *BLACK DOLPHIN*'s mast for sure."

She stood, thought to snatch the pair of semaphore flags from their pocket by the rail because an idea was already forming in her head, and practically ran out, carrying the binoculars as well. She and Gyp reached her boat without being seen, and Sunday was careful not to make any noise as she paddled away from the finger pier far enough to raise her mainsail, thanking God she had followed Ben's advice to dye all her sails black. She dropped sail and anchored about a half mile out in the sound.

With the binoculars, she watched for any movement at the Station House. Seeing none, and convinced there was not enough darkness left for them to put to sea, she assumed the men were all holed up in her own house, or with the two boats under the Station House. She groaned aloud. She'd had very little food and no sleep in the past twenty-four hours, and knew she needed to be fresh both mentally and physically for whatever was to happen when full daylight came, so she lay down in the bottom of the boat for at least a short nap.

It was the noise of a plane that awakened her. The sun was nearly overhead! She glanced to the northwest. Having taken off into the slight southwest breeze, the small, yellow Piper Cub had banked left, and was coming right at her, climbing gradually. Sunday shook the sleep from her eyes, grabbed the semaphore flags, stood, and frantically began signaling:

H-E-L-P G-E-R-M-A-N-S H-E-R-E

With one slight waggle of its wings, the plane kept climbing and continued on toward to the southeast and was soon only a speck in the sky. Crestfallen, Sunday lowered the flags. She gave Gyp a look of hopelessness.

"That's a civilian volunteer pilot, Gyp. He saw us all right, but he doesn't know semaphore from chicken soup! Damn!"

She sat on the thwart, head in her hands, trying desperately to think of what to do next. If she sailed to Roanoke Island and alerted the authorities, an official boat would surely be dispatched, possibly from Elizabeth City or New Bern, and might—just might—reach Pea Island before nightfall and capture them all. But that would no doubt mean certain death for her father. She could gain a little time by sailing past New Inlet, beaching her boat, and chasing down one of the patrolling sentries.

But if she did that, the man's first question would be to ask her where Amos Turner was, and she'd have to tell him, which, of course, would get poor AWOL Amos in a world of trouble. Did they shoot deserters in time of war? Hadn't she read that somewhere? No, that option, plus the fact that she'd also be signing her father's death warrant were chances she couldn't take, no matter what.

"Looks like it's up to us, Gyp."

There was absolutely nothing that could be done during daylight. *Nothing to do but wait for dark.* She knew it would be a long, miserable day, but at least the late-April sun wouldn't be unbearable. Acute hunger and thirst wouldn't be a problem either, since she still had her emergency water jug and a packet of beef jerky, which was always stowed in BLACK DOLPHIN's cuddy. She sighed helplessly. Well, there was nothing for it but to try to get some more sleep. She had a feeling that she would need all her strength when night finally came.

The endless hours dragged by. The longest ones of her life. At last the sun disappeared over the western horizon, partly obscured by some low clouds. She felt a slight chill on her cheek. "That's good, Gyp. There might be a little fog tonight."

She waited until what she judged to be around ten o'clock, sharing the last of the jerky and some water with her dog, then hoisted sail and made for New Inlet. She sailed through, turned right, and beached her boat on the north tip of Hatteras Island. She paused to think for a moment or two, then slowly removed her clothes and boots. "All right, old boy, we've got some swimming to do. You ready?"

She and Gyp easily swam across the inlet, which, since the most-recent hurricane, had shoaled to nothing more than a fast-moving creek. Together, they walked the water line up the beach toward her house. When within two hundred yards south of it, she waded into the surf up to her waist, wanting to get close, but also wanting to offer the smallest possible target.

Gyp, watching her, kept slow pace along the water's edge, his nose up and his ears laid back.

Sunday crept closer. When she was within a hundred yards of her house, she knelt down, so that only her head was above water. A foot at the time, she moved in closer, but saw no sign of life. No movement at all. The two boats were nowhere to be seen either. If she hadn't spotted the strip of light coming from beneath the door of her house, she wouldn't have known there was a soul there. There was only the sound of the ocean around her, gently rocking her in the mild surf.

She glanced at her dog. Gyp apparently also sensed they were in for another long wait, and stretched out on his belly just beyond the tide line.

Sunday had no idea how much time passed. To keep warm, and to keep her muscles loose and tuned for whatever might happen, she ducked under and swam a few yards back and forth every half-hour or so. Gyp watched her, but his training held, and he remained motionless on the beach, like an obscure piece of driftwood.

After another hour or so, Sunday noticed a wisp of fog waft between her and her house, and at almost the same instant, saw the light go out from under the door. They all came out, her father included, once more gagged and tied up, but not blindfolded. The one in charge said something she couldn't hear, and the tall one in the rubber suit untied her father. It soon became clear why.

They needed his labor again. Together with three of the others, he walked back to the Station House. *They've gone to get the boats, Gyp. Don't you move.* Sunday was surprised at how light those two boats obviously were. Four men easily carried them down to the water's edge, and then made another trip back for the large outboard motors. They were surely preparing to leave, and *there was no way she could stop them.*

She was amazed at what happened next. While the three Germans were standing in the surf clamping the motors on, her father seized a chance to escape. Fast as lightning, he nailed the closest one of them with a punishing right cross, a sucker punch that put the unsuspecting man on his back in the surf. Slick turned fast and kneed the next closest one in the groin and took off running down the beach. Sunday held her breath, watching in shocked disbelief, her heart full of pride. Slick abruptly turned to the right, and began climbing the steep dune behind her house. Sunday grinned. *Smart, Daddy! If you can get over that dune, they'll never catch you.*

Just as quick as she had felt sudden elation, her heart sank. She saw the tall man crouch, aim his pistol, and fire. Slick had almost made it to the crest of the dune. Two of the shots went wild, but the third one caught Slick square in the back. Horrified, Sunday watched as Slick threw his one arm up in the air, staggered, and tumbled backwards down the slope. He struggled to his feet, though, and *tried* to run, but stumbled, fell, and began crawling. Sunday was in agony.

She watched helplessly as the stocky man, who now also had a gun drawn, casually walked over to Slick and kicked him over onto his back.

Still, Slick wasn't yet finished. He struggled back up to his knees once more and looked up with defiance at his tormentor, who calmly circled around him, taking his time. Sunday could have sworn the German leader was smiling as he slowly raised his pistol and at point-blank range, shot Slick in the face. Slick toppled over sideways, and was shot twice more—in the head.

Sunday lost control of her bladder. She thought she would also vomit. Or at least scream, but somehow, somehow, she managed to will herself to stay motionless. Then she was distracted by something else she now saw.

Gyp. Running.

She had never seen Gyp move so fast. With an unholy sound that sounded more like a shriek than a howl, he sailed through the air and knocked the German boss man down with the sheer force of velocity. But the Nazi was agile as a crab. He twisted sideways, and shot Gyp in the side. Standing, he fired again and again into Gyp's twitching body, and then turned back to the men who had witnessed the shootings, standing like mute pilings with their feet rooted in the sand.

"*Los!*" he yelled.

Sunday had no idea what that word meant. She only understood that it was an order; apparently a command to move out. She watched the tall man in the black suit run up to his boss and tell him something. The shorter one nodded, gave more orders, and all the others hurried down to where he stood, picked up her father and Gyp and carried them to the boats. They dumped the bodies in like sacks of flour, scrambled aboard, and started the motors. Both boats went rapidly through the surf, heading due east, and were soon enveloped in the fog.

Sunday's emotions galvanized her body. She struggled out of the water and began running back down the beach to her own boat, knowing full well she didn't have a prayer of catching them. With strength borrowed from some inner reserve and boosted by boiling hatred, she literally muscled her boat out far enough to hoist sail. She raised every square foot of canvas she had, sheeted in and bore away, subconsciously sensing the southwesterly would set her on a fast broad reach.

Sunday needed no compass. She knew the course those men would have to take, and that it would also take considerable time for them to ship those boats and board the submarine—or whatever other vessel may have come in to meet them and pick them up. *BLACK DOLPHIN is a pretty fast boat, too, by God.* Maybe there would be enough time, and maybe she would have enough of the element of surprise to wield—just once—the only weapon she had. Her knife. Maybe she could at least kill that one smiling bastard before they killed her.

She could tell, after a while, that she had crossed their wake. She jibed, trimmed sail, and peered under her mainsail for any sign of them. *Not yet.* She drove on, crossing their wake twice more before she felt, rather than heard, what had to be a huge explosion.

All her experience on the water then paid off. She knew the enormous blast had not come from the surface, but somewhere beneath it. She also felt, before she saw it, a rogue wave the explosion had caused, coming right at her. She automatically headed up, dropped her jib, and waited for it. *That must have been their submarine, Sunday, but how?*

The maverick wave didn't take long to arrive, and wasn't severe. BLACK DOLPHIN rode over it with no more trouble than one of her namesakes would have. Topping it, Sunday spotted one of the boats—not more than a hundred yards away. She knew she couldn't have caught up with it. Had it turned around? *No, Sunday, it must have already been to the submarine, and two of the men are coming back to the beach for some reason. They must have heard that explosion, too—they're lying there dead in the water and looking backwards!*

Only then did Sunday notice the second boat, which the Germans had apparently also been surprised to see. They were unable to react in time as it bore down on them at top speed! Closing rapidly herself, Sunday could now clearly see that there was only one man aboard. A man wearing a white cap. *My God, he's—going to ram them!*

Sunday watched the second boat strike the first one with such force it climbed right up the other's transom, flooding out its own motor, and causing both craft to veer sharply to port, beginning a tight, slow circle.

The man with the white cap was trying to climb into the killer's boat. Who was he? He hadn't been in the group that had come ashore. Anyway, it was a miracle that none of them had spotted her, and she was really close now; *only fifty more yards.*

This was her chance . . .

In practically one motion, she released her sheets, put the helm hard over, threw her sea anchor out, and clamped her knife between her teeth. She made a shallow dive toward the boats, knowing BLACK DOLPHIN would head up, stop, and not drift very far.

Sunday surfaced just as she heard shots. She reached her left hand to the rail of the leading boat and pulled herself up just in time to see the stocky German fire again—at the man with the white cap, who had managed to crawl aboard, rocking the boat some. To steady himself for his next shot, the German man who Sunday had learned to hate so much reached for the rail with his free hand. As he took aim again, Sunday seized his wrist and pulled him overboard. Hard.

Before he could realize what was happening, She released his wrist and grabbed him from behind, around his neck. Dragging him under with her, she swam straight down. Deep. He was too shocked at first to struggle much, but quickly began thrashing his arms and legs. Sunday held him tighter still, twisting viciously in the water so that he couldn't grab onto her. She pulled him down, down, knowing he would soon panic and replace the air in his lungs with the warm water that the tide had brought from the edge of the Gulf Stream.

She didn't want it to be quick. She wanted him to *know* what was going to happen to him. She wanted him to be fully aware he was going to die, and by whose hand. She yanked him around and looked into his bulging eyes. *You killed my Daddy and my dog, and somewhere between here and the beach, you threw them both overboard, didn't you? Look at my face, you German son of a bitch. I want you to know what it feels like to die. What it feels like to be chum. Shark bait.*

She pulled him still deeper. Finally, his contorted face momentarily disappeared from view, hidden in the cloud of bubbles erupting from his suddenly gaping mouth. His lungs had burst, and Sunday knew the life had gone out of him. But she wanted to make sure. Make him suffer even after death. She took the filleting knife from between her teeth and slowly cut his throat from ear to ear. Something darker than the water gushed forth, and only then did she release her grip on him, watching his body sink. *Come on, hammerheads. Suppertime.*

Sunday swam back to the surface and treaded water. She waited for the boats to circle toward her, reached up to the rail and climbed into the first one. Its bottom was bloody, most of it coming from the skinny little man who had been on the beach. One quick glance at his face told her he was beyond any help. She turned to the second one. For the first time, Sunday noticed the fancy uniform the man was wearing.

"You an officer, Mister White Cap?"

She saw that he had also been shot, but was conscious, writhing in pain, and holding his throat. There was a sizable hole in his left cheek, but that was not what was causing his agony. Sunday moved to him, pulled his hand away from his throat, and immediately saw what the problem was. The bullet had struck a shiny medal he wore around his neck, and had driven it into his windpipe, blocking most of his breathing, and half of it was still stuck there. Part, or all, of that bullet must have glanced up and to the left, passing clean through his cheek! She tugged on the medal. It came free, but she realized something more drastic would have to be done.

She smiled at him. "Gasping like a gaffed fish, aren't you? Don't worry, you won't die."

She saw his eyes widen as she moved the point of her knife to his throat. "I saw Susan Bearclaw do this one time when Ronnie Wilkins choked on a piece of cornbread."

She felt for the spot, then, deft as any surgeon, cut a hole in his windpipe large enough to stick her finger into. She felt the air rushing in, then out.

"No, sir. You'll live. And I'll tell you something else. When I get you back to Pea Island and nurse you back to health, you got a lot of explaining to do."

She straightened, looking around. BLACK DOLPHIN was drifting only fifty or sixty yards away, to starboard. She felt for and found the cutoff switch for the outboard motor. When its sound died down, she turned her attention to the body of the small man.

"I'll treat you better than you did my Daddy, buddy boy. You're going to get a Christian burial, even if you don't deserve one."

She looked around for lines long enough for a tether, wondering if there was enough wind for her to tow both boats back to shore.

"Well," she said to no one, eyeing the boxes so neatly stowed, now resting in dark, red puddles, "might be possible if we lighten this boat up some."

The boxes were extremely heavy, hard to throw overboard. But, there weren't many of them, and she still had plenty of adrenaline-pumped strength left.

Chapter 15

Sunday stood, testing the wind, and grunted in disappointment. There was not enough breeze to tow the motorboats behind *Black Dolphin*, even if its direction had been onshore. A quick examination of the engine of the boat she was in revealed too much damage from being rammed by the second one. Another decision had to be made. Fast, too, before all three boats drifted too far apart.

Working rapidly, she transferred her human cargo to the second boat, pausing only long enough to pick up the bent, glittering medal that had saved White Cap's life. She stared at the strangely shaped black cross only for a second or two. Sunday didn't own any jewels, but she recognized diamonds easily enough! No time to think about that now. Being naked, she simply clamped it between her teeth while she rocked, tipped, and scuttled the first boat.

The motor of its sister boat started easily, and reminded Sunday of her earlier astonishment at how quiet it was. She glanced once at White Cap, who was holding his hand against his bleeding cheek. Sunday didn't have much sympathy for him, but as she slipped the medal into his uniform pocket she gave him a grudging compliment, "Well, sir, I'll say one thing for you Germans. You know how to build good boats. Engines, too. Never saw any like these before."

With those words, she steered the motorboat over to her own vessel, jumped nimbly aboard, fetched her anchor line and under quiet power, was soon towing her sailboat back to shore, talking to her wounded captive the whole time.

"I'll take care of you and your dead mate, Charlie White Cap. You're not going to die, but I know you're hurting like the devil. Still and all, don't you even think about trying any foolishness. That's right, you just keep right on staring at me like that."

She allowed herself a soft chuckle. "Bet you never saw a naked black woman before, did you? Don't get yourself any ideas about that, either. I want to, I can break what's left of your Nazi neck."

Sunday thought, for the briefest of moments, she saw the hint of a smile on White Cap's face. It suddenly dawned on her that he had understood every word she'd said. "Uh-huh! You speak American?"

White Cap managed a painful nod.

"That's good, though I reckon it'll be some time before you're able to do much talking. That bullet messed your throat up to a fare-thee-well, didn't it? Well, let me tell you something. I'll mess the rest of you up a lot worse with this fish knife if you do anything stupid."

Within half an hour, she beached both boats, left the body of the short man where it lay in the bottom of the aluminum boat, and helped White Cap to her house. Inside, she lit the hurricane lamp and stretched him out on the lower bunk.

"Lie still. I'll be with you in a minute."

She put a kettle of water on, and while it was heating, quite unmindful of her nudity, she reached to the shelf for several jars. She knew White Cap was watching every move she made, and said, "I'm making you some special tea. It's gon' hurt like hell to get the first few swallows down your gullet, but pretty soon you won't feel much of anything at all. Guaranteed! Now, first things first."

She cut a two-inch section from a thin reed, blew through it a couple of times, then stuck it into the hole she had cut in his throat.

"That'll let you breathe a little easier. When the swelling goes down in your neck, I can take it out. You'll heal up fast enough, I think. Saltwater's mean on an open sore, but it kills germs, too. Next, I'll have to get to work on your cheek."

Seeing the apprehension form in his blue eyes, she added, "Don't you worry none, Charlie White Cap, I know what I'm doing."

When the mixture was ready, she helped him sit up, and gently poured a little into his mouth, admiring how, though he squeezed his eyes shut tight against the pain he was feeling, he held the rest of his body steady. Little by little, she emptied the cup into his mouth, wiping away what dribbled out with a clean cloth. "Taste bitter, does it? No matter. Soon you won't feel a damn thing. I promise."

The brew she had made did its job within ten minutes, and she saw his body begin to relax. "Learned about this stuff when I was sixteen. Another five minutes, you'll be fast asleep."

Because of the strength of the mixture she'd made, it took less time than that. When he was out, she turned his damaged face to the light, threaded her needle, and went to work, expertly sewing up the jagged wound in his cheek.

"Humph. You're sure going to have an ugly scar, Charlie boy, and that's a shame. Looks like you were one good-looking joker before."

When her patient was sleeping peacefully, Sunday went outside, stretched, and looked up, to the east. "Dawn in less than an hour, Sunday. Come on, get a-movin'. You can take time out for all your feelings and some rest later."

She hurried back down to the beach, easily picked up the already-stiffening body of the scrawny little man, waded out to *BLACK DOLPHIN* and gently laid him on her deck; then went back, shoved the aluminum boat out into the mild surf, and climbed aboard. The engine started again on the first pull, and she steered due east, at full speed, enjoying the wind on her bare skin and in her hair. When Sunday judged she was in deep enough water, she scuttled the boat, treaded water while watching it sink silvery out of sight, then, with steady, smooth strokes, began swimming back. Helped by the incoming tide, she reached the surf just as the rising sun cast her long shadow on the beach all the way up to her house.

She walked inside, sighed once, and busied herself making a complicated poultice which she applied to her sleeping patient's face, bandaging it with a piece of clean cheesecloth.

"Okay, Mister Charlie White Cap, that'll probably do fine. You'll sleep like a baby for twelve hours or more. That ought to be enough."

Satisfied, she drank a cup of strong tea, gathered her strength for the one remaining task, and went outside again. She picked up the spade she had seen before, took it with her to her boat, climbed aboard, and hoisted sail.

Sunday sailed north, just outside the surf line, until she reached the area where the old CCC camp had been. She beached her boat, and carried the small body up to the base of the dunes. Before the new sun could cause her to seriously sweat, she had dug a hole deep enough.

Pausing to rest, she stared at the freckled face of the man for the first time, noticing he had red hair. Suddenly struck with compassion, she closed the poor creature's sightless eyes, then frowned at the bloody uniform shirt.

"Don't have no idea what your name is, Bud, but nobody ought to be laid in the ground like that, German or not. Let's get you outta that nasty mess. I'll wash you up proper, then say a few Christian verses over you."

Gritting her teeth, Sunday proceeded to unbutton, then remove the wet, sticky garment. Before she had both his arms out, she found herself gaping at two things. The first was a pair of metal objects hanging from a chain around his neck. She squinted at them, not quite believing what she was staring at. *Lord God! These are dog tags. Notched American dog tags, just like the ones Papa Ben and the others wore. Who the hell are you, Buddy boy?*

She read the name and number aloud, "Reams, Bobby Joe US46877520."

She hung them around her own neck. *I'll worry about that later. Don't have time now.*

The second thing that caught her attention was that below the bullet hole in his bloody, skinny chest, he was wearing a belt with a numerous sewn pouches. She unsnapped one of them, and rocked back in total shock when from one of them she removed a wad of red-stained-but-green bills that sported the kindly face of Benjamin Franklin! Deciding she would worry about that revelation later as well, she went back to work with the spade, wishing she had a proper shovel.

She found Slick's body a mile north of the Oregon Inlet. The crabs and small fish had already begun their feasting. Sunday did her best to ignore his gruesome features, and called upon all her remaining strength and

willpower to haul his waterlogged, bloating form onto
BLACK DOLPHIN's deck, forcing back tears of both deep
sorrow and deeper hatred. Before turning back toward
Pea Island, she made two unsuccessful passes up and
down the shore line on the outside chance she might find
also find Gyp's remains.

Cursing under her breath because she had forgotten
to at least put a shirt on, or bring an extra piece of canvas,
she unbent her jib to protect her father's body from the
swarming flies as she dragged her already stinking
burden up the beach to where she had buried the little
man with the money belt.

"Well, Daddy," she muttered, "I reckon this'll have to
be your final resting place. You did a lot of bad things in
your life, but I reckon you did some good things, too, and
I believe God will take it all into account. I loved you, and
I know you loved me. I'm sorry your grave isn't in a
churchyard, with flowers and a real preacher and all, but
I'll do the best I can."

She picked up the spade and settled into a kind of
dull rhythm as she dug:

"Old Slick Everette was a fine old man,
Washed his face in a frying pan,
Combed his hair with a wagon wheel,
And died with a toothache in his heel . . . "

After a while, it was finished. Still kneeling, she
recited the Lord's Prayer and the Twenty-third Psalm, sat
still for another few minutes in silent reverence, then
straightened and stood, sweating profusely under the
increasing heat.

"I'll carve you and your death partner a marker first
chance I get, Daddy, and I'll put some snow pea blooms

on your grave every year, and if anybody ever says a bad word about you, I'll make them mighty sorry—sorry as I am to lose you. Next time I come up here, I'll bring the picture of my mother, and bury her next to you. I reckon you might like that. She was a right pretty woman, wasn't she?"

She sat down again next to the two graves, fingering the money belt, trying her best to figure it all out, talking aloud as if both men could converse with her.

"Mister Red Head, ever since people lived on the Banks, part of what they did to make a living was to salvage stuff washed up on the shore from storms and shipwrecks. You had a lot of money on you, but you sure won't need it now, will you? I reckon you won't mind if I keep it. Ought to be more than enough to buy a decent trawler, soon as I can find myself a good crew—which might be a lot harder than finding a good boat!

"Daddy, I don't know what those Germans were up to, or what they were so busy hiding, but I know where they buried it all. Besides, I've got one of them in my house, and soon as he can talk some, you can bet your boots I'll find out. I might turn him over to the law after a while, but I'm going to get myself some answers to all this mess before I do. Maybe you can rest better knowing I took care of the man that shot you and him and poor Gyp. Whoever that bastard was, he was one sorry excuse for a human being, and I made sure he knew he was going to hell. I hope his body never washes ashore, either, and if it does, I hope the hammerheads had at least a few good meals off of him."

She sat there for another fifteen minutes in silence before slowly rising, and carrying her folded jib sail, trudged back down the beach, grateful that a decent breeze was coming up. She bent the jib back on, raised sail, and set her course for New Inlet.

Halfway there, she was surrounded by her finned friends, and with misting eyes, shouted at the top of her voice:

"Not today, boys. Much as I'd like to, I'm too damn tired, and that's a fact. Besides, I still have a bunch of things to do before I get to sleep. Anyway, I appreciate the offer and the company. Don't y'all laugh too hard at us, you hear? I know you're wondering why we have wars with each other, and in spite of what the Good Book says, we insist on hurting and killing each other for the dumbest reasons you can imagine. I hope to God it'll be over soon. Then, first chance I get, we'll have ourselves a good swim together. Okay?"

Sunday judged it was almost three in the afternoon when she eased her boat into her old slip by the Station House. Feeling sweaty and smelling herself, she jumped overboard in shoulder-deep water and washed before walking up the path. Halfway to the top, some sixth sense caused her to stop and glance back out over the sound. Sure enough, there was a large black smudge on the northwest horizon. Sunday watched it for a moment, then felt a chilling tinge of panic.

"Damn!" she said aloud. "That's Robert Kinch's ferry, and he's making straight for Pea Island, not Ocracoke. What for?"

Without waiting for any answer to her own question, she ran fast as she could back to her house and hurriedly put on a shirt and pants. White Cap was still asleep. Sunday stood there for another few seconds, her brain racing forward to yet another decision. She stripped her inert patient of all his clothes, frowning at the belt, holster, and its ugly pistol.

She was also curious about the small, football-shaped dog tag hanging around *his* neck. It was different than the oblong pair she had removed from the little man named Reams, and was stamped with strange writing she assumed must be German. She didn't have time to study it closely, so she hung it around her own neck as well, stuffed everything else into her footlocker, and stood again, this time gazing at the well-formed, pale white body lying on the bunk. "Ahh, Charlie No-Name, the rest of you is still one good-looking joker, and that's a fact."

She didn't think twice. She picked up a hefty piece of firewood and brought it down sharply on the top of White Cap's head, hard enough to break skin and raise a knot, but not hard enough to do any serious damage— except to prolong his unconsciousness. Without waiting for the bleeding to stop, she picked up the needle and thread and rapidly closed the two-inch gash. Satisfied, she dropped the needle on the table, ran out of the house and up the beach toward the Station House.

When she climbed to the peak of the dune ridge, she noticed Kinch's boat pulling away from the pier. Hands in his pockets, head hanging down, Amos Turner was returning to duty.

Chapter 16

Sunday caught up with Amos just as he reached the steps to the Station House porch. Lost in his own thoughts, he hadn't noticed her—until she spoke.

"You're back. How's your wife?"

Startled, Amos turned sharply around. "Oh. Sunday. Lorraine? She's a lot better. Ain't cried none in three days, so I thought I'd best come on back. How *you* doin'?"

Sunday climbed the steps and sat down heavily on the top one. "Dog tired, and that's the truth. I'm glad you came back, Amos. I sure could have used your help the last couple days. Things have been pretty busy around here."

"Oh yeah? Like what?"

Sunday sighed loudly. Looked down at her bare toes. For the first time in her life, she felt an ugly gnawing in her gut because she knew she was going to tell her first lie. She looked up, hoping Amos could see how weary she was.

"I was out fishing early yesterday morning, pretty close to the Stream. I found three sailors floating on a junk raft. Their ship must have got blown up and sunk. No telling where. Those poor men must have been drifting for days."

"Really? What did you do?"

"Well, wasn't anything I *could* do for two of them. Both dead, and the third one would have been soon if I hadn't spotted them. He'd been hurt pretty bad, but he was still alive. Naked as a jaybird, but still alive. I got him in my house, nursing him."

Amos stared at her. For a minute, he didn't speak. Then he said, "Why didn't you call for some help?"

"Two reasons, Amos. One, if I did, the Coast Guard would want to know where you were, sure as the devil, and I didn't want to get you in any trouble. You know, missing from duty and all. Second, I couldn't have called anybody anyhow."

"Why not?"

" 'Cause somebody broke into the Station House while I was offshore. Cut the wires to the telephone." *Okay, Sunday, that one was only part of a lie.*

Amos' eyes widened.

"What? Broke into—"

He jumped up and rushed inside, Sunday right behind him, made a beeline for the telephone. He picked up the severed ends of the wires, a puzzled look on his face, and then looked at Sunday, his eyes full of the anxiety Sunday had been hoping for.

"Shit! I'm gonna be in big trouble. Anything else tore up or missing?"

Sunday bit her tongue. She nearly said that the Station House had been in such a filthy mess there was no way for her to know. Instead, she shrugged. "I don't know. I had my hands full burying those two sailors and taking care of the other one. I didn't take the time to look around carefully."

Without waiting for any other information, Amos dropped the loose wires and promptly began a search and an inventory, practically ignoring Sunday. Fifteen minutes was all it took. He sat down in the old chair he had once rocked Sunday in.

"Far as I can tell, whoever it was came in here, they didn't take nothin'. Not a damn thing. Funny. Who you reckon it could have been, Sunday?"

"Beats me. Probably some trash kids from Roanoke or Elizabeth City. Maybe some deadbeat crabbers. Who knows? Maybe cut the wire so they'd have plenty of time to get away. Anyway, if nothing's missing, and you fix those wires back, you can't get in any real trouble, and I won't say anything about it to anybody, either. I'm just glad you came back. I was plenty worried about you."

Amos nodded. "I reckon I can splice that phone wire easy enough. Thanks, Sunday. You were right to start with. I never should have left my post. The Coast Guard would have put me in jail for a long time if they knew I had." In relief, he puffed out his cheeks, and then finally thought to ask, "Say, where'd you bury them sailors?"

"Up there where the old CCC camp was. The other one's going to be all right, I think. Took right bad blows on the head and on his throat. Lucky for him I came along when I did. Else he'd soon been dead as his mates were."

Amos stood, slowly shaking his head. "That's my Sunday, all right. Okay, I'd best get to work on that wire. I'll stop by later. Hey . . . wait a minute."

Amos had another thought, one of sudden suspicion. With narrowed eyes, he asked, "Where's Slick?"

Sunday frowned because a second lie was now necessary.

"Oh, it wasn't Daddy, Amos. I took him down to Ocracoke day before yesterday. I don't know if he's still there or not. He might be on his way to Texas by now. No telling where he's off to this time."

Somewhat relieved—for Sunday's sake—Amos chuckled.

"He's a piece of work, sure enough. Always was. Listen Sunday, I gotta thank you for all you did for Lorraine."

"It's all right. I'm mighty sorry we couldn't save the baby, but since you won't have to go to jail for twenty years, I reckon you'll have time to make a bunch more. See you later, Amos. Come by when you get a chance."

"I will."

Having reached the bitter end of her rope of strength, yet satisfied that her lies had been so convincing, Sunday stumbled back to her house, glanced once at her sleeping patient, then climbed to the top bunk and collapsed immediately into the sleep of utter, total exhaustion.

Sunday had no idea how long she slept; only that she felt something pull her arm. At first she thought she was dreaming, but when the tugging persisted, she opened her eyes and gradually, as from a drugged stupor, focused on the bandaged face and wide eyes of her naked guest. It was only then she heard the knocking at her door.

She was instantly alert.

Sitting up abruptly, she said, "Calm down. That's just Amos. Get back in bed—and cover yourself up."

Sunday took two deep breaths. She was fully aware she was still repressing her emotional state. Inside, she wanted desperately to give in to it. To mourn her losses. To vent her pain. Her anguish. But there was no time. Not yet. There was still too much to do. She shook the cobwebs from her head, slid off the bunk and went to the door. "Who's there?"

"It's me, Sunday. Amos. You okay?"

"Yes. Hold on a minute, Amos."

She turned quickly to make sure the German was back in the lower bunk. He had followed her orders, his eyes still locked on hers, showing an undisguised look of fear. She gave him a reassuring smile, then opened the door. "Did you get the telephone fixed?"

"Yesterday. You been asleep all this time?"

"I reckon I have, off and on." She gestured toward the bunk.

"Amos Turner, meet Charlie No-Name."

Amos looked down at the bandaged man in the lower bunk, then back at Sunday. "Charlie?"

Sunday laughed. "He can't talk, so he couldn't tell me what his name is, so I'm just calling him Charlie for now."

Amos bent over for a closer look. "What's that sticking out of his throat?"

"Piece of a reed. Without it, he couldn't breathe. Something must have slammed into his throat real bad. His face and head were a mess, too. Took me a right good while to sew him up. You want some tea? I was just about to make some."

Amos frowned. "No, thanks. I'd best be doing my job."

He jerked his thumb back in "Charlie's" direction.

"If he was in a big ship, might be some more survivors besides him. After I got the telephone line fixed, I called up and down the coast. Nobody's seen no bodies or wreckage lately, but you never know, do you?"

Sunday felt a trickle of sweat under her arms. "That's right. You never know. Stop by again, Amos. Any time."

She hoped her tone sounded casual enough. It must have, since Amos smiled, just as he always had, tipped his cap, and left. Sunday watched him trudge down to the surf line, then start south, binoculars hung around his neck. She turned.

"Amos is one of my oldest friends. He may not be the brightest star in the night sky, but he's not stupid, either. Lucky for you he's had a lot on his mind lately. How you feeling? How 'bout some tea. I could use some myself, come to think of it. Then I need to figure out what to feed you."

Sunday had never heard the word *protein* in her life, yet she knew from long experience that fish and other seafood were chock-a-block full of the strength-building ingredient the human body needs for survival. The stew she made, combined with the pain-killing tea brew she managed to get down her houseguest's mangled throat, had an immediate effect. She could see the gratitude in her patient's eyes, observing as well that each time she fed him, the pain showing in those blue eyes was a little less.

For three days and nights she nursed, washed, and watched him. On the morning of the fourth day, after 'breakfast,' she said, "You feel strong enough to walk outside?"

A barely perceptible but affirmative nod was her answer.

"Okay, let's see, I reckon you can wear some of my clothes."

From her sea chest, she removed one of her shirts and a pair of pants. She handed them to him. "I reckon these will do. Think you're strong enough to dress yourself?"

"Charlie" managed another slight nod, and what she thought was the beginning of a swollen, crooked smile. Sunday turned her head while he put on the shirt and pants.

She opened the door and walked outside, looking up and down the beach. "No sign of Amos. Good."

Walking slowly, Sunday led Charlie down to the border of the retreating tide. She looked around, and soon spotted what she had been looking for: a thin piece of driftwood. This she handed to Charlie, and pointed to the damp, smooth sand. "We got to talk. Sit down and write your name for me."

After a moment's hesitation, he bent over and scratched a word in the sand.

HORST

Then, before Sunday could react to that, he scratched through it, and wrote:

CHARLIE

Sunday threw back her head and laughed. "I saw it the first time. What kind of name is Horst? That something like horse? In German?"

CHARLIE PLEASE

AND THANK YOU FOR

SAVING MY LIFE

Sunday stopped laughing, and allowed her face to become serious. "Well, I did that for a good reason, Charlie boy. Looks like you know American real good. I got a whole bunch of questions for you, and I don't want lies, either. Understand?"

Charlie nodded, but held up one finger, then scratched other words in the sand.

WAIT PLEASE

FIRST MY QUESTION

"Yeah? What's that?"

WHERE IS BORMANN

Sunday pursed her lips. Cocked her head. "Who's Bormann?"

No hesitation this time:

THE MAN WHO SHOT ME

Sunday eyes became mere slits. "You were chasing him, too, weren't you? What were you going to do when you caught him?"

Charlie looked her dead in the eye, his blue ones cold as ice. His gesture of pulling the stick across his throat was plain enough, but he took no chances of her misunderstanding him. In the sand, he scribed:

KILL HIM

HE MURDERED MY CREW

Sunday remembered the underwater explosion. "It was a submarine, wasn't it?"

Charlie nodded. This time Sunday noticed his eyes were wet as he wrote:

MY BOAT

I WAS HER CAPTAIN

Sunday pursed her lips. That would confirm what she had guessed about his fancy uniform and the white cap, now stowed out of sight in her sea chest.

"Well, now, Captain Charlie, you won't ever have to worry about killing your Mr. Bormann or whatever his name was. I did that for you. He killed my Daddy and my dog, and after he shot you, I pulled him under and cut his throat. He was shark bait in two minutes."

Charlie nodded, and stared out to sea for several minutes. Then, as if he'd thought of something he had forgotten about, quickly wrote:

IS THE OTHER MAN DEAD

"You mean the little skinny one? Yep. Your Bormann fella killed him, too. He was shot right through the heart. I buried him Christian."

Remembering the dog tags now hanging around her own neck, she added, "His name was Bobby Joe Reams. That sure as hell isn't a German name, is it?"

Before she could get an answer, instinct caused her to look up. There was a man walking resolutely down the beach. Sunday's eyesight was keen as ever, as was her memory of how he carried himself, but she capped her eyes with her right hand to be certain. Sure enough, though he was wearing street clothes instead of a uniform, the unmistakable figure of Benjamin Searcy was marching steadily toward them, and Sunday instantly realized two things: Amos had called him (that was clear as spring water), and, there was no way on earth she would be able to lie to him.

She turned back quickly to Charlie and said, "We've got company, Charlie, and this time, we've both got a lot of explaining to do."

Charlie glanced at the approaching figure, then looked back at Sunday, question marks in both eyes.

Sunday understood, and said, "He's the man who raised me. More of a Daddy than my real one was. Amos must have called him."

Charlie quickly rubbed out his last words, and in their place, rapidly wrote:

PLEASE DO NOT BETRAY ME

I CAN OFFER YOU GREAT WEALTH

Several new thoughts flew through Sunday's mind as she read this. She responded by erasing all the lines, saying, "Don't you worry, Charlie. I may turn you in, but in my own sweet time. You stay right there."

She waved, and ran to meet her godfather.

CHAPTER 17

"PAPA BEN!"

Sunday flung her arms around the former Keeper's neck, then released him just as quickly. Something was wrong. Bad wrong. She had hugged a . . . sick old man. A shriveled-up shell of a man, whose clothes hung on a scarecrow's body. She drew back, holding him at arm's length.

His eyes told her everything before he even said a word. The wide, but contorted smile on his face was only the longest of many deep lines. His hair and beard, now cotton white, sharply contrasted the hollow cheeks and sunken eyes. His head rested on a neck that was pitifully small, leaving a considerable gap between wattles and collar.

Sunday had seen, smelled, this sickness before; the first time at Ernestine Pike's bedside.

"Ben," she whispered, "what is it?"

The smile never wavered. "Doctors at Elizabeth City tell me it's cancer, Sunday. There's nothing more they can do, so I've come seeking your expertise."

This news, on top of everything else that had happened, was more than she could bear. Her knees buckled.

"Oh, God. Dear, sweet Jesus. Not my Papa Ben . . ." Sunday wailed.

Ben took both her hands in his.

"I'm afraid it's true, honey. And, I need your help now. I want you to show me how to make that special tea, and how to make it progressively stronger. The pain is already pretty bad, and is bound to get worse; I will need to be able to handle it. Will you do this for me?"

Sunday, gradually realizing that Ben had not come because of a call from Amos, was drenched yet again with fresh emotions, of both relief and deep sorrow. For a moment, she was unable to answer. And before she could find the words, she saw Ben's eyes glance over her shoulder, down the beach.

"Who is that?" he said.

Blinking back tears, Sunday tried desperately to shift mental gears. "Him? Oh, that's my new friend, Charlie."

"Charlie? Charlie who?"

"I don't know the 'who.' He's a shipwrecked sailor I pulled off of a raft drifting out in the Stream. He was hurt, and I'm kinda nursing him back to health."

Sunday took Ben by the elbow and started walking to her house, telling him a shortened version of the lie she had told Amos, startled at how much easier it was the second time around—even with Ben Searcy, after all. By the time they reached the door, Ben paused, and looked down the beach at the figure squatting on the sand, the stick still in his hand.

Sunday managed to manufacture a slight grin.

"His throat is hurt bad, so he can't talk. Can't speak a single word, and I've been using the same trick you used to do on me: writing in the sand. But, so far I haven't learned much from him. I think the knock he got on his head must have jiggled his brains, like scrambled eggs. He doesn't remember anything. Not even his name, or what ship he was in."

"What are you going to do after he recovers?"

"Don't rightly know yet, Papa Ben. I reckon I'll just take it one day at the time. Anyway, forget about him. Let's get inside and see what we can do for you."

After handing her old mentor a mug full of what had been left from Charlie's medicine, Sunday busied herself by carefully selecting the ingredients for the painkilling mixture, in enough quantity to last several weeks, explaining, "I'll show you how to measure this stuff out, and then I'll write it down, like a doctor does. I'll bring you some more when this runs out. Are you going to spend the night at the Station House?"

Ben sat down at the rough table, watching her work. He answered in the affirmative, sipping the bitter brew and making small talk about his wife and how they had spent a lot of their recent time traveling.

"There's so much of this fine state I have never seen, Sunday. Of course, the gas rationing limits how far we can go, but we swap other stamps for gas, so Estelle and I have made several trips west. To Raleigh and beyond, even to the mountains once. It's really beautiful up there, but all in all, I suppose there is no place I'd rather die than here, on the Banks. Doctors don't know how much time I have left. It could be a few months, but then, it might only be a few weeks. Anyway, whatever time I have left, I want to be alert, and I know your tea can help."

Like a water dam strained by flood pressure to its limit, Sunday forced her tears back. She sat down across from him, took a pad and pencil, and wrote down the dosage from the various bottles and jars, along with the correct amount of ginseng tea. After making sure Ben understood it, and how to gradually increase it, she placed the entire collection of labeled containers in a small basket, and pushed it across the table.

"You know what I think I'll do? I think I'll cook you and Amos a fine dinner tonight, and maybe make a cobbler, too. How does that sound?"

"Too good to be true. I miss this old place, and I have missed you, Sunday. You know, you ought to start thinking about settling down yourself someday soon. Get married and raise your own family. In hindsight, I wish I had done the same."

Sunday forced a wry smile. "I reckon I've got plenty of time left to think about things like that. Besides, I'm too busy."

Ben changed the subject. "This tea works fast. I feel a lot better already. Say, aren't you forgetting your other patient? Why don't you bring him in. I'd like to meet him. Is he an American sailor?"

"No, I don't think so. He understands American all right, but I think he's some kind of foreigner."

Again Sunday felt a sharp twinge of apprehension, but knew there was nothing for it but to call Charlie in. In too deep with her lie now, there was little else she could do except keep it going. She rose, went back outside, walked down the beach toward the solitary figure still sitting there, and whistled. The German looked up.

"Charlie, come on back up here. I want you to meet Mr. Searcy."

She kept on walking, meeting him halfway.

"Listen quick. I didn't rat on you, so rest your mind about that. I haven't made up my own mind about you yet, Captain Horse. Like I said, I might turn you in, and I might not. Either way, though, not until I have some personal satisfaction about what your boats were doing here in the first place. Ben Searcy's retired now, but he was the Captain of the Life-Saving crew here for a long time. He's the smartest man I ever knew, and he's real sick now, but that don't mean he isn't still sharp as a straight razor. Be careful what you, uh, 'say.' Maybe you'd just better act like you don't remember anything. That's why I whacked you on the head."

Charlie nodded, and once more showed his warped half smile of gratitude.

They reached the door of Sunday's house. She took his arm, led him inside, and said, "Cap'n Ben Searcy, shake hands with Charlie No-Name."

Ben reached his hand out, and Sunday had yet another pang of pity when she saw how frail it was. Ben, ever the professional, said, "Sunday tells me you understand English. What type vessel were you in? Warship? Merchantman?"

He got a confused shrug for an answer.

"You don't remember your ship, or what happened? Torpedo maybe?"

Negative shake of the head.

"Can't you remember anything? Your name? Where your home is?"

Another headshake.

Ben looked at Sunday. "Amnesia's the word. Amnesia is total loss of memory. Chances are he'll get it back. Might come sudden, or it might be gradual."

He looked again into Charlie's blank blue eyes. "Whatever the case, you couldn't be in better hands. Sunday Everette knows more than most legitimate doctors. She'll have your wounds healed up in no time at all. I'm sorry you lost your ship and got hurt, but you're mighty lucky she's the one who found you."

Charlie nodded, then pointed to Ben's mug of tea.

Sunday took the cue. "Looks like you're aching bad again, aren't you? Okay, have a seat and I'll get you some more."

Ben stood. "I think I'll go on up to the Station House now. I need to lie down for a little while. If Amos comes by, tell him I'm here, will you?"

"Sure thing," Sunday said. "He's patrolling down near the inlet, I think. Ben, before you go, I need to tell you there's a little bit more to Charlie's story."

Ben cocked his head. Raised a white eyebrow.

"There were two other men on that raft, but they didn't make it. I buried them up by the old camp."

Ben pursed his lips, took another swallow of the tea, and looked back at Charlie with a genuine look of sympathy. "My condolences for the loss of your shipmates, son. I've seen it happen much too often in my lifetime."

He glanced back at Sunday, opened his mouth to say something, but thought better of it.

He got up, went to the door, holding the basket, and said, "My stomach won't take fried fish anymore, honey. But that fish stew I'm smelling might be something I can keep down tonight, especially if you make a few biscuits to go along with it."

Sunday laughed. "No cornbread?"

Ben shook his head. "I'm afraid not. Can't handle anything greasy, but Amos won't mind whatever you cook. You could fry up cow chips and seaweed and it would be better than anything he ever threw together. See you tonight. Around six?"

"Six it is. Go get some rest. Wait. You want me to walk with you?"

"No, no. I'm fine. Thanks again for the tea. It makes all the difference in the world, honey. You ought to get a patent on it and bottle it. It would make you rich!"

Fresh tears welled in Sunday's eyes as she watched Papa Ben laboriously climb up the dune line toward the Station House. She sighed, took a deep breath, poured Charlie a cup of her brew, set it before him and said, "Soon as the pain dies down, I want you to take that pad and pencil and start writing. Understand?"

Charlie didn't wait. He nodded, and immediately picked up the pencil. With it he wrote, in neat block letters:

YOU DESERVE TO KNOW

I SHALL TELL YOU ALL

THERE IS A PROBLEM HOWEVER

"What problem?"

Charlie held up both hands, waving them in a gesture of frustration, then bent over and wrote:

THERE IS MUCH I

ALSO DO NOT KNOW

Sunday frowned deeply. "Oh, yeah? Well, Mister White Cap, I've got all day, don't I? Drink some more of that tea, then start from the beginning. And just remember, I'll know if you're lying to me."

Charlie looked her in the eye for a long moment, then began writing.

CHAPTER 18

I SHALL WRITE THIS WITH FULL TRUST IN YOU, MISS EVERETTE. PLEASE BEAR IN MIND THAT YOU INDEED HOLD MY LIFE IN YOUR HANDS. SHOULD I BE CAPTURED, I WOULD BE SHOT, ALTHOUGH I AM NOT A SPY. YOU MUST BELIEVE THIS. MY FULL NAME IS HORST VON HELLENBACH. MY RANK IS EQUAL TO COMMANDER IN YOUR NAVY. I WAS IN COMMAND OF A SUBMARINE SENT ON A SECRET MISSION, SENT BY HITLER HIMSELF. DO YOU KNOW WHO ADOLF HITLER IS?

Looking over his shoulder, Sunday answered, " 'Course I do. He's your top boss man. A real Nazi bastard from what I hear."

For the first time, she then noticed he was wearing a shiny gold ring on the fourth finger of his left hand. *So Charlie's a married man! Wonder what his wife looks like?* She started to say something about it when Charlie began furiously writing again.

HITLER IS A MADMAN. TOTALLY INSANE. AND, HIS INSANITY HAS LOST THE WAR FOR US AND DESTROYED OUR COUNTRY. DO YOU KNOW THE NAME MARTIN BORMANN?

"The one I killed? No, not until you mentioned it. Never heard of him."

THAT IS NOT SURPRISING. BORMANN WAS A HIGH OFFICIAL IN OUR GOVERNMENT AND THE MAN CLOSEST TO HITLER. IN REALITY, HE WAS, AFTER HITLER, THE MOST POWERFUL MAN IN GERMANY AND MOST

DEVIOUS AND SECRETIVE. A TRULY EVIL MAN. BECAUSE OF HIS INFLUENCE, HITLER HIMSELF PERSONALLY ORDERED ME TO MAKE THIS VOYAGE. I HAD NO CHOICE BUT TO DO MY DUTY AS A MILITARY OFFICER. I WAS ALSO LED TO BELIEVE WE WERE TO SAIL TO SOUTH AMERICA. BORMANN WAS ABOARD, AND WE WERE CARRYING A CARGO I WAS NOT ALLOWED TO SEE, EITHER BEFORE OR DURING THE VOYAGE. I WAS SUSPICIOUS, HOWEVER, AND CONCLUDED THAT BORMANN HAD TRICKED HITLER AND WAS ATTEMPTING TO ESCAPE GERMANY WITH A FORTUNE IN GOLD. I KNEW THAT OTHERS BEFORE HIM HAD DONE THE SAME, AND REALIZED AT LAST I WAS MERELY AN EXPENDABLE DELIVERY BOY.

"Gold?" Sunday said. "*Gold* was what those men were unloading from the small boats? Is that what you were offering me to keep my mouth shut?"

Charlie looked up at her, his brow furrowed. The pencil flew.

YOU SAW THEM?

"Oh, yeah. I saw them all right. They didn't know I was watching. I hid up on top of the Station House and saw everything. They forced my Daddy to help them, and when he tried to get away, this son of a bitch you're talking about shot him down in cold blood. My dog, too."

Charlie nodded, and dropped his head. Sunday surmised his long pause was more out of respect than to rest his writing hand. Momentarily he continued.

I AM VERY SAD FOR THE DEATH OF YOUR FATHER. AGAIN, YOU MUST BELIEVE ME. I HAD NOTHING TO DO WITH THAT. I WAS STILL ABOARD MY BOAT. DURING THE LAST LEG OF OUR VOYAGE, I WAS AMAZED WHEN BORMANN ORDERED ME TO BRING MY BOAT CLOSE IN TO YOUR SHORE AND WAIT ON THE SEA BOTTOM WHILE HE MADE SEVERAL TRIPS TO YOUR BEACH. I THEN

KNEW HE HAD NO INTENTION OF GOING TO SOUTH AMERICA. THIS ISLAND WAS APPARENTLY HIS PLANNED DESTINATION. HOWEVER, WHAT I CANNOT UNDERSTAND IS WHY. ONE DOES NOT ESCAPE INTO AN ENEMY COUNTRY. WHAT I DO KNOW NOW IS THAT HE ALSO PLANNED TO MURDER ME AND ALL MY CREW AFTER HE TRANSFERRED THE CARGO OF GOLD TO SHORE. HAD IT NOT BEEN FOR YOU HE WOULD HAVE SUCCEEDED.

Reading all this, a new thought came into Sunday's head. "You write like a school teacher. Where'd you learn such good American? I mean, English?"

OUR GERMAN SCHOOLS ARE VERY THOROUGH.

"Must be," Sunday said. "Keep going."

BORMANN MUST HAVE HAD A GOOD REASON FOR CHOOSING THIS PLACE, AND I AM ALSO CERTAIN THE SMALL MAN HAD SOMETHING TO DO WITH IT. HE AND BORMANN BOTH WORE UNIFORMS OF ORDINARY SOLDIERS WHEN THEY CAME ASHORE. THAT IS ANOTHER MYSTERY TO ME. THEIR UNIFORMS WERE THOSE OF GERMAN UNITS BASED IN AFRICA THREE OR FOUR YEARS AGO. UNITS WHICH WE KNEW HAD BEEN CAPTURED BY YOUR SOLDIERS. AS I TOLD YOU BEFORE, THERE IS SO MUCH I DO NOT KNOW. I WAS NEVER INFORMED OF BORMANN'S TRUE INTENTIONS. HOW DID YOU KNOW THE DEAD MAN WAS CALLED REAMS?

Sunday reached under her shirt and extracted both pairs of the dog tags.

"Here's yours. These were around his neck."

Charlie studied them, shaking his head. At last he wrote,

THESE ARE IDENTIFICATION TAGS FOR AN AMERICAN SOLDIER OR SAILOR. THIS EXPLAINS WHY REAMS NEVER SAID A SINGLE WORD DURING THE ENTIRE VOYAGE FROM GERMANY. HE OBVIOUSLY

COULD NOT SPEAK OUR LANGUAGE. HE MUST HAVE
BEEN SOMEHOW IN BORMANN'S EMPLOY.

"But why?"

Charlie pounded his fist on the table in frustration.
His swollen face turned red. He looked up at Sunday
with agonized eyes, and quickly wrote,

I DO NOT <u>KNOW</u>. IT IS ALL LIKE PIECES OF A PUZZLE
AND I CANNOT PUT THEM TOGETHER. NOT YET. REAMS
MUST HAVE BEEN A CAPTIVE. A PRISONER OF WAR. BUT
WHY WOULD AN AMERICAN SOLDIER OR A PRISONER OF
WAR BE ON A VOYAGE WITH MARTIN BORMANN? WAS
HE FORCED? AND IF SO, WHY?

CAN YOU NOW SEE THAT THERE ARE MANY
QUESTIONS I HAVE NO ANSWERS FOR?

Sunday nodded soberly, in complete fascination, but
just as confused as before. Charlie saw this and went on.

WHEN HE AND BORMANN MADE THEIR LAST TRIP
TO THE BEACH, I FOLLOWED THEM. TO FIND OUT. YOU
MUST HAVE BEEN NEAR US WHEN THE DETONATION
CAME.

"I was."

AT THAT MOMENT I KNEW BORMANN HAD
SABOTAGED MY BOAT AND KILLED MY CREW. EVERY
MAN. SO AS TO LEAVE NO WITNESSES TO HIS
TREACHERY AND TREASON. HE ASSUMED I WAS ALSO
ON BOARD. WHEN MY BOAT WAS DESTROYED, MY ONLY
WISH WAS TO KILL HIM. YOU MUST HAVE SEEN ME RAM
HIS BOAT. I TRIED TO BOARD HIM, AND WAS REACHING
FOR MY WEAPON, BUT HE SHOT ME FIRST. THE REST
YOU KNOW. PLEASE, NOW TELL ME EXACTLY WHAT YOU
SAW. IT IS VERY IMPORTANT THAT YOU LEAVE
NOTHING OUT.

Sunday walked back around the table, sat down and
faced him. Marveling at the German's knowledge of

English, she began talking. Taking her time, she related, slowly, and in careful detail, everything she had seen, heard, and done from the time Gyp had started growling up to the moment she had rescued him and then buried her father and Reams. "There's one other thing, Charlie. That little fella had a belt around his waist."

She stood, turned her back to him, unbuttoned her shirt and removed the money belt. She fastened her shirt again, turned back around to face him, and held the belt up.

"There's fifty-thousand dollars stuffed in this thing. All in American hundred-dollar bills. It don't look to me like Reams was forced. If he really was working with that Bormann guy, he sure got paid a lot for it."

With wide eyes and a slack jaw, Charlie stared first at Sunday, then at the money belt, then back at her again. Sunday could tell he was as surprised as she had been.

REAMS IS THE KEY, OF COURSE. HE MUST HAVE BEEN BRIBED. BUT FOR WHAT REASON?

Charlie paused for a moment, then wrote,

WHERE DID THEY HIDE THE GOLD?

"They buried it. All around this house, and in the one-holer."

Confusion now showed in Charlie's eyes.

ONE WHAT?

"The privy. Toilet."

Charlie nodded, then stood. He walked to the window, rubbing his hands. When he turned back to face her, he was once again slowly shaking his head and hands in apparent helplessness. Then, as if he had thought about something else, he sat back down and wrote:

DO YOU HAVE RECENT NEWSPAPERS?

Sunday shook her head. "No, I don't. But, I've got something just as good."

She pointed to the small radio resting on her lowest shelf.

"If it's news you're after, we can hear it loud and clear tonight, around five o'clock."

Charlie attempted another smile with his swollen lips. Then he wrote:

EXCELLENT. MAY I PLEASE HAVE SOME MORE TEA? I AGAIN HAVE MUCH PAIN.

Sunday grinned.

"Sure. I'll make some more. I reckon your fingers are hurting just as bad as your face. You'd best not drink too much of it at one time, though. That'll make your brains slow down, and I'm thinking you are going to try powerful hard to figure this mess out. I sure hope you can. I lost a lot that night, too, on account of your Mister Bormann."

She looked deep into his eyes, lowered her voice and its tone for sincerity's sake and said, "I believe what you've told me, Charlie, and I don't think you came here to fight or kill people. Besides, there is nobody here on Pea Island to fight *with* except me. And maybe poor old Amos. Closest other folks live on Hatteras Island, south of New Inlet, some twenty miles away. Well, none of that matters much now, does it?"

She stood. "I'll make you up a new batch of tea. Why don't you lie back down for a little while. You get excited, blood rushes up to your head, and that makes the pain worse. Go on, lie down."

Wearily, Charlie got up, walked over to the bunk and stretched out.

Sunday watched him until she was sure he was asleep, and then placed the money belt and dog tags into her sea chest. She stood there for a moment with her hands on her hips, shaking her own head, trying to digest it all.

She sat down and read all of Charlie's notes, going all over again in her mind their strange conversation, word by word, sentence by sentence. None of it yet made much sense to her, but something deep inside her stirred a different series of emotions. *"Sabotaged my boat . . . Killed my crew . . . Every man . . . "* She was absolutely certain Charlie had not lied to her, and felt even more sympathetic toward him, because his mental suffering was surely no less than his physical pain.

On another sudden impulse, she walked outside, grabbed the spade and began digging at the east corner of her house. It didn't take long before she uncovered one of the wooden crates. Reaching down, she brushed the sand away from the stout rope handles and pulled, surprised yet again at how heavy it was. She brought it inside and placed it on her table. Using the sharp edge of the spade, she pried the nailed-down lid loose and peered inside.

She caught her breath. What she was looking at didn't look like gold. The box held four black bricks!

She took one of them out, turning it over and over, and muttered under her breath how clever the Germans had been to paint them all. She picked up a knife and scraped some of the paint away. The color that gleamed up at her was undeniable. She remembered how small the twenty-dollar gold coins left to her by Susan Bearclaw had been, and did some rapid, silent calculations.

"God Almighty! One of these bricks must be enough to make hundreds of those coins. Maybe more. If there are fifty or so of these boxes, with four bricks in each one, there has to be . . . Lord, no telling how many millions of dollars worth! No wonder Bormann was willing to kill a bunch of people. But why here on Pea Island?"

Unable, or unwilling, to spend more energy thinking about this fantastic discovery—a thousand times more than old Blackbeard must have amassed in his pirate days—Sunday placed the cover back on the crate, lifted it, and stowed it under the table for the time being. With shaking hands, she busied herself with preparations for the dinner she had promised the others.

Her thoughts were racing through her head faster than her dolphin friends could swim, and she felt almost dizzy with the knowledge that right outside her door was a king's fortune! Two king's fortunes. *But hold on here, Sunday Everette. That gold is painted with more colors than just black. There's a lot of red covering each one of those damn bricks. Forget it. You'd never in this world be able to enjoy one penny of that kind of blood money. Daddy would look down—or up—from wherever he is now and rebuke you for the rest of your life. He wouldn't mind you keeping the cash money, probably. 'Finders, keepers,' he'd say. But all that blood-soaked Devil's gold? No way in the name of Jesus will I touch it. Ever again.*

She worked steadily. Thinking of the cash reminded her that the little man, the Bobby Joe Reams fella, had been an American soldier boy. A traitor to his country? No doubt! Another thing: he sure wasn't a Yankee, either. Never heard of any Yankee boy with double names like Bobby Joe.

Aloud, she said, "Plenty of them down here, though. Boys *and* girls. Bobby Joe, Billy Ray, Bobbi Sue, Willa Jean, Annie Mae—lots and lots of them in North Carolina. For that matter, some right out here on the Banks. For all I know Mister Bobby Joe Reams might have been born somewhere within spittin' distance of here."

Before she knew it, time had slipped away. It was almost five when she finished the cobbler. She went over and roused her sleeping guest, handing him yet another cup of her potent tea brew.

"Charlie, it's time for the evening news on the radio. You want to listen to it?"

Charlie instantly sat up, rubbing his eyes. Some kind of guttural, rasping sound came from his shredded throat, and he winced at the pain it produced. He looked up at her with pleading eyes. Sunday nodded, turned and walked over to the small radio and turned it on, happy that since the coastal weather was good, reception would be also.

Sunday watched his face as they listened to the announcer joyfully describing, in considerable detail, how the Allies were advancing on both fronts:

In the South Pacific, fierce fighting raged on the Island of Okinawa, only 350 miles from Japan itself. Although the Japs were fighting furiously to protect the backdoor of their home islands, and their Kamikaze planes were inflicting severe damage to the American warships, the final outcome was hardly in doubt. Thousands and thousands of Japs had been killed, the announcer said, while American casualties were "moderate."

News from the European theatre was even better . . .

Allied armies had practically cut off Berlin from the Bavarian mountains, where it was rumored that Hitler and his Nazis had planned to make a last-ditch stand. Berlin itself was under siege from the Russians, and Mussolini had been captured and executed by Italian partisans while trying to escape into Switzerland. In fact, Adolf Hitler himself was reported to have died while "defending Berlin from the onrushing Russians," and weak peace overtures had been attempted by Heinrich Himmler, Chief of the dreaded Gestapo. These President

Truman had firmly rejected. Nothing less than unconditional surrender was expected within a matter of days. Perhaps hours.

At those words, Charlie gave Sunday a look of total surprise, reached for the pencil and pad of paper and rapidly wrote:

TRUMAN?

WHERE IS ROOSEVELT?

Sunday frowned. "He died almost a month ago. Ben took me to see his funeral train. Didn't you know?"

Charlie shook his head and turned back to the radio, listening intently.

" . . . *And best of all,*" the announcer was saying, "*today, May 3rd, 1945, is an important day. A day of celebrating, folks, because less than twenty-four hours ago, all German forces in Italy have surrendered. The war in Europe will soon be over, fellow Americans! Nazi Germany cannot possibly hold out much longer. As a matter of fact, Hitler is so desperate, he is shoving thousands of old men and young boys into battle. Pathetic cannon fodder! More hard evidence of his cruelty against even his own people . . .* "

Sunday watched as Charlie stood, turned to her with tears in his eyes, then walked to the door and stood outside, facing the ocean.

She wondered what kind of thoughts must be going through his head now. Thoughts that were hurting him more than his physical wounds. She thought of saying something to him, but changed her mind—it wouldn't do any good. She wondered what he was thinking about. Who was he mourning? His countrymen? His shipmates? His wife? *How would you feel in you were in his place, Sunday?*

No. There was nothing she could say that would help him. She began ladling the stew into a large pot. The biscuits were just about done, and the cobbler had already cooled.

CHAPTER 19

SUNDAY TOOK the fish stew dinner and fixings to the Station House, much to Amos' delight.

"I can't stay long," she said. But, she lingered throughout the meal anyway, first to hear the war news, then listen while Ben, now in far less pain, began to muse aloud on his predictions of the imminent post-war period on the Banks and other barrier islands.

"I see a very bright future for you, Sunday. You, too Amos." With a mock frown at his former surfman, he added, "That is, if you can manage to stay at your post from now on."

Amos' jaw dropped and he gave Sunday a quick look of sheer mortification. Sunday grinned. *Amos, you should know by now that not much ever happens on the islands Ben Searcy doesn't know about.*

"I think maybe you've learned your lesson," Ben went on. "You should stay in the Coast Guard, Amos. Now that you have a family that is bound to grow, you will need the security of those steady paychecks, just like before. Plus, if you keep your nose clean and do your duty properly, you'll get decent medical benefits as well as regular promotions and a good pension when you retire."

He turned his attention to Sunday.

"As for you, I know it will take practically an Act of God to get you off Pea Island, and whether or not you do leave, I have no doubt you will make out just fine in the coming years. Better than ever. There will soon be lots of men coming home from the war. Discharged men, looking for jobs. They will find them, too. New families and homes will be established, and there is talk now of a new bill in Congress that will assist any of those former servicemen who wish to go to college. I foresee a tremendous surge in education, not only here in North Carolina, but all over the country. And with all that will come a new economy. People will have money to spend. The only negative for you is that the Banks will never be the same."

He sighed, paused for another sip of coffee, then said, "You watch. I'll bet my last dollar there will be considerable commercial growth out here, too, at least on the northern Banks. Cottages and hotels, restaurants, amusement parks, and the like will spout up like garden weeds. Tourists will be flocking down here for extended vacations, more and more each year. It'll take time, of course, but progress will eventually spread out here, on new roads, and modern civilization in all its rolling, automotive ugliness will overrun our islands like a slow tidal wave."

"Will it be all that bad?" Sunday wanted to know.

"For me it would be, but I won't be here to see it, thank God. But if you're as smart as you always have been, you will cash in on it. There will be a healthy growth in the commercial fishing industry, as well, so I would advise you to start shopping for a trawler soon. Right away in fact. Mark my words, it will not be long before you will also see a similar interest in sport fishing, especially among the old wealthy and the new rich."

Ben stretched, leaned back in his chair and chuckled. "If I were a young fellow again, with my knowledge of boats and these coastal waters, I'd keep an eye out for one of those surplus PT boats. My guess is they will go cheap. I'd buy one, and convert it into a charter vessel for all those fat-cat vacationers who want a marlin or swordfish trophy to hang over their fireplaces."

He winked knowingly at Sunday. "Something to keep in mind a few years down the road, honey."

Sunday nodded, knowing Ben Searcy had never given her bad advice, and wasn't doing so now.

As if reading her mind, Ben added, "Of course, more and more medical doctors will find their way out here as well, so my guess is that your healing practice may shrink steadily as time goes by. Now, that might not be a bad thing, either. The way I see it, one of these days, you're going to seriously think about finding a mate and raising your own family."

He held up both hands to ward off the instantaneous protest he knew she would voice, then said, "I know, I know, all things in good time. Lord, I'm tired. All this good stew and talk has made me pretty sleepy. Think I'll go to bed. Wake me at six prompt, please, Amos."

"Yes, sir. I will."

"And Amos," Ben shot back as he reached the hall, "Thanks for cleaning the old place up a little. I'm downright proud of you."

As though he had still another afterthought, he glanced at Sunday, not smiling. "Do me yet one more favor, honey."

" 'Course. Anything."

"Do you think Charlie will be well enough to travel by next week?"

"Probably in just a few days. Why?"

"I'd like it if you could come over to Manteo to spend a day with me, and I think it might be a good idea if you could bring him along with you."

Sunday gave her mentor a quizzical smile, wondering what had prompted the unusual request. Whatever his motive was, she wasn't about to refuse. "Sure, Papa Ben. What about next Tuesday, the seventh?"

"That would be fine. Estelle and I will look forward to it. Count on staying overnight."

When Ben was finally out of sight, Sunday got up to leave, too. "I reckon I'd better go take care of my patient. He's bound to be hungry, too, and his bandages need changing."

Amos let out a slow breath. "You think Cap'n Ben's right about all that stuff?"

At the front door, Sunday turned and gave him her answer, "Have you ever known him to be wrong about anything?"

"No, I guess not. I'm glad he didn't tell nobody I was AWOL."

"I'm sure he had his reasons. See you later. I hope you enjoy the rest of the cobbler."

She took her time walking back to her house, her mind overflowing with unanswered questions. Nagging questions, about her own actions.

Why had she not told Ben Searcy—and Amos, too, for that matter—the truth about Charlie, the crates of gold, her Daddy, and the others? Why hadn't she simply turned the German submarine captain over to Amos? Why had she worked so hard to help Charlie? Yes, she had killed Bormann, but there was no law in the land that would fault her for doing it, given the circumstances. He had been a vicious killer himself, right? And what was the American boy, Bobby Joe Reams, doing helping Bormann?

Anyway, she was too tired to think about it now. Maybe Charlie himself would figure it out, given enough time, and a little time was something only she could give him. It wasn't like he might try to kill her and escape. Her instinct told her he just didn't seem like the murdering type, and besides, where could he escape to? Especially hurt like he was. No, as she had told Ben, it was best to just take it one day at the time, at least for now.

When she got back to her house, Charlie was sleeping peacefully. Sunday sat down and watched him for a while. She wondered what kind of home he came from. What kind of family. What was his wife like? Was she pretty? Did she know English as well as he did? Charlie must have been a good sailor man, too. Not many men his age got to be captain of any kind of ship.

She got up and walked to her chest. She quietly lifted its lid and removed the bullet-bent medal he'd been wearing. Turning it over and over in her hands, she examined it closely. This shiny black cross framed with diamonds he'd been wearing around his neck wasn't some cheap toy. Nor was it any kind of religious token. Must be some kind of high honor, and the fact that he hadn't mentioned it showed he wasn't full of what Ben always called vanity. Stood a lot of pain, too, didn't he? She knew he'd have to be hurting real bad before he'd ask for more of her special tea.

What would happen to him if she did turn him in? Would they really shoot him? What does a spy do anyway? But Charlie certainly wasn't a spy. He was captain of a ship of war. Still, much as Americans hated Germans and Japs, things probably wouldn't go well for him, captain or not. Plus, would the authorities look after his wounds properly? She doubted it. And since he couldn't talk, they'd most likely be meaner to him than most of the other prisoners, wherever they took him.

Well, there was plenty of time to worry about all that later. No, sir. Captain Charlie White Cap wasn't going anywhere. Not for a while . . .

She ate three spoons full of stew that had already gone cold, sighed, and climbed up into her bunk. In a matter of seconds, she was in deep, dreamless sleep.

Sunday would never be able to pinpoint during the days that followed exactly when she and Charlie discovered they could silently converse by Morse. It seemed to her, when she thought about it later, that it must have been one of the times she was changing the bandage on his cheek. Or maybe it was the night she removed the reed from his neck.

He had blinked rapidly, and whether it was from intuition or from some predestined, unseen force, she quickly recognized that some of his blinks were long, some short. It simply evolved. One minute she was chattering away at him, working on his wounds; the next minute they were sending each other short eye-messages, one long blink for a dash, a short one for a dot.

A-R-E Y-O-U I-N P-A-I-N?

V-E-R-Y L-I-T-T-L-E N-O-W. T-H-A-N-K Y-O-U.

G-O-O-D. H-U-N-G-R-Y?

Y-E-S.

Sunday was delighted! It was like a child's game. At first, the two of them purposely constricted their sentences and the thoughts behind them to a bare minimum of words. Within a day or two, they had honed their technique to such a degree that Charlie could 'talk' to her without resorting every other minute to the pad and pencil. This made it possible to chat while taking long walks up and down the beach—as long as they kept eye contact.

And it was on one of those leisurely walks Sunday learned that Charlie had some family; a mother, a brother, and a—fiancée! Because of the ring he wore, Sunday was at first confused—then certain—Charlie was lying through his teeth about that. She asked about it.

"Wife?"

Charlie replied:

NO, ELISABETH WAS NOT MY WIFE. WE WERE BETROTHED, AND OUR WEDDING DAY WAS TO HAVE BEEN THE VERY DAY HITLER SENT ME ON THIS VOYAGE.

"That's a damn shame. Was she pretty?" It struck Sunday that they were both talking about her in the past tense.

SHE WAS BEAUTIFUL.

"I bet you loved her a lot."

Charlie stopped walking. Looking away from her, he stared out at the ocean for a few minutes, then turned back to face her, his eyes working rapidly.

IT WAS VERY COMPLICATED, MISS EVERETTE. SHE LOVED MY BROTHER AND ME EQUALLY, AND WE BOTH LOVED HER. SHE CHOSE ME BECAUSE I WAS MORE . . . MORE WELL-KNOWN IN GERMANY.

"Was your brother also an officer?"

NO. HE WAS A PHYSICIAN. A SURGEON.

"I don't understand. Surgeons are important, aren't they? At least they are in America. They make a lot of money, too."

BUT THEY ARE NOT IN THE PUBLIC EYE.

"And you were? You mean you were famous or something?"

Charlie's face colored.

OR SOMETHING. YES, IN A WAY.

Unconsciously, he touched his throat.

I WAS RECENTLY DECORATED BY HITLER HIMSELF AT A HIGHLY PUBLICIZED CEREMONY. ELISABETH WAS VERY— HOW DO YOU SAY, IMPRESSIONABLE? YES, THAT IS THE WORD. IMPRESSIONABLE. SHE WAS MORE INTERESTED IN STATUS THAN CHARACTER. IF HITLER HAD DECORATED MY BROTHER, AND IT HAD BEEN HIS PHOTOGRAPH IN THE NEWSPAPERS AND IN ALL THE FILM THEATRES, ELISABETH WOULD SURELY HAVE CHOSEN HIM OVER AN OBSCURE, MID-RANK NAVAL OFFICER. AS IT WAS, OUR ENGAGEMENT WAS HER IDEA. SHE INSISTED, AND I SUPPOSE I WAS UNABLE OR PERHAPS UNWILLING TO ARGUE HER OUT OF IT.

"I don't get it. Didn't you *want* to marry her?"

I SUPPOSE SO. I THOUGHT I DID AT THE TIME. WE ALL GREW UP TOGETHER. HER PARENTS AND MINE ALWAYS ASSUMED SHE WOULD MARRY ONE OR THE OTHER OF US. IT WAS AN EXPECTED THING.

He stopped again, his eyes full of a different kind of pain.

PLEASE SUNDAY, THIS IS ALL SO VERY DIFFICULT TO EXPLAIN. NOW THAT I AM AWAY FROM HER, I CAN PERCEIVE FOR THE FIRST TIME HOW SHALLOW SHE REALLY WAS.

What do you know. He called me by my first name! Sunday kept pushing. "I reckon you miss her a lot, though, don't you?"

They walked another fifty yards before Charlie answered.

I THINK WHAT I MISS IS THE HABIT OF HER. THE . . . CONVENIENCE . . . OF HER.

With this, Sunday felt her own face burning, realizing he was talking in a polite, roundabout way about sex. Suddenly embarrassed, she decided to drop the whole subject, though she was still positive he was lying. *Fiancée, my foot! That ring he's wearing is no diamond engagement ring. That's a wedding band if I ever saw one!*

What Sunday also realized, to her undying shame, was how easy it was to picture this tall, handsome man before his wounds. Before his loss. Before his war. And, it was also an easy thing to admit to herself how attracted to him she was.

Sunday kept the two of them busy every waking hour, and in spite of natural pride in her healing skills, Sunday was nevertheless surprised at how fast Charlie was recovering. Since she had removed the reed from his throat and had stitched the hole carefully, they had spent most of their time outdoors. Salt spray from BLACK DOLPHIN's bow waves, along with the early May sun, did wonders for his throat and cheek wounds. All the swelling went down, and on several short trips they made together to tend her crab pots (as well as several more for fishing in both the sound and the ocean), she was genuinely impressed at how well Charlie handled her boat, proving over and over his expert sailing skills. ("Oh, you're a man born to the water, all right, Charlie White Cap, that's a plain fact.") She was happy to see him laugh for the first time, and even happier to see a new light behind those blue eyes of his.

On the sixth day, on a pleasure sail, she took him almost to the Stream to visit her dolphin friends. She caught herself stopping just short of stripping and diving overboard, although she couldn't help but admire the fresh muscle tone in Charlie's torso when he removed his borrowed shirt. A light tan was definitely replacing the man's pale skin. *You're looking a lot better, Charlie boy.*

Last week, your skin looked a lot like one of my pie shells. Now look at you. Your athlete's body is getting downright healthy again. Sunday became aware her thoughts were drifting once more in the wrong direction. *Change the subject again, girl!*

"You know, I've been thinking a lot about that Reams boy," she said. "It may be he was from somewhere around these parts."

WHY DO YOU SAY THAT?

She chose her words carefully, "Because he had double first names. They were not nicknames. His dog tags said 'Bobby Joe Reams,' not 'Robert Joseph Reams.' Only people who live down here in the South have crazy names like that. I've got an idea for when we get back to Pea Island."

WHAT IS IT?

"Tell you later. Ever been frog gigging?"

NO. WHAT IS FROG GIGGING?

Sunday giggled. "Catching frogs to eat. We've got some powerful big bullfrogs up there in the marsh."

Charlie made a face.

YOU EAT FROGS?

Sunday laughed. "Just their legs. I think they taste better than chicken. Lot's of folks do. Tell you what: let's borrow Amos' gig and go up there tonight and get us a few."

AS YOU WISH, BUT I DO NOT THINK I WILL EAT ANY, THANK YOU JUST THE SAME.

"Want to bet? My Daddy taught me how to cook them real good. You just lop off their legs and fry them up in a pan of butter and spices. It's fun, too, 'cause the legs keep on jumping around in the frying pan for a while like they were still alive. Anyway, that's what we're having for supper tonight!"

Amos was only too happy to loan Sunday his rubber boots and his gig—a small trident attached to the end of a long handle. Charlie tried on the boots, commenting,

A LITTLE LARGE, BUT I CAN WALK IN THEM, I THINK.

He hefted the gig.

THIS IS VERY MUCH LIKE A SMALL HARPOON.

Sunday took the gig from him, showing how to make short, quick thrusts. "Yep. Works about the same way for flounder, too. Tears a bullfrog's body up nasty, but it's only his legs we want, anyway. Come on, bring the flashlight and sack. It'll be dark soon. By the time we're done, you'll be mighty hungry. I promise."

Charlie wasn't so sure.

"Bringing me a few, Sunday?" Amos begged.

"Sure I will. Say, by the way, there's something else you can help me with."

"Yeah? What?"

"Instead of paying me by the month for my miserable failure with Lorraine, I'd like for you to make a call for me."

"Sure. Who you want me to call?"

"Commander French."

Amos was completely taken aback. "French? But— he's my boss man!"

"I know. And he has a lot of influence. A lot of pull."

"Reckon he does, but what do you want from him?"

Sunday took a deep breath, knowing she was about to plunge into a serious gamble.

"One of those dead men on that raft was an American boy, Amos. I have his dog tags." She took them from around her neck and handed them to the flabbergasted coastguardsman, who stared at them with blank eyes.

"I want you to call Commander French and see if he can run a trace on him. Army, Navy, Marines, all branches of the service. If we can find them, the boy's folks might want to know where he's buried."

She watched as Amos studied the tags, and tried to appear nonchalant. As though it was a trivial thing. "Just let me know what French says first chance you get. How many frog legs you want?"

That night, under a full moon, Sunday and Charlie stalked, blinded, and bagged two dozen enormous victims, the long legs of which Sunday immediately amputated. "That ought to be enough. Let's go home. I'm hungry. How about you?"

Charlie still wasn't so sure. Nevertheless, just as Sunday had promised, he found them to be delicious, as were the hush puppies and fried green tomatoes—which he had also never tasted.

"We'd best turn in early, Charlie. Tomorrow, we're going to sail over to Manteo and have supper with Ben and his wife. Special invitation."

Charlie did not respond at all to that remark, and soon both he and Sunday went to bed with full stomachs. Also, Sunday thought, in good spirits. For the first time since his rescue, Charlie had forgotten about listening to the nightly radio, broadcasting—for him, at least—its grim news. It was also the first night he needed no medicine.

CHAPTER 20

MAY 7, 1945 dawned on Pea Island clear as cut glass, but as soon as Sunday walked outside and sniffed the wind, she knew the sunshine wouldn't last. She called inside to her houseguest, "We're going to get us a thunderstorm, Charlie. We'd best have a quick breakfast and shove off. With luck, we can make it to Wanchese before it comes."

Charlie came out and also looked up at the sky, scanning the horizon with the eye of an experienced sailor. He nodded and rapidly blinked,

YOU ARE CORRECT. I BELIEVE THE RAIN WILL COME BY MIDDAY, FROM THE SOUTHWEST.

"Well, if it catches us, we'll be sailing northwest. Could be a fun, fast ride and won't be too cold. Anyway, sailing BLACK DOLPHIN across the sound will be a lot more fun than taking Robert Kinch's ferryboat. Besides, if we did, we'd first have to walk up to the Station House and have Amos call Robert on the radio to make a detour. His boat only stops by once a month nowadays. Come on, let's make some oatmeal and biscuits. Something that sticks to the ribs."

After they ate, Sunday went fishing in her sea chest for something decent for Charlie to wear. Charlie sat at the table, watching her remove his old uniform, cap, the black pistol and its holster. Sunday glanced at him, but his eyes showed no sign of either emotion or need for conversation. She dug deeper and extracted her best shirt and trousers.

"You weigh a lot more than I do, Charlie, but we're almost the same height. Here, try these boots on. I've got such big feet, I'll bet they'll fit, or be close enough for you to wear them without them pinching."

The boots did fit, more or less, as did the shirt and pants, and with Sunday's extra slicker and sou'wester on his head, Charlie was completely outfitted for wet sailing weather and in Sunday's mind, quite presentable for any social visit, even if they had been going to church! They set sail shortly after eight o'clock.

BLACK DOLPHIN, splendidly sailed by her expert two-person crew, made the trip across the sound in, by Sunday's reckoning, record time, reaching the Wanchese docks just minutes before the first thunder and lightning rolled in. They hitched a ride to Manteo with a local fisherman, and shortly after noon, were knocking on Estelle Carson Searcy's door.

Estelle herself greeted them, "Come, in, come in. Ben's in town at the doctor's, but I expect him back before dinner."

Sunday made the introductions, and was careful to explain that Charlie could converse in English just fine, but that she, using Morse code signals from him, would have to be his "voice."

"Yes, I understand completely, Sunday," Estelle said. Then, looking Charlie full in the eye, said, "Ben told me all about your misfortune, sir. Has there been any improvement at all in your memory?"

Charlie returned her warm smile, but shrugged and shook his head fatalistically.

"I'm so sorry. Perhaps one day soon . . . Please, come in and sit down. Sunday, it's wonderful to see you again, and I want to thank you from the bottom of my heart for your, ah, medicine. It's helping Ben so much. We're both very grateful."

"I'm glad I could help, Estelle."

"You surely have. He's . . . He seems so much better, now. Oh, do excuse me. I'm forgetting my manners. Would you like some tea? How about some lettuce and tomato sandwiches. I imagine you haven't had lunch yet, have you?"

"No, ma'am. That would be fine. Let me help you make the sandwiches."

After lunch, while Ben's graceful wife poured more tea, Sunday said, "Say, while we're waiting for Ben, why don't you tell Charlie some of the stories you've collected. On the way over here, I told him you had been a schoolteacher, and were writing a book about famous stories of the Banks and Roanoke Island."

Estelle Searcy gave Sunday a smile sweeter than the sugar she was passing over, but her eyes were saying, *How clever of you, Sunday Everette, to divert any conversation away from your rescued sailor and his condition. All right, I'll play along.*

"Oh, my," she said, as if suffering from academic modesty. "That little thing? It's merely an amateur trifle. Besides, most of those stories have come from Ben. You know what a wellspring of knowledge he is concerning the Outer Banks."

"He sure is," Sunday agreed. "But from what I hear, those old yarns are only part of that book."

"That's true, I suppose." Teacup and saucer in hand, she faced Charlie. "My chief contribution is a history of the attempt to organize an independent, incorporated Negro town here at Manteo after the War Between the States—what mainlanders around here still call the War of Northern Aggression. Their effort was a noble attempt, but one that failed."

With a tinkling little laugh she added, "It seems that Sunday is a great deal more interested in such subjects now than when she was my pupil. In those days she preferred fisticuffs over history, although I have to admit her language usage has improved remarkably."

Sunday had to laugh, too. "I'll bet you were happy to be rid of me back then."

"No. On the contrary, you would have been a worthwhile project for me. A real challenge for my abilities as a teacher, but there were a dozen or so young boys in my school who were *very* happy you left. Anyway, which story do you think Mister, ah, Charlie would like?"

"What about the White Deer? I already told him about Blackbeard, and Old Quark, and the fire ship of Ocracoke."

Estelle nodded, and again she faced Charlie. "Those are strange and often fanciful legends, but every Banker will swear they are true. The tale of the White Deer is really the story of Virginia Dare, the first English child born in America. Her fate, and that of her parents and all the rest of that unlucky colony here on Roanoke Island is a real, ongoing mystery, Charlie. The legend I'm writing about is the one told about Virginia from the native Indian point of view. It's very romantic, a truly beautiful story in its own right. It seems that—"

Estelle didn't get to even begin her narrative. Ben burst through the door—dripping wet, and with more energy than Sunday had seen in years.

"Quick, Estelle, turn on the radio. The Germans have surrendered. The war in Europe is over!"

They all instantly clustered around the radio and listened in stunned silence.

On every station they could raise, the fantastic news was being broadcast with great excitement. VE Day . . . Victory in Europe . . . interspersed with blaring music of

John Phillip Sousa and the national anthem, Germany's unconditional surrender was being shouted over the airwaves by ecstatic announcers, national and local. Allied armies victorious . . . Russians and American forces had linked up at Torgau . . . Berlin had surrendered to the Russians on May second. Hitler and Himmler rumored dead . . . Admiral Karl Doenitz had succeeded Hitler . . . General Alfred Jodl of the German High Command signed terms early this morning at a little red schoolhouse in Reims, France. Eisenhower's Chief of Staff, General Walter B. Smith, had signed for the Allies . . . The free world is in jubilant celebration . . . President Truman will make a speech soon.

On and on it went, with much repetition and endless commentary. Sunday gradually became aware that outside there were other noises augmenting the frequent thunderclaps. She looked through the window. The street outside was full of people oblivious to the stormy weather, all banging pots, pans, shouting, and throwing firecrackers.

"News travels fast these days," Sunday thought aloud.

Then she glanced at Charlie, and nearly fainted. His eyes were glassy. Veiled with tears. His face was blanched to beyond pale, and he was gripping the sides of the armchair he was sitting in so hard his fingers and knuckles had gone white as his face. He was not looking at her, either. He was staring straight ahead, seeing nothing. Or maybe imagining something that was thousands of miles away.

And with a furrowed brow, Benjamin Searcy was staring right at him! Sunday's heart fluttered to her throat. *Oh, my God. He knows!*

But the moment passed as fast as it had occurred. Ben jumped up, hugged his wife, then hugged Sunday.

He grabbed Charlie's hand and pumped it up and down vigorously. Then he announced, "Listen up, all of you. This news is cause for celebration. Extravagance even."

He looked at his watch once, and went on, his voice shrill, "Estelle, you're not going to cook tonight. Not one morsel. We're going to take the four o'clock boat to Elizabeth City. I'm taking us all out to dinner. Damn the expense. Then I'm treating all four of us to the movies."

"Movies? A real picture show?" Sunday asked. "I've never seen one. Not in my whole life."

"Well, honey," Ben said, "You'll love the one that's on at the Carolina. They show first-run movies there, and this is the second night *Lassie Come Home* is playing. It's a story tender as those Estelle writes."

Jim Carew's Catfish Shop had never served one single catfish. Its unique location (just beyond the western edge of Elizabeth City's town limits, by the farthermost docks) guaranteed daily access to the freshest and tastiest seafood selection to be found in North Carolina, or so Jim said. And, because of the way his wife prepared the food, few of his customers disagreed. Jim's establishment was hardly what could be called a proper restaurant: a pair of small rooms containing five red-and-white-covered tables, all on the left side of the frame house. The two rooms on the right, with separate front and back entrances, served as the Carew's living quarters. The common kitchen was at the rear. The wide front porch could be also be hastily set up for large crowds, provided the weather was satisfactory. No one knew how Eunice Carew kept flies and other insects away from her meals and customers, but she somehow managed that in addition to never making their clientele wait more than ten minutes to be served.

To Jim's knowledge, they had never served a single meal to a white man either. However, his old friend Cap'n Ben Searcy, having called ahead, had warned him that there was one coming, and also made an unusual request. With them were Ben's handsome schoolteacher wife and the tall, beautiful girl they called Sunday. Jim Carew had known Ben Searcy far too long to question the former Keeper's judgment, and if Ben wanted to bring a white man to eat with them, he must have had his reasons. Anyway, that was his business. There would be no questions asked. He'd simply serve them at table number nine, in the back of the west room.

There was no such thing as a menu at Carew's. Every man or woman who ate there regularly knew what seafood was in season, and the shrimp, oysters, trout, snapper, blues, ocean perch, flounder, or sea bass entrees, supplemented with cornbread and appropriate vegetables, were filling and delicious, with portions large enough for Joe Louis.

Ben ordered for everyone, and no one complained about his choices. Sweet iced tea by the pitcher washed it all down, and Eunice Carew's famous banana pudding dessert added yet one more notch to her reputation. Estelle, making dinner conversation, told Sunday that no bribe or coercion could ever persuade the three-hundred-pound cook to reveal any of her recipe secrets, but Sunday scarcely heard. She had noticed, all through the meal, that Ben glanced occasionally at Charlie, who was still having some difficulty chewing and swallowing.

The meal lasted over an hour. Ben, with a final gesture of dropping his napkin on top of his plate said, "Half an hour before the movie begins."

With no little effort, he stood. "Charlie, would you mind coming with me? You, too, Sunday."

Ben led them back to the steamy kitchen. Jim was waiting there for them, holding a faded raincoat and an equally ancient slouch hat. "Will these do, Cap'n?"

Ben took the articles from him. "Admirably, Jim, and thank you. I'll return them tomorrow. Do you have the other stuff?"

Jim grinned, showing several gold-framed teeth. "Yes, sir. You want to do the job, or you want me to?"

"You can." To Charlie, he said, "Son, the movie house we're going to has a separate entrance for coloreds like us. We have to sit in a partitioned-off balcony area. We want you to sit with us, so we're going to fix you up so that you look like a black man. If you stand behind us, and with this coat and hat on in this rain, I don't think the ticket girl will notice. Jim here is going to put some coloring on your face."

Charlie nodded, and stood stoically while Jim Carew carefully spread the mysterious brown mixture on his face, covering every inch of skin that would show between the hat and buttoned-up collar.

"Can't do nothin' 'bout them blue eyes, but it'll be dark, and if you keep your head down, it should work."

Eunice giggled. "Looks like he's getting ready for a minstrel show."

"Sure does," her husband agreed.

"Don't forget to keep your hands in your pockets till you get inside, Charlie, and when you do, for God's sake, keep that hat on. I have never yet seen a black man with blond hair. Not even an albino."

The disguise worked, and as they climbed the steps leading to the left balcony, Sunday paused midway up, in awe. The lobby was luxurious. Magnificent twin chandeliers hung from its high, ornately decorated ceiling. Rich maroon carpet covered the floor. At the top, when they entered the balcony, she was further impressed with the brocade, the vaulted dark-blue ceiling that featured lights behind pinhole openings, simulating twinkling stars in the night sky. False, draped boxes protruded from the terra cotta walls, and a thick velvet curtain hung over the wide, gilded stage proscenium.

"It's beautiful," she whispered to Estelle.

"Yes, it is," Ben's wife whispered back. "You can almost forget it's segregated. Almost."

"What's that smell?"

"Popcorn. Shhh . . . I'll tell you about that later. Look, the curtain is opening. The movie's about to start."

Sunday glued her eyes to the immense white screen, which was quickly filled with images of Coming Attractions. After a few minutes of holding her breath, she leaned to her right and whispered to Charlie, "My God, everybody's so big!"

Sunday was totally entranced, and when the animated cartoons (several of them complete with music as funny as they were) filled the screen, she laughed and clapped her hands in childlike pleasure.

But then came the Pathé *News of the Day* discovery of hell.

After two minutes of the nightmare she was watching, Sunday wished with every fiber of her being that they had never come. She dared not glance sideways at Charlie, who had grabbed her hand. Squeezing it tight. The grainy images on the screen, accompanied by the somber voice of the professional announcer were far beyond rational belief.

One grisly scene followed another: skeletons of human beings—barely alive—by the hundreds. By the thousands. Most in black-and-white-striped rags. The barbed wire. The filth. Filth and misery so stark you could nearly smell it. The open graves. The stacks and stacks of corpses. Piles of human hair. Shoes and clothes. Suitcases. Jewelry and personal effects. Adolf Hitler's hell.

There were occasional shots of American soldiers, their grim faces full of shock, disbelief, and gut-sickness. The only few words Sunday would remember, being uttered in deep, resonant tones by the narrator, were the same ones every other soul inside the Carolina Theatre would remember the rest of their lives: death camps with strange names—in Germany, and other countries Sunday had only hazy knowledge of. Jews. Gypsies. Undesirables. Murdered. Shot. Strangled. Hanged. Gassed. And burned. Burned in iron furnaces. Murdered and burned up like dirty piles of trash. Millions of them. *Millions?* Was that even possible? Horror was the nicest word Sunday could think of for the endless stream of starvation, suffering, and death she was witnessing. Was this how the Germans made war?

Suddenly she became aware of Charlie squeezing her hand, this time in Morse, a short squeeze or a long one.

S-u-n-d-a-y, I m-u-s-t g-e-t a-w-a-y f-r-o-m h-e-r-e. I c-a-n-n-o-t b-r-e-a-t-h-e. I b-e-g y-o-u. P-l-e-a-s-e t-a-k-e m-e o-u-t.

Sunday led him out of the theater. They staggered in the rain down to the waterfront. Charlie never let go of her hand, although he transmitted no more messages. They tread in an eerie silence Sunday would have never thought possible. It was as if her whole world had come to an abrupt stop. Its entire population mute as Charlie. Even crickets were holding their breath. The only thought that Sunday was conscious of passing through her mind, piercing the indelible images now burned into her brain, was that Ben Searcy had done this on purpose. *Damn you, Papa Ben; why'd you have to do this? You knew what was in that movie didn't you? You knew! I sure hope you enjoy watching* LASSIE COME HOME. *Damn you. I loved and trusted you so much. So much.*

She had no idea of the passing of time. No idea of how they had made their way to the ferry landing. No idea of when Ben and Estelle joined them in the ether of the trip back to Manteo. She was aware, however, that none of them—Ben, Estelle, or she herself—chanced a look at Charlie's blackened face. She would later have no cognizant memory of when they arrived at the house, or of saying goodnight. She would not even remember how much time passed before she crept into the room they had given Charlie. She would only remember saying one thing to him: "Charlie, I know in my heart that you had nothing to do with any of that. It wouldn't be possible. Not for you."

She also would remember how pitiful was his painful sobbing, inconsolable sobbing that came forth like the warm spring rain falling outside. But until the day she would die, she knew she would treasure the memory of how she finally did stop it. How she removed all her clothes. And his. And smeared her own face with shared tears and the bootblack from his. And the kisses. First tender, then deep. And when their two bodies became one.

CHAPTER 21

THE SUN was already high when Sunday opened her eyes and glanced out the window, remembering with a low chuckle that they had not even bothered to pull the shade down. She turned, still wrapped in Charlie's arms, and gazed into his face. His blue eyes were open—*had he slept any at all?*—and there was a contented smile on his lips.

In a rush of memories of the night before, ranging from horror to ecstasy, Sunday pulled away from his embrace, looked into those blues and said, almost in a whisper, "Listen to me, Charlie. We'll talk about 'us' another time. Soon, I promise. But, right now you're going to have to pull yourself together about what we saw in that movie house last night. I don't know what Ben has in mind, but we have to be ready for it, no matter what. Let me do the talking, okay?"

Charlie's smile became a frown. His eyes blinked: *O-K.*

"Good. It's late. We better get dressed and see how the land lies."

In less than fifteen minutes, they walked into the aromatic kitchen where Estelle was busy toiling over her stove, making breakfast.

"Good morning," she chirped, as though it was a perfectly normal one. "I hope you both slept well. Can Charlie manage scrambled eggs and bacon, Sunday?"

Sunday smiled. *Not a word about the disaster of the night before.* "His throat can't handle bacon just yet, Estelle, or hard toast either, but the eggs and maybe some biscuits would be fine for both of us. Grits, too."

Estelle kept on stirring furiously. She still hadn't looked at either of them. "Coming right up. Why don't you go on and sit down at the table. I'll only be a few minutes."

"All right," Sunday said. "Um, where's Ben?"

"In the parlor. He said he had to make a few telephone calls."

Sunday's heart skipped a beat. She gave Charlie a quick look she hoped was one of confidence, as if to say, *Don't worry, Ben Searcy won't—what's that word you used? 'Betray?' No, he won't do that. Not my Papa Ben.*

But to Estelle she said, "Sure I can't help you in here?"

"No, no. I'm almost finished anyway. We all slept late, didn't we?"

Sunday grabbed Charlie's hand, squeezed it reassuringly, and led him into the dining room. They had no more than taken their seats when Ben came in, smiled broadly at the two of them, and sat down at his place at the head of the table.

"Glad to see you looking better, Charlie. Jim Carew's spicy food a bit too much for you, was it? That's a shame. I'm sorry you missed the feature movie."

Sunday took the cue. "Me, too. I think Charlie's much better this morning, aren't you?"

Charlie smiled again and nodded.

Sunday leaned back and offered a smile of her own to her old mentor. *No finger-pointing about our sleeping together last night, either.* "Well, that trout was pretty greasy. So were the hush puppies. No wonder he got sick. By the way, how are you feeling these days? I haven't even had a chance to ask you." *Take advantage of the moment, Sunday.* "How's the medicine working?"

Ben's gaze and fixed smile were steady. "I'm holding my own."

At that moment, Estelle brought a huge platter of eggs and biscuits, which she placed before Sunday. She sat down and said, "I'll bring the rest in a moment. Ben, will you say grace?"

Sunday shot Charlie a quick wink and a look that said, *Lower your head, like this.*

"Heavenly Father," Ben intoned, "grant us thy blessings today and all the days of the rest of our lives. Bless this food to the nourishment of our ailing bodies, guide us down the right paths today, and grant us wisdom to make our future steps sure and just. We ask this in the name of your son, Jesus Christ. Amen."

When Ben finished his prayer, and was certain all eyes were on him, he grinned and said, "Eat a big breakfast, you two. We have a long drive ahead of us today, and we're getting a late start on it."

Sunday caught herself just before replying that she and Charlie had planned to shove off right away for Pea Island. *Ten-to-one, as Daddy used to say, those phone calls have something to do with this.* "Where to this time, Papa Ben? Sure we haven't worn our welcome out?"

"Of course not. We're driving to New Bern and Morehead City. There are a couple of boats I heard about for sale I thought you might want to take a look at. Estelle's going to pack us a picnic lunch, so why don't you two take turns with your bath, and we'll get right on the road. Charlie, you'll find an extra razor and toothbrush in the bathroom. Now, please eat up."

Sunday picked up her fork and dug in, thinking, *Maybe I was wrong. Maybe this trip to look at a couple of trawlers really is all he has in mind. Like a kind of final farewell present.*

"You heard what the Cap'n said," Sunday said, laughing, "Orders are orders. Eat up."

Except for two hasty bathroom stops for poor Estelle, they drove the first leg—to Williamston—in very good time. However, before they crossed the bridge over the Roanoke River into that small lumber town, Ben pulled the Chevy over to the side of the road. From under his seat, he extracted a pair of binoculars, opened his door, and said, "Sunday, there's something over there I want you and Charlie to see."

He led them through gnarly underbrush and scrub pines to the top of a slight knoll.

"From here, we have a good view."

He handed Sunday the binoculars and pointed the two hundred yards across the fast flowing river.

"Take a look."

Sunday put the binoculars to her eyes, focusing with the ease of well-practiced experience, and stared—at the barbed-wire-enclosed compound, the wooden guard towers and barracks, the sizable playing field, and then at the men milling about inside. She lowered the glasses and gave Ben a look of confusion. "That's a prison, isn't it?"

Ben took the glasses from her and handed them to Charlie. "That's what it is, all right. Have a look, son."

Ben waited until Charlie was absorbed in gazing across the river, took Sunday gently by the elbow and led her several yards back.

"Sunday, those are German prisoners of war. You have lied to me, honey, for the first time in your life. I have no doubt the story you told me of Charlie's rescue was partially true, but you certainly lied to me about a great deal of it.

"Where, for instance, was Slick? I know he was visiting you at the time. Where was your dog? Gyp never leaves your side. I made several inquiries, honey. Neither the Navy nor Coast Guard has a record of any ships being sunk anywhere close to our coast at that time. Those men you found had to have come from a submarine. Not one of ours, either. I checked."

Sunday listened, holding her breath and staring at her toes.

"Your Charlie," Ben went on, "is a sailor man, sure enough, but his skin showed me he was not from any surface ship. That kind of pallor only shows up on submariners. Sailors who don't get their bodies in the sun very much. Or even their faces. In addition, I knew Charlie was not an American from the way he eats—sort of left-handed, European style. That, plus his close-cut blond hair and those blue eyes make me think he just might be a German."

He turned back to watch Charlie, who still had the binoculars trained on the compound across the river. "I'll be very interested in his reaction to those men he's watching."

Sunday let her breath out in a long, slow sigh. "You don't miss much, do you?"

"I try not to. I didn't miss anything last night, either."

"All right, Papa Ben. I should have known I could never fool you. What are you going to do? His war is over now."

Ben rubbed his chin.

"I don't know yet. Much depends on you. Before I can make any decision, I want the truth from you. All of it, the whole story, but not right now. Tonight, when we get back home. Oh, and Sunday, it was extremely clever of you both to figure out the Morse code system you're using, but if I were you, I wouldn't say anything to him yet about this conversation we're having right now. Understand?"

Sunday's subdued reply was like that of a rebuked child. "Yes, sir. I do."

"Fine, then. Let's be on our way." He turned once again. "Hey Charlie, let's go. We have a lot of miles to cover before lunch."

Charlie sat like an expressionless wooden Indian all the way to New Bern. Estelle, ever the genteel diplomat, filled the silence by chattering away about the history of that quaint town, the second oldest in the state, and its first capitol. Sunday paid Estelle's historical ramblings no attention whatsoever, her apprehension growing by the hour. And, just as she expected, Ben wasn't finished with his preplanned itinerary yet. Not by a long shot.

They ate a hasty picnic lunch on the grass in the charming little De Gaffenried park, which Estelle informed them was named for the Swiss Baron who founded the town. Ben then drove, a few miles north, down a road that paralleled the broad Neuse River, to a secluded pine forest where they came upon a much larger POW camp.

"There are nearly five thousand prisoners here, Charlie," Ben said softly.

"Like those others you saw back at Williamston, these men are treated very well indeed, and are even allowed to work on farms if they want to. Rumor has it that many of them like it here so much, they plan to come back someday after their repatriation.

"Sunday, you remember going with us to Rocky Mount, don't you? There was a much smaller camp located there, too, for a while. Those prisoners were offered work in the tobacco warehouses, but most couldn't take the stifling heat. The main camp is located in Durham. That's where the officers and those who are hard cases are kept, under a good deal more security."

Sunday didn't dare ask where Ben had obtained so much information about German prisoners of war, for fear he might actually tell her, and maybe spook Charlie into doing something rash. So far, Charlie had not made any kind of overt reaction to the sights he had been subjected to, and Sunday wondered how long he could hold his emotions in check.

"Look, Ben," Estelle said, pointing down the road.

They all turned and watched as a military convoy of trucks, bumper to bumper, came rumbling toward the main gate of the camp. At the same time, a burly American soldier with an MP armband around his left arm—which also shouldered a rifle—walked toward them, a serious look on his face.

He was polite, though, "Sorry folks, you'll have to leave this area. Just please turn your car around and drive on out of here."

"What's going on, Sergeant?" Ben wanted to know.

"We're moving a lot of these boys out to the depot in New Bern. They'll take a special train down to Morehead City for boarding."

"Boarding?"

"Yeah. On a turnaround troopship. About half of them will be on their way home tomorrow. The rest will be gone by next week this time. Now, please do as I ask. Get along with you."

Sunday gritted her teeth. *Damn you again, Ben Searcy. You knew about that, too, didn't you. Trawler, my eye!*

Sunday was only half right. There actually were two used trawlers for sale, berthed side by side in the basin at Morehead City, that Ben had wanted her to look at. He also knew that making any kind of inquiry regarding those boats was the furthermost thing from her mind, and when she expressed no interest in boarding or surveying either one of them, he casually suggested they go watch the prisoners boarding.

Sipping Coca-Colas they had bought, they all stood behind the ropes on the quay at the railhead, and stared like children at a parade as the hundreds of prisoners, like so many trained animals, filed over the gangplank of the old Liberty ship.

"You reckon they're glad to be going home, Charlie?" Ben said.

Charlie didn't answer.

There were two other pairs of eyes watching the steady procession. Leaning over the rail of the ship's quarterdeck, smoking cigarettes, two off-watch merchant seamen were laconically waiting for chow call. One spoke.

"Helluva note. Nursemaiding a thousand sonsabitch Krauts all the way back to Bremerhaven. Lucky us. Some fucking duty, and not but one free night in Baltimore to boot. At least we'll get paid."

His partner started to reply and then suddenly stiffened. He tossed his cigarette butt over the rail, leaned farther over and said, "Well, I'll be damned. I'll be God-fucking-*damned!* Talk about luck!"

"What is it? What are you looking at, Bummy?"

Seaman Second Class Calvin "Bummy" Keene pointed. "Look over there. See that tall, good-looking nigger woman?"

"Yeah? So?"

Bummy smiled and crossed his arms. "That's the same black bitch I told you about. The one who shot me."

"No kiddin'? You sure?"

"Oh, yeah, I'm sure."

Chapter 22

"I THINK we've seen enough of this," Ben said, glancing at his watch. "Come on, let's go. You can finish your drinks in the car."

It took him less than half an hour's driving to locate the Morehead City Public Library. Winking at his wife as he parked the car, he turned to his backseat passengers.

"We won't be long, and we'd best leave Estelle here. If she goes inside, I'll never get her out. Besides, we still have one more errand to run after this stop."

That said, he led his two bewildered guests up the steps and through the front door.

Seated behind the main desk, the prim, elderly librarian looked up from her work. Her mouth dropped open at the same speed her eyebrows shot up in astonishment at seeing three strangers—two of them *colored people*—brazenly marching directly up to her sanctified station like they owned the place. The old Negro man spoke right up, too!

"Ma'am, we need to see where you keep the Morehead City High School yearbooks."

Still speechless, all she could think of to do was point toward the west room, which housed most of the reference material.

Gesturing for Sunday and Charlie to take chairs at a vacant table, Ben began searching through the shelves. When he returned, he had four large books in hand, which he silently placed on the table before sitting down.

They were leather bound high school annuals for the years of 1941 through 1944.

"I don't think this will take long," he muttered, and opened the first one.

Sunday and Charlie exchanged several questioning glances while Ben thumbed deliberately through the books. And, it didn't take long for him to find what he was looking for. With an eyebrow arched in tacit triumph, he twisted the 1942 yearbook around so that they could see what his forefinger touched. The small, senior-class photograph of a grinning boy dressed in bib overalls was underlined with his name: Bobby Joe Reams. In a whisper, Ben asked Sunday, "Is this the boy you buried?"

Her nod was positive. "That's him, all right, but—how did you know?"

She got only a grim smile for an answer. She and Ben both glanced at Charlie, who was staring at the photo as if he were seeing a ghost.

Ben said nothing more, but got up and returned the books to their well-dusted shelf. Then he motioned for them to follow him outside, pausing briefly at the desk to quietly thank the still-flustered librarian.

Walking to the car, he continued mystifying Sunday and Charlie by saying, "We have just one more stop to make, and then we'll drive back home. Don't ask me any questions now. We'll talk about it all then and there!"

Ben's second stop was at the local newspaper office. He asked the others to wait while he went inside. He returned a few minutes later and passed back a copy of a small clipping. This was a grainy, black-bordered photo of the same Bobby Joe Reams, only this time in the uniform of a corporal in the United States Army Air Corps. The text revealed that he had been listed as

Missing in Action after a bombing sortie over somewhere in Germany during the fall of 1943.

On the interminable drive back to Elizabeth City and ferry crossing to Manteo, the interior of Estelle's Chevy was quiet as a church is on Monday. Sated with a liberal dose of Sunday's medicine from his thermos, Ben slept fitfully during the entire trip, with his stoic wife driving. In the rear seat, Sunday and Charlie were equally silent, completely absorbed in lead-heavy individual thoughts, until both were bordering on mental as well as physical exhaustion. Safe once again in Charlie's assigned room, they tumbled fully clothed into bed, grateful to be together, but far too tired to speculate on how much longer they might still be.

Late the following morning, a seemingly rejuvenated Ben Searcy spoke another brief blessing over breakfast, chattering cheerfully during the meal, which was mostly ignored. Once Estelle had cleared the table and discretely left the room, he held serious court.

"All right, let's get down to it. Earlier, I mentioned to you that I had made some calls. Matter of fact, I made a lot of calls. Some of them were to several towns in our general area. I was inquiring if there were any families named Reams. I found quite a few, but only one Robert Reams, a fisherman in Morehead City, who turned out to be Bobby Joe's father. He had no other family."

Ben turned and smiled at Sunday.

"Honey, you asked me how I knew. Simple. For once, Amos did do his duty properly. He called me right after you asked him to get in touch with Commander French. He told me about your 'casual' request, and gave me the boy's name and his dog tag number. I haven't made up my mind about reporting Reams. Not yet, anyway."

Sunday looked Ben in the eye. Softly, and, for the second time in as many days, she asked, "What are you going to do, Papa Ben?"

Ben pursed his lips and replied, "I haven't made up my mind yet. Right now, as I told you, I want the truth."

He turned his attention to Charlie.

"Young man, Sunday has lied to me about you, and, more or less by proxy, *for* you. From practically since she was born, I have loved this young woman like the daughter I never had, and I always will. One reason I care for her so much is that she had never in her life lied to me about anything. I have never known her to do anything without good reason either, and I have a sneaking suspicion of why she did lie. I'm going to take that into careful consideration in my decision making, but for the present, I want to hear about the whole stinking business that happened, even if it takes the two of you all day and night."

He grinned at Charlie before continuing.

"It was smart of you both to think of using Morse in order to talk to each other. I daresay I can manage that, too, Charlie, if you like, just as soon as you admit that you are a German seaman and that you don't have half an ounce of amnesia. But first, I want to hear it from Sunday."

He lowered his eyes at her.

"All of it, too, honey. Don't leave anything out. Then I'll listen to Charlie's story. After that, let us see if we can't untangle this nasty ball of twine."

Sunday shifted in her chair and cleared her throat. "Okay, Papa Ben. I'm sorry about the lies. Truly I am. You deserved better than that from me."

She looked down, then back up at him with moist eyes. When she spoke, the words came in a rush, her voice cracking.

"It all started the same night I sailed back from here with Gyp after tending to Amos' wife. Daddy had stayed behind to watch the Station House. Soon as we tied up BLACK DOLPHIN, Gyp smelled something and started acting funny. I was tired, but suspicious right off that something was bad wrong. What happened that night and the next was ugly and it isn't easy for me to talk about it because my Daddy and my dog were both killed that second night. Shot down in cold blood right in front of my eyes and all I could think of was getting revenge. All I wanted—"

"Whoa, Sunday," Ben gently interrupted, placing a gnarled hand over hers. "I know this can't be easy for you, but try to slow down and rely on some of your famous inner strength. Just tell me, step by step, minute by minute, exactly what happened."

In a more controlled voice, Sunday's recitation took the better part of an hour. In all that time, Ben's eyes never wavered from hers, and at the end, his were also wet.

His voice was as soothing as it had been up in the crow's nest on the night of George Harris' sudden departure, "Honey, I don't believe there are more than a handful of people—either men or women—in this whole world who could have done all you did that night, and Charlie here, or whatever his real name may be, is living proof of it."

He stood, stretched, and walked to the stove in the kitchen to fetch the two teapots being kept warm, one of which contained Estelle's normal strong blend. The other pot was mostly filled with Sunday's secret narcotic mixture. Ben poured for all three of them, went back into the kitchen for a pencil and pad, which he handed across the table to Charlie.

He sat down again, and said, "Charlie, only a top officer could have escaped from the conning tower of that submarine before it submerged and obviously exploded underwater. Sunday says you were her captain. Is that true? Take your time. Write if you wish, or blink. My Morse may not be quite as fast as it used to be, but I reckon it's still good enough. Why did you come to Pea Island? Exactly what was your mission?"

Charlie paused for a moment, then wrote, in block letters:

AS I TOLD SUNDAY, MY NAME IS HORST VON HELLENBACH. YES, I WAS THE U-BOAT'S CAPTAIN AND WILL TELL YOU ALL I KNOW, BUT FIRST, I HAVE A QUESTION. DO YOU KNOW WHO MARTIN BORMANN WAS?

Ben answered, frowning, "The man Sunday killed? I know almost nothing about him. I remember reading somewhere about Bormann being among Adolf Hitler's close friends."

As he continued writing, Charlie produced a sardonic grimace:

HE WAS MUCH MORE THAN THAT. NEXT TO HITLER, BORMANN WAS THE MOST POWERFUL MAN IN GERMANY. I BELIEVE BORMANN KNEW, POSSIBLY FOR YEARS, THAT THE WAR WAS LOST, AND CAREFULLY PLANNED TO FORSAKE HITLER AND ESCAPE CERTAIN DEATH BY STEALING A FORTUNE IN GOLD AND MAKING HIS WAY SECRETLY TO PEA ISLAND. I BELIEVE HE SOMEHOW MANAGED TO DUPE HITLER HIMSELF, SINCE IT WAS HITLER WHO PERSONALLY ORDERED ME TO COMMAND THE VOYAGE. I DISCOVERED BORMANN'S PRESENCE ABOARD MY BOAT ONLY AFTER WE WERE ALREADY AT SEA. I WAS GIVEN ORDERS TO SAIL TO SOUTH AMERICA AND WAS ASTOUNDED WHEN

BORMANN ORDERED ME TO STOP HERE. PEA ISLAND HAD APPARENTLY BEEN HIS ULTIMATE DESTINATION ALL ALONG.

Charlie paused to put his pencil down, flexing his fingers. He picked up the pencil again and wrote:

THE DEATH OF SUNDAY'S FATHER AND HER DOG WERE NOT THE FIRST NOR THE LAST OF BORMANN'S HIGH CRIMES. HE SABOTAGED MY BOAT AND MURDERED MY CREW, TO THE LAST MAN, ALL BUT ME AND THE YOUNG REAMS BOY. I ALSO WISHED TO HAVE REVENGE, AND TRIED TO KILL BORMANN MYSELF. I FOLLOWED HIM, BUT I COULD NOT—

At this point, Charlie dropped the pencil and covered his eyes, slowly shaking his head.

Ben coughed once quietly and told him, "Son, in my time, I have also been a man of the sea, both a sailor and ship's officer. Rest assured that I have some idea of what it is like to lose and mourn for lost shipmates. Please take all the time you need, but like Sunday has, tell me the whole story from your perspective. Then we will stop for lunch."

Although it was somewhat disjointed because of his disability, Charlie got through his own mute monologue also within an hour's time. Sunday noticed that Ben's face remained impassive during Charlie's tale, and didn't interrupt him even once. When at last Charlie put down his pencil, no one moved or spoke for several minutes. Suddenly, Charlie grabbed the pencil again and scribbled:

I WAS A NAVAL OFFICER DOING MY HONOR-BOUND DUTY, BUT I WAS NEVER A NAZI. YOU MUST BELIEVE THIS.

Ben, whose eyes were fastened onto the pad while Charlie wrote, straightened in his chair and clasped his hands together on the table.

Then he raised his head and said, in almost a whisper, "Only a few short years ago, I stood at my post on top of my Station House, watching the fireballs of the terrible slaughter you and your colleagues wreaked off our coast. I cursed you and all you represented to the hottest part of hell.

"Now, thanks be to God Almighty, the war is over. Well, at least your part of it is. Mine, too. I am an old man, probably a dying old man, and I have no more hatred left in me. I do believe you were an honorable officer, and that you have told me the truth. We are no longer enemies. Retribution accomplishes absolutely nothing. So, then. Let's stop for now and eat a bite of lunch. Afterwards, we can try to make sense of all this."

All three of them stretched, and smiled at Estelle, who, as if on cue, appeared with a tray of egg salad sandwiches, which, with surprising appetite, they all consumed in silence. Ben noticed Charlie blinking a rapid message to Sunday before walking away from the table. "I didn't quite catch that, honey. What did he say?"

A lopsided grin broke across Sunday's face.

"He has managed to teach me a few words of his own language, Papa Ben. He said, 'Ich muss mal,' which means he has to go pee. He'll be right back. By the way, that was a mighty cruel thing you did the other night, taking us to that movie house. You had seen it all the night before, hadn't you?"

"Yes. I regret having to do that, Sunday, but I wanted to see his reaction. Just recently, I have read a great deal in the newspapers and listened to a lot of news broadcasts on the radio, and the consensus of opinion is that not many people, even inside Germany, knew about those concentration camp horrors. It's quite possible that Charlie had no knowledge of what was going on there either, but I had to simply judge for myself.

"Incidentally, it also hasn't escaped me how you two look at each other, and I know you have slept together. I think you have fallen in love with him. Be careful, Sunday. I know you are a grown woman, but I don't want you to get hurt."

Sunday felt herself coloring in embarrassment.

"I'm not sure about my feelings, Papa Ben. For one thing, I think Charlie lied to me about something really important."

"What?"

"He told me he was just 'engaged,' but that ring be wears is a wedding band, for sure."

For the first time in two days, Ben threw back his head and laughed heartily.

"Oh, Sunday, my precious and still ignorant Sunday. Charlie didn't lie to you. I happen to know that in many European countries, Germany included, engagement rings as we know them are not traditionally used. Couples who become engaged simply buy a single gold band that is worn on the ring finger of the left hand until the marriage ceremony, when it's transferred to the right hand.

"He didn't lie to you, honey, and I don't think he has lied about anything else, Tell you what, let me get another sip of your wonderful medicine, and then we can all go sit on the back porch and drink iced tea. I'm sick and tired of this table."

Sunday followed him out, feeling just a tiny bit lightheaded.

Twenty minutes later, when all three of them were seated comfortably, cold tea glasses in hand, Ben became serious again.

"Well now, we have all the separate pieces of the puzzle clearly before us. All that remains is to put it together. Let's review:

"Martin Bormann decides to double-cross Hitler and escape the lost cause of the Third Reich with his life and a fortune in gold. He devises a complicated, even brilliant plan to divert a submarine, ostensibly to South America, but in reality, he plans to land here. Why? That is mystery number one. Mystery number two: Why was a young American soldier, no doubt one held in Germany as a prisoner of war, also on board the submarine, and carrying fifty-thousand dollars wrapped around his waist?

"It's apparent to me that the two elements are connected. Now, Charlie has told us that in the final moments of transferring the gold, both Bormann and young Bobby Joe Reams were wearing regular army uniforms, uniforms of the German soldiers in Rommel's Africa Corps. Again, why? It's quite clear why Bormann sunk the submarine. Dead men tell no tales. Trouble was, he didn't count on Charlie figuring out what he was doing, and escaping before the boat blew up."

Ben Searcy was in his element now. His eyes were bright as new pennies. Almost feverish. It also seemed to Sunday that his voice was stronger than it had been in years as he went on:

"All right, first things first. Why Pea Island? Well, there aren't many places in the civilized world where you can hide tons of gold bullion. Our Outer Banks, Pea Island in particular, has little or no indigenous population, yet as the crow flies, it is not very far from several sizable cities. Not even the shrewdest pirate could have found a better hiding place. However, Bormann would need a lot of help getting to where he wanted to go. A guide. Somebody who knows the area well. Okay, Sunday, who would that be?"

Sunday's answer was quick. "Bobby Joe Reams, that's who. The son of a local fisherman would know these waters well, rivers and sounds, not to mention the area mainland."

"Right," Ben said. "And, Bormann's fifty-thousand-dollar bribe to a poor fisherman's son would most likely be more than enough to bring him home in a hurry, no matter *what* he had to do for it. Still, I doubt if Bormann's scheme would have ever allowed the boy to live long enough to spend a dime of it. Which brings us to another question."

Ben glanced hard at Charlie. "Bormann couldn't hole up for very long on Pea Island, gold or no gold, so where exactly was he trying to go?"

Charlie smiled and blinked rapidly.

INLAND, I THINK. MOST OF THE SOLDIERS IN THE PRISON CAMP ACROSS THAT RIVER WERE WEARING THE SAME UNIFORMS BORMANN AND REAMS WORE. WHAT WAS THE NAME OF THAT TOWN?

"Williamston," Ben told him.

YES. WILLIAMSTON. NOT TOO FAR ACROSS THE SOUND AND UPRIVER FROM THE COAST. BORMANN WOULD HAVE HAD A BOAT AND WITH REAMS FOR A GUIDE, HE COULD HAVE MADE HIS WAY THERE EASILY, MOTORING AT NIGHT AND HIDING DURING THE DAYLIGHT HOURS.

"Yeah," Sunday put in, "but *why?*"

"That's easy," Ben said. "Sunday, I'll bet that if you had cut his uniform off after you cut his throat, you would have found another money belt, probably with a great deal more than fifty-thousand dollars stuffed in it. With that kind of money, a man could bribe his way into or out of practically any place.

"Don't forget, Bormann no doubt knew the war would end soon, and as we recently saw, a lot of prisoners were being returned home. With false identification and uniform, what was to stop him from being repatriated along with the others, as just one more common soldier, and someday, perhaps even years from now, make his way back to Pea Island and calmly dig up his cache of gold? This is all mere speculation, of course, and chances are we will never really know for sure, no more than we know why he shot the poor kid who was supposed to help him."

All three paused for several minutes, digesting Ben's theory as to its plausibility. Sunday and Charlie both slowly shook their heads. There seemed to be no other rational explanation than the one Ben had suggested.

After several long minutes, Charlie got Ben's attention and blinked, *SIR, I MUST NOW ASK YOU THE SAME QUESTION. WHAT WILL YOU DO?*

Ben answered first with a deep sigh.

"Nothing, Charlie. I shall do and say nothing at all, and neither will Estelle. That decision is Sunday's. I have trusted her all her life, and I will trust her for the rest of mine. Go home in peace. I have found mine, and God knows, the rest of this world could use a little more of that right now."

With effort, he stood. "If you will please excuse me, I am very tired, and need to rest."

He reached his hands to the both of theirs. "Goodbye and good luck."

Estelle wordlessly drove them back to Wanchese.

Sunday had never felt so wrung out in her life. The sail back to Pea Island could have been, and *should* have been lovely. The water wasn't rough, and the warm eight-knot wind was from the right quarter. BLACK DOLPHIN literally danced across the sound all the way home, but Sunday had to do all the boat handling by herself. Charlie sat slumped in the forward part of the cockpit, motionless, his back to her, and Sunday couldn't tell if he was asleep, angry, or merely brooding. In any case, he hardly shifted his inert position during the whole voyage, which, because of the fine weather, was mercifully short.

Continuing in his sullen stupor, Charlie left Sunday to settle her boat down alone, trudging up and over the dunes to her house in total silence. After she made her vessel snug, Sunday followed, thinking she would find Charlie inside her shack, but she spotted him halfway to the beach, sitting hunched over on the bare sand. She prudently decided not to call him to bed, but to leave him to his private meditations.

She undressed, crawled into the upper bunk and was asleep in seconds, but some innate instinct forced her awake less than an hour later. She looked around the dark cabin, rubbing a hand over skin covered in goose bumps, feeling instantly that something was wrong. In the next moment, she realized that Charlie wasn't there. She got up, lit the lantern, and immediately noticed that the lid of her sea trunk was open. She didn't bother to check its contents, somehow *knowing* what was missing.

Nearly naked, she flew out the door, running hard to the murmuring surf. Sure enough, she spotted Charlie standing at the water's edge, staring out to sea. The ugly pistol was in his hand. She reached him, grabbed him by his right arm and viciously twisted him around so that the moonlight lit his face. "What in hell are you doing with that gun, Charlie?"

His wet eyes blinked sadly.

I KNOW YOU WOULD NEVER BETRAY ME, BUT IF I TURNED MYSELF IN, I HAVE NO COUNTRY TO GO BACK TO. ADOLF HITLER AND THOSE LUNATICS AROUND HIM HAVE CAUSED THE HOMELAND I KNEW, LOVED, AND SERVED TO BE DESTROYED. IF I DID GO BACK HOME, I WOULD LIKELY BE ARRESTED AND EITHER EXECUTED OR PUT ON TRIAL AS SOME KIND OF WAR CRIMINAL. SUNDAY, YOUR OLD FRIEND BEN WAS QUITE CORRECT. I AM SURELY RESPONSIBLE FOR THE DEATHS OF MANY OF YOUR OWN COUNTRYMEN, AS WELL AS MANY ENGLISHMEN. I DO NOT KNOW IF I CAN LIVE WITH THAT ON MY CONSCIENCE.

Sunday stared at him for a full two minutes, watching the tears roll unabated down his moonlit face. She backed away from him a foot or two and crossed her arms. Her voice was like acid.

"Okay, Charlie, if you want to shoot your brains out, go ahead. I'm going to be standing right here watching you do it. And you know what else? The last thing you know when you pull that trigger is that what I'll be feeling is nothing but disgust and disappointment. I can't feel a damn bit sorry for the suicide of a coward. I could never love a coward."

Charlie looked up suddenly and stared at her hard, his lips forming the word *love* into a question.

"That's right, Charlie White Cap. I never figured you for a yellow-belly. I figured you loved me and would want to stay here with me and gut it all out. Together. I figured you would help me find a good trawler and then join me—as my mate. Listen to me, Charlie, I've never needed anybody in my whole life, but now I do. I need you. I don't know for sure yet whether or not I really do love you, but if you blow your head off, neither one of us will ever find out, will we?"

With a gurgling sound coming from his mangled throat, Charlie dropped the gun and seized her, holding her so fiercely she could hardly catch her breath. Sunday knew in that instant that the only trigger he would pull would be the one that released his passion.

"Love me, Charlie. Stay here on Pea Island and love me and live with me and make a life—"

She didn't finish. Charlie's kisses smothered any further conversation. As they fell to the sand, ripping off each other's clothing, Sunday had one other conscious thought before passion overwhelmed her own mind and body. *You didn't come 'down the road,' that's for sure, but you'd damn well better stay here, my German Captain, and be a good Daddy to the baby I'm already carrying.*

CHAPTER 23

BUMMY KNEW he'd have to sweeten the deal. The thousand dollars he promised Merchant Seaman Randy Wilkinson after they had watched all the prisoners board was probably enough to enlist his reluctant help, but Bummy had to make sure.

"You won't be sorry, Randy, old buddy. Five hundred now, five hundred after the job's finished."

He grinned at his old friend, counting out the crisp bills, which he handed over. "With what you just got paid this morning, I'm betting that's more money than you've ever had in your pockets at one time. Am I right?"

Randy had to admit that was the truth. "Sure is. Jesus! Okay, Bummy, now what?"

"First things first. Ain't no hurry. Besides, I know you pretty damn well, and we've been at sea for just about three and a half months. Let's go to Sadie's. You can have all you want to drink, and your pick of the ladies. Get yourself an all-nighter if you want to. My treat."

That cinched it. Randy's eyes lit up like twin spotlights. Sadie's was the best (and most expensive) whorehouse in Baltimore. Girls who worked there were, for the most part, clean, and the booze Sadie served was high-quality liquor, uncut. Randy laughed. Slapped his thigh. "Hot damn! You paying for the taxi, too?"

Bummy looked up at the sky and rolled his eyes.

"Give a fucker an inch, sonofabitch takes a mile! Okay, taxi ride's on me, too, but damn your eyes, if you pick an all-nighter, you'll pay for the hotel room out of your own pocket, mister."

Bummy didn't mind in the least springing for a taxi. His plan, so carefully thought out, was working so far like clockwork. And, the clock was ticking. He was certain Randy would choose a whore who would take him to some sleazy hotel for the night, and by the time Randy woke up, the ANDREW CARNEGIE would have long since sailed. From then on, poor old Randy, once the inevitable hangover subsided, would be totally dependant on him.

Predictably, Randy Wilkinson went through all the evening's activities at Sadie's like a trained monkey. Bummy accompanied his friend to the hotel, even—to the annoyance of the greedy redheaded prostitute—into the dingy room where he tactfully relieved Randy of his overstuffed wallet and paid the lady out of his own pocket. He jammed his nearly comatose shipmate's wallet into his own coat pocket, tipped his cap sarcastically at the frowning redhead and said, "You're not gonna roll *my* buddy, sweetheart. Not tonight. Just screw him and get the hell out."

Bummy left the two of them to their business, went downstairs and paid the sleepwalking night clerk five bucks to let him nap in the lobby. Catnaps were all he allowed himself, though. No way was he going to chance Randy's slipping out of his sight and control. He kicked off his shoes and leaned back in one of the ratty armchairs, crossing his feet on the equally ragged ottoman. He lit a Lucky, inhaled deeply, closed his eyes, and went over his plan again and again. Good old Randy, he thought, *You sure as hell were named right! Well, have yourself a ball.*

With a scowl and a beer-flavored grunt, Bummy remembered the many times in various whorehouses and hotels how he himself had fared with ladies of the night. Not good. All he could do, with his equipment, was watch them slowly strip, then fondle them all over for the balance of his allotted time. Intercourse was—*damn it to hell*—impossible. Not that he hadn't tried it, but after that Filipino bitch in Hawaii had taken one look at his grotesque half-scar-half-stump, the bitch had thrown his prepaid money back in his face and run out of the room screaming. No, thanks to Miss Sunday Everette, it had never been good. No sex life at all. It even hurt when he jerked off.

Shoving those painful memories back inside his mental footlocker, Bummy glanced at his watch. It would be a long night. He dozed off and on for the rest of it, and when he noticed the redhead stalk through the lobby on her way out, Bummy stood and went up to the room to wait for Randy to sleep it off. Within twenty-four more hours, old Randy Wilkinson was practically good as new, and ready to follow orders—after a big breakfast, of course, and two pots of coffee.

The second phase of Bummy's plan worked just as well, although it was rather more expensive than he had calculated. The used Ford and the two off-the-rack suits of decent clothes he bought (plus one for Randy) took a chunk out of his budget. Still, the spending of money gave him no deep concern. Money was a means to an end. For years he had saved and saved, carrying all his cash with him wherever he went, hoarding it solely for this opportunity.

Dressed in their new duds, with everything else packed in the Ford trunk, Randy said, "Where we going?"

"Washington, D.C. We're going to get us a room in a cheap hotel and do some detective work."

"Why Washington?"

"Because that's where we will most likely find Dr. George Harris, who don't know it yet, but is gonna tell me where his snot-nosed son is."

"Oh, yeah. George Harris, Jr. That's the black boy you told me about, ain't it? The one the nigger gal liked so much."

"That's the one."

"Okay, Bummy. You're driving."

The phone book in their room at the Christopher Columbus yielded several George Harrises.

"But which one is it?" Randy wanted to know.

Bummy smiled and pointed. "This one here on Walker Street. See? It's the only one with MD behind the name. We're in luck, too. The phone number for the office and the house are the same. Looks like old Doc Harris runs his practice out of his home."

"So. We gonna drive over there now?"

"Naw, stupid. I told you before, there ain't no big hurry. I'm gonna call his office and make a regular appointment. Time I had my eyes checked, don't you think? Come on, we've got one more piece of shopping to do."

"What for this time?"

Bummy tapped the phone book. "Let's look in here and find the nearest pawn shop. We need guns."

Dressed to the nines, shoes polished, hair trimmed and combed, clean-shaven and splashed liberally with Yardley's, Bummy waited his turn, ignoring shy, curious glances thrown his way by other patients in the waiting room. Bummy hid his grin behind the magazine he pretended to read. That he was the only white man in the waiting area didn't bother him in the least. He knew the half dozen nigger patients in Dr. Harris' spic-and-span office were wondering why he was there, but he didn't give a happy damn. His wait was not a long one, either. Within half an hour, the black no-nonsense nurse approached him with a manufactured smile.

"Mr. Calvin Keene? Doctor will see you now. Come right this way."

If the stout, elderly doctor was as curious as his patients, he didn't show it. He offered Bummy his hand and a warm smile, glanced down at the folder on the table and said, "Mr. Keene, my nurse says you need an eye exam. We'll fix you right up. What brings you to me, if I may ask? Did someone refer you?"

Bummy began his well-rehearsed speech. *Act like a regular gentleman, Bummy boy.*

"To tell you the truth, Doctor Harris, I'm not really here for an exam. My eyes are fine. I wanted a chance to talk to you privately, and this seemed like the best way. I know you're a busy man, so I won't waste much of your time. Here's the thing. I have recently been discharged from the Navy, and pretty soon I'll be starting to work on my new job. Some years ago, I was in the CCC camp on Pea Island down in North Carolina. I knew your son, George, Jr., down there. We were all good friends in that camp. Real close buddies. Most of us joined the service when the war broke out."

"Really? So why have you come to see me?"

"Because a lot of us have kept in touch with each other. We're planning a little reunion, to sort of celebrate and remember those who didn't make it back, but we have lost touch with George. Is your son here in Washington? We sure would like for him to join us."

"I remember that work group down there," the good doctor said, with a frown. "It wasn't the best experience my son could have had at the time, but he was adamant. However, to answer your question, no, he isn't here. He's in Alabama."

"Alabama?"

"Yes. Tuskegee, Alabama. George, Jr. went against my advice a second time right after Pearl Harbor and enlisted in the Army. He wound up with a commission in the Army Air Corps. They turned him into a fighter pilot, and thank the Good Lord, he survived a number of combat missions with the Tuskegee fliers. Maybe you heard of them. They were all black men."

"Sure, I've heard of them," Bummy lied again. "I'll bet old George won a lot of medals, too."

"Well, a few. The last year and a half, he's been training other young black pilots down there. He and his family have a little house, off-base."

Bummy felt his pulse quicken. "George has a family of his own?"

"Yes. A wife and a little boy." Dr. Harris pointed to a framed photograph resting on his desk.

"May I see that?" Bummy asked.

The elderly physician walked to his desk, picked up the photo and handed it to Bummy. "That was taken last summer. Little George the Third is almost two, now. My stubborn son married a Tuskegee girl. I expect he will also be discharged soon."

Bummy studied the picture closely. There was George, Jr., all right, in the smart uniform of a captain in the Air Corps, looking snobbish as ever. Beside him stood a pretty black girl, holding a laughing child in rompers.

"He's a cute little guy isn't he?" Bummy commented, his mind weaving like a snake through a new idea. He handed the photo back.

"Dr. Harris, this is some kind of coincidence. We were planning to have our reunion down in Atlanta. It might be that George could make it, too, at least for one day. Would you mind giving me his address and phone number?"

"Not at all. Just a minute." Dr. Harris went back to his desk and jotted the information down on the reverse side of a prescription page, which he handed over.

Bummy read it aloud carefully so that he would make no mistake: "1209 Sycamore Avenue, Tuskegee, Alabama. 3389. Great. Thanks a lot. Say, Doc, if I do get up with him, anything you'd like me to tell him for you?"

The senior Harris snorted. "You may tell him I said it's high time he got back in school. I can't wait forever for my retirement. Now, if you will excuse me, I have other patients waiting who do have problems."

"Sure, sure. And thanks again. I'll be sure and tell him."

"Alabama?" Randy said. "Christ, Bummy, that's one hell of a long drive. Think that old Ford will make it?"

"It'll make it. If not, we'll get another one. Come on, let's get packed and check outta here. We can take turns driving. I want to be in Tuskegee by Wednesday night. Thursday at the latest."

"Okay, you're the boss. What are we gonna do down there?"

"You'll see. All in good time, Randy boy."

Careful not to exceed speed limits, they made it to Tuskegee early on Thursday morning. They rented a room in one of the new motor hotels near the Tuskegee Institute campus, and slept the rest of the day.

While Randy ate enough supper for both of them at a nearby café, Bummy studied the city map he had picked up at the gas station while the attendant filled the Ford's tank. He had no trouble locating Sycamore Avenue. Over coffee, he oriented himself from where they were sitting, and as soon as it was dark, they drove there. Cruising, they were only halfway down Sycamore when they spotted number 1209, the third house from the corner of Locust, on the left-hand side. The small, white, frame house with its tiny, neat lawn sat back only a few yards from the curb.

"That's real good," Bummy said. "Pretty quiet neighborhood and the houses ain't too close together. That's good, too. Okay, Randy, lets go. I've seen enough. We'll relax tonight and get a good night's sleep. Tomorrow we'll have to do more driving, and there's still more shopping to do, too."

In high spirits, Bummy began whistling. His original plan would have to be altered, but the fact that George Harris, Jr. now had a wife and kid made it easier. "Hey, Randy, stop by that store over there. I need to get some more road maps, and a beer or two . . . "

At that same moment in time, Sunday was returning home from the Station House. Charlie looked up when she came in.

"I talked to Nat Poole and Simon Teague on the telephone," she announced. "Nat said he'd be glad to help us survey those trawlers, and Simon said he'd take care of all the banking stuff."

EXCELLENT, Charlie blinked.

ARE YOU READY FOR BED?

Sunday laughed. "Yes, sir, Cap'n. But no fooling around tonight. We've got a long sail ahead of us tomorrow."

WHERE TO THIS TIME?

"Around Harker's Island to Beaufort and Morehead City. My old Papa Nat said he'd call a friend of his who'll give us a temporary job on his shrimper. She's a fifty-five-footer, and we need to know exactly what a trawler crew has to do, don't we?"

YES. I AGREE.

"You feel strong enough?" Sunday snickered. "You ought to. The way you've been holding on to me every night tells me you're plenty strong enough to do some honest work for a change. Still and all, I reckon one goodnight kiss or two won't hurt."

CHAPTER 24

ON THREE voyages to the South Pacific and four across the North Atlantic, Bummy Keene had had countless hours during his off-watch time to formulate dozens of imaginary scenarios. In his warped fantasies, he had wreaked his festering revenge on Sunday Everette in so many different ways he had lost count. There had always been one common thread woven through the fabric of every one of his secret schemes: he had always known he would have to use George Harris as bait. The black bitch had been head over heels in love with George, and most likely would never be able to resist seeing him again.

The fact that good old George, Jr. had a wife and kid of his own made this current variation of his plan easier in many ways, although it would require a little more patience, very careful planning, and a good deal of extra traveling. No matter; after so many years, a few weeks more were nothing. The only problem now was to keep Randy from becoming bored to the point of doing something stupid. The trick was to kill two birds with one stone. The first part was easy.

Every day and night, they parked the Ford in a different area, checking—and making notes—on the movements of the Harris family: what time George left for duty in his Chevy coupe, what time the pretty little nigger wife took the kid out in his stroller for a walk, a pacifier jammed in his fat jigaboo mouth. What time

George came back home. Which days the wife drove George to work so that she could have the car for grocery shopping and errands. Which nights they went out to the movies. Which church they went to on Sunday, and which service.

It took less than two weeks to establish the fact that George and his wife kept to a pretty regular routine. No matter what, George always left his house at seven in the morning and got home at six that evening. Clockwork.

One afternoon, while Mrs. Harris and the kid were shopping, Bummy and Randy visited a surplus store on the edge of town and bought two complete army uniforms; one with sergeant stripes, the other with the two stripes of a corporal—plus MP armbands, web belts, and holsters. Randy was surprised that those items could be bought with no questions asked. ("War's over, Randy. Nobody gives a damn about who buys stuff like this anymore, and money talks.")

Every other night, Bummy treated Randy to a movie, whether they had seen it already or not, and on alternate nights while Randy sucked on his beer, Bummy studied his maps, planning routes, timing, and moves.

At last he made his decision. "Okay, Randy, here's what we're gonna do. Take a look at this map."

He pointed to Tuskegee. "Here we are, and way up here is Pea Island."

He moved his finger slowly over the chosen route, marked in red pencil. "We'll take back roads through Macon, east-south-east from there to Savannah, then up the coast to . . . right about here. This town is halfway."

"Charleston, South Carolina."

"Right. Should be able to make it in one day. Tomorrow, we're gonna drive to Charleston and find us a hideout."

"Shouldn't be too tough. We've both docked at Charleston before. What kind of joint will we be looking for, another cheap hotel? House we can rent?"

Bummy looked up, a sly grin on his face. "Naw, nothing like that. We're gonna snoop around real quiet till we find us a boat."

"A boat! Oh, yeah, man. That's smart! There's hundreds of 'em there. All kinds. What will we be looking for?"

"You'll see."

The classified section of Charleston's newspaper advertised three boats of the type Bummy was looking for. One of them was tied up in a quiet creek about seven miles up the Cooper River.

"Houseboat!" Randy said, admiration in his voice. "Perfect."

Bummy looked around at the dense, surrounding woods. "It'll do fine. Probably used for a hunting cabin. Nobody within miles of here, and only twenty minutes back to that dinky store we passed. There's bound to be a telephone there. We'll make sure of it when we get the groceries."

He jerked his thumb back to the faded, clapboard shack-on-the-water. "Bet that piece of crap hasn't been moved from the day she was hauled up here. Come on, let's go back to town and make a deal on her."

"You gonna buy her, Bummy?"

"Nope. We're just gonna rent her for a month." He winked. "Time enough to find out if we like her or not. If we do, then we'll make an offer, right?"

Randy laughed. "I get it. You're one smart guy,

Bummy Keene."

Bummy gave his sidekick a sharp look. "Goddammit, man, how many times do I have to tell you about names? Just remember your *gun!*"

Randy squinted. "Oops, I forgot. I'm Mr. Randolph Smith, you're Mr. Calvin Wesson."

"Right. Just like in every different place we've registered. No more fucking slip-ups, pal. Come on, let's go."

The deal on the decrepit houseboat was made without much haggling, and the rest of the day was spent cleaning her up inside. In town, in addition to the rope, tape, and padlocks they needed, they bought sheets and blankets for the four bunks, and groceries enough for two weeks, including three assorted boxes of Gerber baby food. There was indeed a pay phone outside Taylor's Country Store, where they bought ice for the ancient icebox in the houseboat's galley, and where Bummy reminded his friend, "You'll have to make trips back here every other day for ice and milk."

"My beer, too. I know. Don't worry, I won't forget."

"And you know what time to make the call?"

"Yeah. Midnight. Sharp. I got the number memorized." To prove it, he rattled it off three times in quick succession.

"Okay. Good. Now, let's get some shuteye. Back to Tuskegee first light tomorrow. We'll rest up all day Thursday and make our move on Friday. No one will miss old Captain Harris till Monday morning."

Randy grinned. "Like I said, Mr. Bummy *Wesson*, you're one smart cookie."

When Barbara Harris heard the doorbell ring at

seven-thirty on Friday morning, she was glad she was dressed decently. Unexpected company? She dropped the dishtowel on the kitchen table, walked to the front door, opened it, and instantly drew back in apprehension when she saw the two MP's standing there. "Something wrong, Sergeant? What—"

The sergeant saluted politely, but his face showed a pained, sympathetic look. "Sorry, ma'am, but there's been some trouble. An accident. It's Captain Harris. He—"

"Oh, my God! Where? What kind of accident?"

"Ma'am, you best get your little boy and come with us. Right away, please."

Barbara Harris flew into the bedroom, yanked her sleeping child from his crib, and ran back out, following the two enlisted men to the car. She was already so distraught she didn't notice that the car was not a Government-Issue Plymouth. Didn't notice it was not painted olive drab. The poor woman was so worried and upset she didn't realize their route was not directly toward the air base at all, but to the other side of town. Motel? Room 121? What on earth could George be doing here? Another question began to form on her lips, but was stopped by several thoughts racing through her brain, none of which she dared admit to.

"My husband's in there?"

The serious-faced sergeant opened the car door for her. "Please hurry, ma'am."

The smiling corporal held the motel room door open for her, and she walked into a nightmare . . .

Half an hour later, she was dressed in men's clothing. Her hair had been cut short. Military style. A baseball cap had been placed on her head, and tape across her mouth. Horrified, with a pistol an inch from her face, she watched as little Georgie was carried back outside by the corporal.

The sergeant spoke to her sharply, "The kid will come to no harm as long as you do exactly like I tell you to. Understand?"

She nodded rapidly.

"Corporal Smith is gonna take you for a long ride. Like a soldier and his buddy on a trip together. Little Georgie will be snug as a bug in the bed we made up for him in the trunk. Don't worry, we fixed it so he gets fresh air. Now listen up. I'm gonna untie you and take that tape off your mouth, but if you make so much as one itsy-bitsy peep, that kid of yours will be dead the next minute. We don't want to hurt you either, and we won't if you cooperate with us. Do as we say, and you both will be back home in no time, safe and sound. If you *don't* do exactly what the corporal tells you to—and I mean *exactly* what he tells you to—he's gonna cut your baby's throat right in front of your eyes, and then yours, too. You got that?"

A frantic nod showed how willing Barbara Harris was to follow any instructions.

The sergeant reached for the tape. "Not one peep, now."

Barbara Harris wouldn't have been able to protest aloud anyway. She was too terrified to scream. She was vaguely conscious that she had wet her pants, and her numbed mind could only register two coherent thoughts. *George? Where are you, George? Oh, dear God, please don't let them hurt my baby.*

Randy stopped a block from George's house. Bummy reached into the back seat for the small suitcase he had prepacked, and leaned close to the window with last-minute admonishments.

"Okay, Randy, you know what to do. Soon as you get

fifty miles away, let her hold and feed the kid. No stopping for nothing but gas and a Coke. We packed plenty of food in the trunk, and when you do stop, she stays in the car. When you have to make pit stops, pull over somewhere out in the country, by some woods, and don't forget to go with her."

"Don't worry. I won't let her out of my sight."

"Good. No speeding, and don't forget to make that call at midnight."

"Gotcha."

Bummy watched the Ford until it was out of sight, then walked leisurely to George's house. Once inside, he went all through the house pulling shades and curtains. He changed clothes, raided the well-stocked icebox, frowning because it contained no beer, and settled down to wait.

At five minutes after six, Captain George Harris, dog-tired from long, highly concentrated hours in the air, walked through his front door and tossed his cap on the hall table.

"Barbara? I'm home. Why are all the curtains closed?"

A sarcastic voice answered him. A man's voice. "Come on in the living room, honey pie."

George's confusion turned quickly to anger and then to shock when he hurried through the living room door and found himself staring straight into the muzzle of a Smith & Wesson .38 caliber revolver.

For a moment he was struck dumb. George looked from the gun's barrel to the face of the strange man who looked somehow familiar, and who smiled as he spoke, "Remember me, George? Pea Island? The CCC camp?"

Recognition came slowly. Too slowly for the man holding the gun.

"I guess you were too busy fucking that tall nigger girl to pay attention to anybody else in the camp. You and me worked in the same gang."

George's voice was a whispered croak. "You're Keene. They called you Bummy."

"That's right."

"Where's my wife? What have you done to my wife and son?"

The gun waggled. "Oh, they're okay. They're both on a long trip with my buddy. Nothing's gonna happen to 'em unless you try something stupid."

George's face turned deathly. He couldn't find his voice again, but his eyes asked all the questions: *What? Where? When? How?* And the most important one— *Why?*

Bummy told him. "Might as well relax, old pal. Come midnight, you and me are gonna start on a long trip, too. Back to Pea Island, and if you ever expect to see your wife and kid again alive, you'll do exactly what I tell you to do and exactly when I tell you to do it."

George's reply was flat, devoid of real understanding, "Pea Island?"

"Yep. I got a long-time-coming date back there with your old girlfriend. You do remember Miss Sunday Everette, don't you?"

"I remember Sunday. What are you going to do?"

"Not me. You. You're gonna romance her again, just like before, while I watch. Then I'm gonna kill the nigger bitch."

George shook his head. "No. *No!* None of this is true. I don't believe you. Where's my wife?"

"You'll get to talk to her at midnight, but only for a few seconds. She can tell you herself."

Chapter 25

AT HIS landing pier at Elizabeth City, Robert Kinch frowned and shook his head at the two men in uniform who had come across his gangplank with an unusual request. "Sorry, I go to Roanoke Island, Hatteras Village, and Ocracoke. I don't make stops at Pea Island any more. Neither do any of the other ferryboats from here."

The sergeant spoke. "It's real important for us to get over there. Army business. Can't you make a special stop? We'd be glad to pay you extra. Would fifty dollars apiece be enough for you to drop us off there and pick us up tomorrow?"

Robert scratched his beard. The sergeant was carrying a suitcase. Two servicemen on some kind of special mission? Military surveying, maybe? Hell, a hundred bucks was more than enough to make a pair of slight detours. Don't have that many passengers on this run anyway.

He eyed the black officer. "Well, Captain, since this must be some kind of emergency, I reckon fifty each would just about cover it. Can you be ready to leave the island by four o'clock tomorrow afternoon?"

The Negro captain glanced at his sergeant, as if to ask if that was satisfactory.

His white sergeant answered for him, "That will be fine. We can be ready to go by then, can't we, Sir?"

The captain gave a half-smile and nodded.

Noticing a few more passengers coming up the gangway, Robert pocketed the crisp bills the sergeant handed him. "Okay, take your seats. We'll be shoving off in two minutes."

Once he cleared the harbor and headed toward Manteo, Robert gave the military men another thought or two, this time aloud, to his mate, "Know something, Andy? Those two soldiers sure look familiar. I could swear I've seen them both before. Just can't put my finger on it. Not yet, anyway."

Aft, George leaned over. "I think that guy recognized me. He keeps looking back at us. He's the same man who picked my father and me up from the camp that summer back in '37."

"Don't sweat it," Bummy answered. "What if he does? Ain't no harm in a war hero coming back to visit an old girlfriend. Just act natural. And don't forget what you got waiting for you when all this is over, provided you play your cards right."

George gritted his teeth. The sobering telephone call three nights ago had proved how serious this crazy man was. Barbara and Georgie had been alive, thank God, but Barbara had been hysterical. Close to a total breakdown. Being already AWOL from his duty was the least of his worries. The one look he'd been allowed at his sobbing wife and child through the grimy window of that dilapidated houseboat in South Carolina had further convinced him that he'd have to play out this macabre charade to whatever nasty, insane end, whatever the cost.

As if reading his thoughts, Bummy said, "Thinking about your precious jewels? Don't forget, if I don't show up back there in three more days, that knife my buddy had under your wife's chin will slice through her throat like a soft stick of butter. So, behave. You've done good so far. Don't screw it up now."

Shirtless, with a red bandana tied around his forehead, Charlie handed a fresh-sawed board up to Amos, who laughed, admiring the man's sweaty, bronzed muscles. "Tell you what, Charlie. You look a damn sight better now than you did when I first saw you. Old Sunday's got you back in good shape, for sure. 'Course, I 'spect y'all workin' on that shrimper for a few weeks helped. Anyways, I really appreciate you helpin' me fix this porch. Should of done it years ago. There's rotten spots all over it."

Amos' continuous, one-sided chatter, interrupted only by his hammer blows nailing down new, fitted planks, was contrived so that his mute helper only needed to nod or shake his head in response. Charlie had indeed gotten his strength back, and physical labor seemed to suit him just fine. Amos grunted. It was too bad about that scar on his cheek, which still stood out like a purple crayon mark on his tanned face.

Amos started to say something else, when something—perhaps from old habit—caused him to straighten, then, look out over the sound to the northwest. Apparently, Charlie had sensed it, too, and didn't turn back around when Amos said, "Now, what the devil is Robert Kinch comin' here for? You and Sunday been expectin' him? To deliver somethin', maybe?"

Curious, they stopped working and watched the boat's gradual approach. Charlie, remembering Amos' question, shook his head in the negative as the boat slowly eased up to the pier. Both he and Amos watched as two men, one of them carrying a suitcase, hopped onto the finger pier. Two men in uniform.

"Those guys ain't coastguardsmen, Charlie. They look like army-types. Wonder what they're doin' here?"

The hammer still in his hand, Amos walked to the edge of the newly repaired porch to greet the approaching pair, "Can I help you boys with something?"

He bent down, squinting as slow recognition came. "Well, I'll be blessed if it ain't George! George Harris!"

Robert Kinch was only half a mile away from Pea Island when faces and names matched up in his gnawing memory. "Damn!"

Right away, he picked up the radio telephone transmitter, keyed it, and within minutes, was talking to Ben Searcy. "Cap'n Ben, I'm mighty glad to hear you're back from your trip. How you feeling? Over."

"I've been better, Robert, but thanks for asking. What's the occasion for this call? Over."

"I just dropped off two passengers in army uniforms at the dock at Pea Island. One of them was that colored boy Sunday was so hot for back then. Over."

"George? George *Harris?* Are you sure? Over."

"Yes, sir. I don't remember the other one's name, but he's the one who raped her. I'd bet my life on it. Over."

There was a long pause before Ben came back on. "Robert, who has the fastest motorboat in Elizabeth City? Over."

"Tim Suggs, Cap'n. She'll do better than twenty knots. Over."

"Thanks. I'm going to call him right away. Sheriff Stanley, too. Thanks a lot for this call. I'll be back in touch soon. Over and out."

The two uniformed men climbed the steps.

"Hello, Amos," George said, offering his hand and something that looked like a smile.

Amos, remembering how George Harris had left Pea Island and acutely aware that Charlie was standing not six feet away, chose his words carefully. "Hello, yourself. Been a long time. What brings you back to Pea Island?"

The sergeant answered for George.

"He's come to see Sunday. What else? Me and him serve in the same outfit, and had a little furlough coming, so, here we are. Say, could you boys spare us a cold drink of water?"

"Sure," Amos answered. "Come on in. Charlie and me were about to take us a break anyway."

It was only after they were all four inside and Amos had gone to the kitchen to fetch a pitcher of water that it dawned on him that the sergeant had been lying. George Harris was in the uniform of a captain in the Army Air Forces, but the sergeant was wearing Provost Marshall insignia. Military Police. *What is going on, here?* He carried the pitcher and glasses into the sitting room. "Here you go."

"Where is everybody, Amos?" George said.

"All gone except for me. Reassigned." He inclined his head toward Charlie. "He's helpin' me with a few chores around here. He can't talk, though. Got his throat hurt bad in the war."

George looked around. "You mean Sunday doesn't live here any more?"

"Nope," Amos told him. "Not for some time now." He pointed south. "She's got her own house down the beach a ways."

"Is the lady at home?" the sergeant wanted to know.

"Yeah, she's at home. What you got in the suitcase?"

"Some presents for Captain Harris' old sweetheart," the sergeant said. "Want to see?"

With that, he hoisted the suitcase onto the table, turning it so that the Amos and Charlie could not see inside, and deftly sprung the two latches. Quick as a cat, he reached inside and Amos found himself staring at the business end of a snub-nosed .38. Amos dropped the glass pitcher and raised his hands. The pitcher shattered at his feet.

The sergeant then waved the gun in Charlie's direction. "Down on the floor, both of you. On your belly. Move!"

Both Amos and Charlie had no choice but to do as the man commanded. From the corner of his eye, Amos watched the sergeant reach back into the suitcase and remove several lengths of half-inch rope, which he tossed to George.

"Okay, Captain Marvel, take your time and tie 'em both up good and tight. And tape this one's mouth up, too. Nice and snug. Never mind about that one. He can't talk anyway."

With his partner looking on, making sure of it, George did exactly as he was instructed.

Within ten minutes, Amos was expertly hogtied. Wide adhesive tape was stretched across his mouth. All Amos could see, from the position he was in, were the feet of the invaders, and between them, all the way across the room where he had been dragged, Charlie's trussed-up figure—and those cold blue eyes of his.

Bummy checked the knots. "Good job, George. They ain't going nowhere for the time being. I'll deal with 'em later. Let's have a look around. What's upstairs?"

Pushing George ahead of him, Bummy climbed the stairs to the second story, glancing into every room, making sure they were all empty. Eventually they reached the crow's nest. Bummy pointed south.

"That must be her place down there. Ain't much to look at, is it? Looks like one of those stinking railroad shacks I was born in."

George didn't answer.

With a laugh, Bummy led the way back downstairs, past the tied-up men on the floor, and walked down the hall to and through the kitchen to the back porch. With George at his side, he took a peek inside the empty boat shed. "Where's the surfboat?"

"I would imagine the Coast Guard reassigned their boat as well."

"Uh-huh." Bummy sniffed, then spotted three five-gallon cans that were stacked in the far corner. "Didn't take all their gas, though."

He hefted one of the cans. "Full. Must be enough here to burn down a barracks. Maybe even—"

He stopped short of finishing his sentence. Another thought had sprung into his fiendish mind. "Wait a minute! I got an idea. Come on."

Urging George ahead of him with the blunt nose of the .38, he walked around the house to the front porch, eyed the two sawhorses and the half dozen planks lying across them, then looked on the porch deck where Amos had dropped the hammer. Nearby was the discarded carpenter's apron, full of twenty-penny nails. "Perfect. Fucking perfect!"

He grinned at George. "Go back around there and bring that can of gas, old buddy."

George didn't move.

Bummy enjoyed the stricken look on his face, knowing George had already figured out what he had in mind.

"I can't do this thing, Keene. I won't."

Bummy's grin changed to a sneer. "Oh, yes you can, and you will, goddamn you. 'Cause if you don't, I'll blow your black nigger brains out right now, and when I get back to South Carolina, I'll cut little Georgie's throat myself. Now, you want to call my bluff? No? Then do what I told you. Now!"

He watched the look on George Harris' face change from anguish to fury, and then to abject hopelessness. To drive his point home, Bummy raised the pistol to George's forehead and pulled the hammer back.

"I can do all this by myself if I have to, you know," he hissed.

He felt a minor spasm of power, of triumph, as George turned and began trudging back around the Station House. Bummy eased the hammer back, jammed the gun in his belt, bent over and picked up the hammer and carpenter's belt.

To George's retreating back he added, "When you get back with the gas, pick up three of these two-by-fours. I'll get the suitcase."

Suddenly remembering something he had noticed before, but had momentarily forgotten, Bummy hurried back inside. He carefully sidestepped the two inert forms lying on the floor, and ripped the telephone from its perch on the wall.

On his way out, he couldn't resist saying, "We're gonna have us a hot dog party down the beach with Miss Everette, boys. A real, black weenie roast. Too bad you ain't invited."

Randy Wilkinson "Smith" was not a man of great patience, and what little he had was rapidly vanishing. Trust in his fellow man was not one of his long suits either, and his faith that Bummy Keene was actually coming back for him was fading faster than he could drink beer.

What's to keep Bummy from doing whatever he wants to do on that island, and take off to God knows where, leaving his good ol' dumb-ass buddy Randy holding the bag? And a shitty bag it is, too. It wouldn't be so bad if we had thought of bringing some diapers. Yeah, sure, smart-guy Bummy. You thought about baby food for the little nigger, all right, but you didn't think about what was just as important. What goes in that fat little brat's mouth comes right out the other end—at least five or six times a day. And what goes in his mouth is one hell of a lot!

After the Harris woman had actually gotten down on her knees and begged, Randy had given in, and driven back up to the store, cursing all the way, but he should have known that a rundown, two-bit, one-pump country gas station like that wouldn't stock such things as diapers. Besides, he was sure that the store's owner, having seen him—a total stranger—in and out so often, had most likely become suspicious. *Was the old fart going to maybe call the police?* Nervous as the devil already, Randy was imagining all kinds of things. *Man, I could get myself arrested for kidnapping, tried, and sentenced to death while old Bummy is out there somewhere free as a bird!*

Not one of the windows in the houseboat would open, either. Randy was used to clean berths in clean ships, and being cooped up in this stinking houseboat with a woman who cried all day and all night was driving him crazy. The woman had already ripped up most of the sheets to substitute for the forgotten diapers, all the while whining, and begging him to let them go. There was no way he could allow her to even go outside to wash the makeshift (and loaded) diapers in the river. Bummy had told him not to let her out. Not for *any* reason.

Eating nothing but sandwiches and going almost three days and nights with practically no sleep was making Randy mean enough to do almost anything short of murder, and when the toilet finally stopped up—at practically the same time his beer and cigarettes ran out—Randy decided he'd had enough! As soon as it was dark, and while his two prisoners were asleep, he slipped out, got in the car and headed for Charleston, where he was pretty sure he could sign on in one ship or another.

For miles, he kept muttering, "To hell with you, Bummy Keene. Five hundred dollars in my hand is for damn sure worth a thousand in the bush."

Sunday finished mixing the last batch of medicine she had promised Ben and washed her hands, glancing at her clock. Almost noon. *Better get busy with those boiled eggs, girl. Charlie and Amos will want their lunch pretty soon, and are both bound to be mighty hungry.*

She took a step toward the stove and stopped dead in her tracks. Just the simple thought of boiled eggs brought on a fresh wave of dizziness and queasy stomach. *Damn! That's the third time this morning. Won't hurt to lie down for five minutes first. Who's going to know?* Sunday eased herself down on the lower bunk and stretched out her full length, allowing herself a hypocritical chuckle.

Aloud she said, "With all you taught me about healing and medicines, Susan Bearclaw, you never told me one little thing about the morning sickness, did you? Why not? Because you were never pregnant?"

She patted her stomach. "You behave, Mister. Or Miss. Whichever you are. Which . . . ever . . . you . . . "

Fists pounding on the door awakened her before she had slept ten minutes, judging from her angry look back at the clock. Not in the best of humor to begin with, Sunday didn't appreciate Charlie's little joke; banging on the door like that either. He knew that door had never had a lock on it.

"Come on in, funny guy," she snapped. "and duck when you do!"

Anticipating her handsome sailor man's sweaty embrace, she rolled over and sat on the side of the bunk, rubbing the sleep from her eyes. When she focused on the two male forms that entered, she automatically muttered, "Charlie, you and Amos are a whole hour early, what are you—"

But after two blinks—her only two—she knew it wasn't Charlie and Amos standing there. One face she found herself staring into was black. Familiar. Handsome as the angel Gabriel. The other one was white. Also familiar. The face of Lucifer himself. Rising, she spoke first to the black face. The handsome face.

"George? George Harris? Is that really you? Why are you crying?"

Immediately, she transferred her gaze to the other face. A hated face that now showed a sneer.

Bummy raised his right hand. The hand that held a gun. "So, Miss Annie Oakley Everette, ain't you gonna even speak to me?"

After many tries, Amos snagged the tape on a raised nail. It came loose but he stopped his steady stream of profanity when he saw Charlie start rolling across the floor toward him. Amos knew there was purpose in Charlie's movement, and, on every other roll, those icy blue eyes, fixed on his own, showed something much different than his own frustration. Amos had seen that kind of look many times before. The look of resolution.

The look of authority. The look of command. Keeping his voice low, Amos asked, "What you got in mind, Charlie?"

When Charlie was within five or six feet, Amos noticed something else in those eyes. He shuddered involuntarily in spite of his trusses.

Amos saw that Charlie was blinking. *Why?*

"What is it, Charlie? You tryin' to tell me somethin'?"

Amos kept watching. Several minutes passed before he realized that there was a pattern to Charlie's blinking. Some long, some short . . .

"Be damned. You tryin' to send me *Morse?* That it?"

With effort, Charlie smiled at him and nodded his head. Then he blinked:

G-L-A-S-S. B-R-O-K-E-N G-L-A-S-S.

Amos saw Charlie's head jerk sideways twice.

"Right! The water pitcher I dropped. Broke to smithereens."

Charlie smiled back at him. Another nod, then another signal:

T-O C-U-T R-O-P-E-S.

Amos needed no more signals. Feeling a rush of adrenaline, he glanced back to where he had dropped the pitcher. Sure enough, there were shards and fragments lying all over the floor, some large enough to do the job. Without hesitating, he began rolling, too, and soon, his nose was inches away from what he was looking for. Luckily, a two-inch piece was still attached to the handle!

"Perfect! This'll do, Charlie, but how am I gon' pick it up?"

Charlie opened and closed his mouth several times, showing his teeth.

"I get it!" Amos almost yelled. "Now, if I can do this without cuttin' my lips off, we're in business. Roll on over here and get sideways. I'll drop it right by your hands."

Both men were sweating profusely from their exertion, but with a great many minor adjustments, eventually dragged and rolled their bodies into position, back to back. Amos could no longer see Charlie's face, but soon, he felt a scraping pressure on the ropes around his wrists.

"You got the right spot. Work steady, Charlie, so your fingers don't cramp up, and for God's sake, don't drop that piece of glass. These ropes are brand new. Ain't never been wet, so they'll cut easy."

But Amos knew it would not be easy. It could take an hour at least. Maybe longer . . .

Ben Searcy, carrying a flask of Sunday's medicine, struggled to keep his balance as he hurried down the gangplank of the Manteo-Elizabeth City ferry. Tim Suggs had not answered his telephone, but maybe, Ben prayed, just maybe, he was at the boatyard. If not, Ben knew he would have to 'borrow' Tim's boat. Too, if he could find Tim, he'd ask him if he owned some kind of gun. Pistol, rifle, shotgun—anything would do.

He walked fast as he could toward the boatyard docks. The pain was bad, real bad, but he tried his best to ignore it. *Don't take a swallow of this medicine until you absolutely have to, Ben. You have to make it last, and there's no telling how long all this is going to take.*

Cursing under his breath that he had not been able to reach Sheriff Stanley directly, he had left a message with a deputy. He'd had better luck with Commander French, who had promised to redirect one of his boats to Pea Island. ETA somewhere around five o'clock. Ben turned the corner around the large building that was the terminal for the ways. Breathed a huge sigh of relief. Tim Suggs was standing there talking to another workman, both of them loafing, smoking cigarettes and drinking Pepsi-Colas.

Ben yelled, not a bit surprised that his voice was weak as a baby's, "Tim! Tim Suggs! I need your help. It's a matter of life or death."

Sunday knew, the moment she saw the gun, that she would need all her wits, all her cunning, to stay alive. *Where was Charlie? Amos?*

She shifted her glances from one to the other; the tear-streaked face of her first love, and the ugly face of the hated creature who had raped her. And, for the moment at least, it was the latter who held the power.

"What do you want here, Bummy Keene?"

The sneer became a voice. A voice full of pure venom. "What I'd like to have is something you took away from me with that shotgun. I was in the hospital for two months. Three operations that hurt worse than your shot, and I still had to piss through a tube. Take a look at what you done to me."

Shifting the gun to his left hand and keeping his eyes locked into Sunday's, he unzipped his pants, pulled down his shorts, and pointed to his grotesque, misshapen half-organ.

"Pretty, ain't he? And just about as useful as a strip of beefsteak. Now, you take old George, here, I'll bet his tallywhacker's just as good as it ever was. He's got a wife and kid to prove it, too, don't you George?"

Sunday turned back to George even before Bummy pulled his shorts back up. Never in her life had she seen such pain on a human face. She forced herself to smile.

"You have a wife and child, George? Why, that's wonderful."

George finally managed a hoarse whisper, "He forced me to do this, Sunday. His accomplice is holding them hostage. They threatened to kill them if I didn't bring him here. What did he do to you?"

Understanding washed over Sunday like the first big wave of a hurricane. She took a deep breath, trying desperately to think of how to respond. *So it's revenge Bummy's after. Retribution.* But first, she had to answer George's question. "It happened after you left the camp. He and three of his friends raped me. I whipped the other three and shot him with a rock-salted shell."

She turned to Bummy. "So, if you can't rape me again, what do you want?"

Bummy's face became even uglier. "First, take all those clothes off. I want to see your naked body in plain daylight."

Sunday clenched her teeth. *Where is Charlie? Has this bastard shot him and Amos? No, I would have heard the shots.* "All right, if that's what you want."

Slowly, Sunday began undressing, all the while judging how far it was to the table where her knives were, and if she could reach one before . . . No, too far. She would have to think of something else.

In a few minutes, she stood nude, her clothes around her feet.

"Hey, George," Bummy said, his ferret's eyes roaming all over Sunday's perfect body. "I gotta hand it to you. It must have took a lot of guts to run out on a woman like that. 'Course, I guess you didn't have a whole hell of a lot of choice about it, did you? I remember what a sweet piece of ass she was then, and from the looks of her now, I'm guessing it'll be even better. Go on. Help yourself. I'm gonna enjoy watching you."

"What?" George said.

Bummy waggled the pistol in his face. "You heard me. Get naked and screw her right there on the floor. It ought to be something to see."

George hesitated, but when his tormenter stuck the barrel of the pistol up under his chin, he reached for his buttons with trembling fingers.

"Aw, shit!" Bummy said, spitting on the floor. "You're sure one nervous fucker. Sunday, help the poor nigger out."

Moving deliberately, Sunday complied with Bummy's order. *We need to make Bummy's torture last as long as possible. Keep stalling, Sunday. We have to have more time.* Undressing George, she took as much of that precious time as she thought she could get away with. At last, with eyes squeezed shut from shame and fear, George stood naked before her. Sunday tried not to look at him—in the way she once had—and kept presence of mind enough to suggest the bunk instead of the floor. The foot of the lower bunk was only two feet from the table.

Bummy didn't object, and Sunday laid back on the quilt, opened her arms, and, not knowing what else to do, said, "George, better do as he says. Just try to remember our dolphins."

But George couldn't move. His whole body began shaking from his sobbing, and Bummy, looking down, could plainly see that there was no way on earth George could perform any kind of sexual command.

"Christ," Bummy said, in honest disgust. "Well, looks like you two ain't gonna give me a kootchy show after all. What a joke. I thought all you nigger boys could get it up anytime, anyplace. So be it. George, get your black ass out there and bring that suitcase in."

George did as he was told, and Bummy sat down on one of the chairs by the table. "Put it here."

He opened it, removed several more lengths of rope, tossed them to his reluctant assistant, and ordered, "Tie her to that bunk. Spread eagle, and don't be too gentle about doing it."

Waving the pistol with his left hand, he reached into his pocket for his Luckies. While George was busy tying Sunday to the bunk, he lit one, puffed a few times, and reached back into the suitcase. George, with his back turned to him, didn't see what Bummy had taken out, or the loop of Bummy's swing, bringing the Military Police billy club down hard on his head. He collapsed in a heap by the bunk.

Bummy, the cigarette dangling from his lips, looked down at Sunday. "Too bad, honey child. If you hadn't shot my pecker off, it would have taken you a lot longer to die."

With those words, he walked outside and returned with the can of gasoline. Suddenly remembering he had a lighted cigarette in his mouth, he quickly dropped it on the floor next to the naked, unconscious George, and stepped on it, grinding it out. While he was at it, Bummy used his foot to turn George's body over onto his back.

"I promised those boys up there we were gonna have a weenie roast," he told Sunday. Snorting, he added, "But old George's weenie ain't hardly big enough now to roast, is it?"

Sunday's mind was racing like a riptide. She had smelled the gasoline, and knew instantly what Bummy was going to do. *Charlie and Amos are both alive! He hasn't killed them . . . yet. Time, Sunday. Stall for some more time. It's all you can do.*

"Bummy, I'm truly sorry I shot you. You would probably have whipped me good if I had fought fair. You're still quite a man, you know, even if you can't . . .

you know. Come on, now, you really don't want to do this. I could make you a rich man. Richer than you could ever imagine."

Amused, Bummy played along with what he assumed was surely a lie. "You? Make me *rich?*"

He spread his arms theatrically. "You, a jigaboo woman who lives in a shithole like this can make me a rich man? What do you take me for, a stupid fool?"

"Listen to me, Bummy Keene. Look under the table, there. See that crate?"

"Yeah, I see it. So what?"

"Take the lid off and look inside."

Not quite so certain anymore that she wasn't sincere, Bummy dragged the crate from under the table. He examined its contents for a good five minutes before he spoke, "Is this shit real *gold?*"

"It's real, all right. Stolen German gold. What's in that box is worth maybe a million dollars. If you let me go, I can show you where there are thirty more crates just like that one. It's all yours if you let us live."

Bummy sat silent for a few more minutes. Then he stood and placed the shiny brick back into its crate. He turned to face Sunday, who was smiling at him. His return smile was the cruelest thing Sunday had ever seen, and his answer made her heart sink to the bottom of her soul.

"I ain't greedy, honey. *One* million is plenty for my needs. Besides, how could I take thirty crates away from here? This one's heavy enough to haul around. No, you've just given me enough to pay for a lot of hurting. Tell you what I will do, though, since you just gave me a small fortune. Instead of dousing both of you with this gas, I'll just drop a little dab in here, and use the rest on the walls of this shack. If old George wakes up in time, or if you figure out some way to get loose, who knows? Maybe you'll have a chance to get out before you roast alive."

Sunday bit down hard on her lip, knowing it would be futile to say more. She had won more of a concession from him than she had might have hoped for. Yet, she tried one last ploy. "You've got that gun, Bummy. For all that gold, you could at least just shoot us in the head and make it quick."

Bummy picked up the gas can, tipped it, and poured a small puddle under the table.

"Yeah, but that would be too nice, honey pie. I want you to have time to *think* about what you did to me. So long, Sunday Everette. I'll see you in hell someday."

Sunday watched him pick up the crate of gold and the can of gasoline, walk through, and slam her door shut. A few moments later, she heard the unmistakable sounds of hammering.

CHAPTER 26

BUMMY DROPPED the hammer and stood back from the door, pleased with his work. Even if George came to and freed Sunday, they would not be able to budge it from the inside. He picked up the can of gas and began on the south side of the house, dousing the walls liberally. He worked his way around, clockwise.

On the north side, something caused him to trip and nearly stumble and fall. He cursed at the frog gig that had been leaning against the wall, and gave it a vicious kick, knocking it a few feet away. When he reached the door, having completely circled the house, he realized he had used up all the gas. He splashed the remaining few drops against the boarded-up door and tossed the can aside.

Bummy reached into his pocket for his smokes and lighter. He plucked the last of the Lucky Strikes from the pack, stuck it between his lips and crumpled the empty pack in his hand. Standing back a safe distance, he lit the package, then threw it against the wall.

With a soft *whump,* the gasoline ignited, shooting flames all around the house. Bummy was surprised at the intensity of the heat. He picked up the heavy box of gold and backed away several yards from the house, and then laughed at the repetition of his own prejudiced joke.

"Damn, Bummy boy, that's gonna be some weenie roast." He watched the fire grow for another moment or two.

Again aloud, he said, "Better not hang around here too long, son. Best you get your ass on back up there to the Station House. There's two more cans of gas left in the boat shed. Ought to be enough."

He glanced at his watch.

"I reckon there won't be nobody left to mind if I borrow that little black sailboat. Bet I can get halfway across the sound before dark, and make a safe landfall before morning. Shit, this was all too fucking easy!"

Hefting the heavy box, he turned to go.

Bummy Keene may or may not have ever known that, in certain circumstances, three seconds could be a very long period of time. Quite enough time to realize he had made three serious mistakes.

In the first second that it took him to recognize the blond, shirtless man launching himself through the air at him in a flying tackle, Bummy realized his first mistake was to have not shot those two guys in the Station House to begin with. In the next second, as he dropped the box on the sand, simultaneously yanking the gun from his belt, he instantly understood his second mistake—he couldn't shoot worth a damn with his left hand. When he pulled the trigger and nothing happened, he cursed himself for a third mistake: buying a gun from a pawn shop instead of a hardware store. It had either a missing firing pin or bad ammo. Whatever the case was, he didn't get a chance for another shot. His time—his three seconds—were up.

The speed and weight of the man's tackle knocked him up against the burning house, banging his head hard enough to momentarily stun him. From instinct, he raised the gun to fire again, but there was not enough time. The blond man with crazy blue eyes had picked up the frog gig . . .

Charlie made two quick thrusts. The first drove into eye sockets. The second, delivered with twice the force, slashed arteries as it sliced through the neck, pinning his prey to the soft planks of the wall. Charlie ran around to the door, but Amos was already there, with the hammer.

"I'll have these boards loose in one minute, Charlie," he yelled, "Find somethin' to bust in one of the windows."

Charlie looked around frantically. He spotted the box of gold, ran over to it and picked it up, as if it weighed no more than a loaf of bread. He rushed around to the west side, removed one of the gold bars, and threw it through the window, producing two immediate results: smoke poured out through the sizeable hole, and he also heard Sunday's voice.

"*Hurry,* Charlie. I know it's you, but hurry, *please!*"

Charlie threw a second gold bar, producing a larger hole. More smoke was escaping the interior, pouring through the window in a thick, black plume. Gathering all his strength, Charlie seized the ropes, swung the lightened box around him like an Olympic hammer, and released it. It crashed through the window, leaving enough of an opening for his body. Without any hesitation, he backed up three steps, got a running start, and, with arms over his face, hurled himself through the jagged opening. He landed on his shoulder and rolled, just as he had been taught to do as a cadet. On his knees, he looked around. Through the searing smoke, he heard Sunday's voice again.

"I'm on the bunk, Charlie. Get a knife from the table. Quick!"

His lungs filling with smoke, his eyes smarting, Charlie grabbed the knife and crawled toward the bunk. Just as he reached it, Amos flung the door open, creating a sudden, violent draft, which fanned flames inside the house, but also blew away enough of the smoke for Charlie to see that the naked black army captain was lying on top of Sunday, and had protected her from the burning top bunk that had collapsed and fallen on top of him.

Amos was beside Charlie in an instant. Using his only tool—the hammer he still had in his hand—Amos clawed the burning debris from George's back, and pulled him from Sunday's body. As Charlie, nearly blinded now, felt for, and then cut the ropes that held Sunday to the bunk posts, he was aware that Amos was dragging George through the open door.

The moment Sunday's wrists were free, she sat up and seized Charlie's face. "Save my sea chest if you can." With those words, she ran out behind Amos.

Charlie, knowing the iron handles of Sunday's sea chest would be blistering hot, picked up the hammer Amos had dropped, made his way to the chest, hooked the claw on one of the handles and pulled. It took all his remaining reservoir of strength to drag the chest that held Sunday's most prized possessions from the inferno. He made it twenty feet toward the ocean before falling backwards on his back, badly burned in a dozen places, smoke-blinded, and totally exhausted. Before he fainted, he heard the roof of Sunday's house fall in.

They all converged within half an hour on either side of five o'clock. It would be the largest gathering of people on Pea Island since the CCC gang left: Ben Searcy, the burly Tim Suggs, Commander Willis French in his launch, the five-man crew of the cutter French had dispatched, and Robert Kinch, ferrying two dozen people from both Ocracoke Island and Hatteras Village, including two Dare County deputies. Aghast at what they found (and soon to be hypnotized by what they were about to see), none of them would leave until well after midnight.

French and his crew were the first ones on the scene, Ben and Tim Suggs a step or two behind them. The house, or what was left of it, was blazing away like some iniquitous bonfire set on the beach of hell. The charred body of a man was pinned through the neck to part of one wall that was still standing. Amos Turner was dragging a half full tub of lard, unable to speak because his throat and lungs were still full of swallowed smoke. A sea chest that had been dragged a few yards toward the beach sat like a lonely, miniature shipwreck.

And, down by the tide line, Sunday Everette, on her knees and bent over two other naked forms—one black, one white—was singing!

No, *not* singing. It was some kind of chant. Quiet. Eerie. Not of this world. It was a scene like none of the hushed crowd had ever seen. A scene none of them would forget. Ever. Sunday kept chanting, long after the sun went down. Long after the embers of her house were the only light against the dark void of the reposing Atlantic.

> *"Old Dan Tucker was a fine old man,*
> *Go away fire, go away burn;*
> *Washed his face in a frying pan,*
> *Don't cry, Susan, now it's my turn;*
> *Combed his hair with a wagon wheel,*
> *Get away fire, get away pain;*
> *Heal this skin like a soft cool rain,*
> *And died with a toothache in his heel;*
> *Go away burn, give up your fight,*
> *Nobody dies on my beach tonight;*
> *Old Dan Tucker lived a right long life. . ."*

On and on she went. Relentless. With soft voice and softer fingers. It was a beautiful sound to hear and a wondrous sight to watch. Listen and watch they did. All of them. Mesmerized. On and on she chanted. Hour after hour.

Shortly before midnight, the white man sat up, and Sunday gave him a drink of water. Everyone watching knew they had witnessed some kind of miracle. Sunday Everette's legend was born then, full-grown, like Venus when she emerged from the sea. When the black man groaned and moved his head, the lard on his horribly burned back shining like glass, the crowd broke out in a cheer that could be heard at Cape Hatteras.

Somebody handed Sunday a slicker to cover her nakedness. She thanked the man, a coastguardsman, and looked around, as if she was only just now seeing the crowd gathered around her. Then she smiled.

"Anybody bring something to eat? I'm mighty hungry."

EPILOGUE

CHARLIE WAS well enough to accompany Sunday to Manteo for Ben Searcy's funeral. Ben was laid to rest not five hundred feet from an unmarked grave in the indigent area where Bummy Keene's pine box had been unceremoniously dumped two weeks before. Estelle hugged Sunday, and informed her that Ben had passed away quietly in his sleep, and had been in no pain.

After the service, they were approached by Sheriff Stanley and were told that Bummy's accomplice, one Randolph Wilkinson, had been arrested in Charleston trying to board a freighter for Caracas. He had confessed the entire plot, including the fact that having lost his nerve, he had abandoned George's wife and baby in the houseboat, had driven the Ford to Charleston, and had signed on aboard the freighter, hoping to escape both the law and Bummy's wrath.

With her baby in her arms, Barbara Harris had walked to the country store and, in spite of still being in a numbed state of shock, had managed to contact both the South Carolina authorities and George's father. Working together with local police and Alabama law enforcement, The FBI had quickly unraveled the scheme, and had taken Barbara, her child, and her father-in-law to the naval hospital in Norfolk, where George had been transported.

All concerned had been astonished when George needed only two weeks of treatment, and, smiling broadly, had walked out under his own steam, unscarred physically, but branded forever by his ordeal; a very personal experience with a psychopath. This would serve him well in later years in a highly successful practice in New York City. He never saw Sunday again.

It was a strange thing that none of the Bankers who had been witness to Sunday's fire talking ever thought to go back to Pea Island and poke through the ashes of her house. It was, perhaps, as if all who had been there considered the place some kind of shrine. For her part, Sunday wanted nothing more to do with the bloody gold still buried there. Content to leave Hitler's treasure where it lay hidden, she permanently stowed the memory of it into the most remote closet of her mind—where only the deepest secrets were kept. Charlie, sensing her feelings, never once referred to it either.

As a matter of fact, Sunday and Charlie were, as Ben had predicted, the last known inhabitants of Pea Island, since Amos had also been taken to the hospital in Norfolk for treatment. He never returned to active duty.

Two of his former Station House colleagues, however, Clem Hardison and Joe Freeman, left the Coast Guard and were the first two deckhands Sunday hired for her new trawler. Named *Black Dolphin II*, the fishing boat was a practically new, fifty-foot Desco; a single rig vessel, powered by a dependable Gray Marine gas engine (which would soon be converted to diesel). She was freshly painted white, with a distinct black-dolphin logo that would soon be well known in east coast commercial fishing waters. In later years, a second boat would join the Black Dolphin fleet, and when one became available, a converted PT boat was added, with Charlie as Captain. Ben's prophecy about sportfishing turned out to also be accurate.

Clem and Joe were aboard when *BLACK DOLPHIN II* took her first cruise—but not for fishing. It was a relatively short pleasure trip out to the Gulf Stream. Sunday, according to Clem Hardison (whose memory of the event would remain sharp the rest of his life), politely but firmly told her mate and crew, with outstretched arms, "Boys, this is my church. And as half owner and captain of this vessel, I have the right to perform marriage ceremonies."

Then, Clem swore, she took Charlie's hand and led him to the bow.

"Lord, If you don't mind, we're going to use my name for this. Do you, Charlie Everette, take me, Sunday Everette, to be your lawful wedded wife, in sickness and in health, till death do us part?"

Charlie nodded his "I do."

Sunday said, "I vow the same. Clem, hand me those two rings."

Thus, Sunday and Charlie became man and wife, at least as far as they were concerned, and no one who ever knew them thought otherwise. *BLACK DOLPHIN II* was berthed permanently at Wanchese, and with the kind assistance of Sunday's old Papa Nat Poole, along with her working crew, the trawler's superstructure, wheelhouse, and cabin were altered to make snug living quarters for Sunday and her husband.

Their daughter, Susan Bearclaw Everette, was born aboard a few months later.

Seasonal fishing, along with Sunday's healing practice and some shrewd investments counseled by Simon Teague, all proved to be profitable, guaranteeing security and steady financial success for the Everette family. They never had to borrow a dime.

And Sunday's legend grew.

AUTHOR'S NOTE

Pea Island is no longer a separate island. Hurricanes and other acts of nature closed the inlet between Pea Island and Hatteras Island just as capriciously as they had opened it more than a century ago. Pea Island is now part of the first National Seashore, and is also a wildlife sanctuary.

Until the mid 1940's, there were more than twenty Life-Saving Stations along the eastern shore. Several of them were on North Carolina's Outer Banks, and it is true that the Pea Island Station had an all-black crew. Their heroic exploits are well chronicled. For dramatic purposes, I have taken a few geographical and historic liberties regarding some elements of this story.

The terrible loss of life and shipping off the coast of North Carolina is well documented. More than six hundred ships lie on the bottom there, many of them sunk by German submarines during both World Wars, and that stretch of ocean near Cape Hatteras was aptly given the nickname "Torpedo Junction."

The German prisoner of war camps in this novel are also factual. As a very young boy, I myself talked to several of the prisoners during their work breaks. I know for a fact that many of them eventually did immigrate to the United States.

With the exception of Martin Bormann, all the characters in this book are fictitious. Any similarity to names and families of actual persons is purely accidental and unintentional.

Much has been written about Bormann's possible escape from the Hitler bunker during the last hours of the Third Reich, and, given his well-known gifts of intelligence and an instinct for survival, who is to say he didn't? With literary apologies to any surviving members of Bormann's family, my own ideas of how he may have escaped appear in the second book of this trilogy. Bormann was indeed "Hitler's Judas."

T.L.